AFTERGLOW

Also by Phil Stamper

The Gravity of Us
As Far as You'll Take Me
Golden Boys

AFTER

GLOW

PHIL STAMPER

BLOOMSBURY

NEW YORK   LONDON   OXFORD   NEW DELHI   SYDNEY

BLOOMSBURY YA
Bloomsbury Publishing Inc., part of Bloomsbury Publishing Plc
1385 Broadway, New York, NY 10018

BLOOMSBURY and the Diana logo are trademarks of Bloomsbury Publishing Plc

First published in the United States of America in February 2023 by Bloomsbury YA

Text copyright © 2023 by Phil Stamper
Illustrations by May van Millingen

Bloomsbury books may be purchased for business or promotional use. For information
on bulk purchases please contact Macmillan Corporate and Premium Sales Department
at specialmarkets@macmillan.com

Library of Congress Cataloging-in-Publication Data
Names: Stamper, Phil, author.
Title: Afterglow / by Phil Stamper.
Description: New York : Bloomsbury Children's Books, [2023] | Series: Golden boys ; book 2
Summary: After a life-changing summer, Gabriel, Reese, Sal, and Heath are finally ready for
senior year, but as graduation nears and the boys prepare to enter the real world,
it is clear their friendship will never be the same.
Identifiers: LCCN 2022036055 (print) | LCCN 2022036056 (e-book)
ISBN 978-1-5476-0738-9 (hardcover) • ISBN 978-1-5476-0868-3 (e-book)
Subjects: CYAC: Gay people—Fiction. | Best friends—Fiction. | Friendship—Fiction. | LCGFT: Novels.
Classification: LCC PZ7.1.S7316 Af 2023 (print) | LCC PZ7.1.S7316 (e-book) | DDC [Fic]—dc23
LC record available at https://lccn.loc.gov/2022036055
LC e-book record available at https://lccn.loc.gov/2022036056

Book design by John Candell
Typeset by Westchester Publishing Services
Printed and bound in the U.S.A.
2 4 6 8 10 9 7 5 3 1

To find out more about our authors and books visit www.bloomsbury.com
and sign up for our newsletters.

To Caitlin.

A thousand thank-yous doesn't come close.

• The Story So Far •

GABRIEL + HEATH + REESE + SAL

> Activity time!!!!!

> Aaaaat the risk of being too sentimental... give me one rose and one thorn of the whole summer. Ⓖ

> aw gabriel's getting sappy!!!

> thorn: coming back from Daytona to a new apartment, my parents divorce being final, and no longer living on a beach

> rose: coming back from Daytona with a hot new boyfriend

> (thats you reese)

(in case you needed the clarification)

also! reconnecting with my cuz diana was great

To be fair you did kiss multiple boys in Florida so I appreciate the clarification 😐

That's my thorn. Lots of roses though... I loved learning how to sew, I think my designs got way better in Paris, also, you know, I got to live in Paris which is objectively the coolest of the cities we all went to.

Hey, Boston was fun! My rose was learning I could actually make friends who aren't you guys. I wasn't sure I could do it lmao. My thorn is coming back and still having 6.5 months before I find out if I got into Ohio State.

Pro: I figured out I really do like politics ... just not DC politics. Con: My spectacular breakdown.

its roses and thorns not pros
and cons

H you have no whimsy

Special bonus rose that
we're all still friends after
that wild summer. But also
a thorn because we weren't
really great at keeping up
with each other.

And that kinda scares me,
since this is probably our
last year living in the same
town... ever. G

CHAPTER ONE

REESE

OCTOBER'S ALWAYS BEEN MY favorite month. There's a hint of change all around me—the breeze becomes slightly cooler, the trees change color, my allergies finally chill out, and high school football season gets into full swing.

Well, okay. That's a Heath thing. For me, that means high school football *concessions stand* season starts, and I get to have cheesy fries every Friday night.

After leaving Paris this summer, I came back with a strange new set of responsibilities. As the overall art guru, I've already been put in charge of designing this year's prom. I have a whole new set of classes, each of them more challenging than the last. Also, for the first time in history, I get to play the role of boyfriend.

I'm someone's boyfriend, I think as I slip on a chunky knitted sweater. *I'm Heath's boyfriend!*

Outside, I hear the crunch of gravel followed by three sharp beeps, Heath's code for *I Love You*—specifically, code for "I love you but will not be coming up to the door to pick you up."

I throw on my shades, say my goodbyes to Mom and Mamma, then walk out the door into the fading sun.

From the moment I step into his truck, the scent of Heath's deodorant hits me, and I know that if I were standing, I'd go weak at the knees. It's marvelous and ridiculous and dangerous the power this perfect boy has over me.

"Mi amor," he says, in a bad French accent, in place of hello.

I cringe. "I think you mean *mon* amour?"

He winces. "Ah, right. Guess that's what I get for trying to impress my well-traveled boyfriend."

"Yet, somehow, I'm *still* attracted to you," I say, flipping my scarf over my shoulder.

As we make our way to the high school, we talk like that—inside jokes and conversation that wouldn't make a bit of sense to any passersby, in our own language. Two months in, everything with Heath still feels new and tentative, but simultaneously old and safe.

I look at him, but his eyes are fixed on the road.

"What're you thinking about?" he asks.

"Honestly? How this still doesn't feel real. You and me." I pause. "After all this time."

He pulls the truck to a stop and grips me smoothly under my arm. He pulls me toward him while leaning in, and our lips meet. It's a quick kiss, but it's firm too. It tells me one thing: *I'm here, and I'm not going away.*

"Did that feel real?" he asks.

My lips still tingle. "It's feeling realer by the second."

"Good," he says, giving me a beaming smile.

We drive the rest of the way in near silence, until we start to approach the school. Through the open windows of the truck, I hear faint echoes of our fight song being played by the band, and as we pull into the parking lot, I hear the commotion of the crowd. Their energy gets absorbed into me, and my heart rate spikes in excitement.

Gabriel, Sal, Heath, and I have been so busy since the school year started. Heath with weight training, Gabriel with his new LGBTQ+ Advocacy Group, and Sal with student council, that some days even our group chat falls into silence.

But at the homecoming game tonight, the four of us will be inseparable.

• • •

Heath and I walk into the field hand in hand, and I observe my surroundings keenly. In Paris, no one would've batted an eye at us, but in Gracemont, Ohio? Things are a little different here.

We pass a ton of people, parents I know, old teachers, I even give a polite smile to the middle school janitor. Her eyes flick to our clenched hands before meeting my gaze, and as I feel my breath get stuck in my throat, she gives me a look that can be only interpreted as: "*ooh la la!*"

I blush and lead Heath toward the bleachers.

"The guys are over there, but I'll catch up with you in a

second," Heath says, walking backward and pointing to a few of his baseball friends. "Gonna say hi to them first. Want anything from the concessions when I come back?"

Cheese fries, I answer in my head. But then I remember that if I get them now, I'm going to also get them in the third quarter when I start to get bored, and my stomach is going to hurt.

"Just a Sprite?" I say unconvincingly.

He narrows his eyes. "Right. Cheesy fries and a Sprite, coming up."

I head up to the bleachers, and the cool breeze on my freshly un-held hand makes me kind of miss Heath. I shake my head. After all that yearning, actually having someone plays with your brain just as much, and I curse my silly little brain for being so cliché.

"Reese!" Gabriel shouts as he comes down the stairs, phone in hand. "Say hi to Matt!"

I lean back against the chain-link fence, a little disoriented, as I force a smile and wave to the guy on the other side of his Face-Time call.

"Sal's up there," he says. "I'll be back in a second, service is terrible."

I wade through the crowd, eventually spotting Sal looking bored out of his mind, scrolling some sort of social feed, his face softly reflecting his phone light. I squeeze past a couple of first years and take a seat next to him, nudging him softly with my shoulder.

"Reese," he says. "Where's Heath?"

"With his baseball friends," I say. "Why's Gabriel choosing right now to FaceTime his boyfriend?"

"They're in love, or something." Sal just shakes his head.

The two of us sit there, not really talking, just scrolling our Instagram feeds. While everyone around us is clad in school hoodies, varsity jackets, and the rare T-shirt and shorts combo of the midwestern teen who swears he's "never cold," Sal's in a button up and slacks, and I'm in a fashionable sweater and jeans.

"Do you ever get the feeling we don't really fit in here?" I ask finally.

He sighs. "Every single day."

We sit in silence after that, while the crowd around us comes to life. We go through the motions, standing for the national anthem, cheering as our team receives the opening kickoff and charges toward the 40-yard line, singing the fight song.

Eventually, Sal nudges me. There's a smirk on his face when I turn to him, but his gaze is focused on something in the distance. Gabriel and Heath, laughing, push their way through the crowd to get to us, giant sodas and mountains of cheesy fries clenched precariously in their grasp.

They take their seats by us, and for as "othered" as I felt minutes ago, it really feels like home when Heath hands me my soda and puts his arm around me. Gabe instantly launches into a story about how his sister was able to sneak booze into an Ohio State game, and we listen intently between bites of food and the random obligatory cheer.

For so many years, the four of us actively rejected activities like this, but now that our days here are numbered... it's like we all feel this drive to make the most out of this year.

Gabriel and Sal are laughing about something so hard it looks like their eyes are starting to water. Meanwhile, Heath tries to feed me a cheese-covered fry, and drips a little on my lips—maybe on purpose—and uses that as an excuse to kiss my lips clean.

So many things changed this summer, but the four of us fall right back into the rhythm we've had since preschool. I might feel out of place in Gracemont, Ohio. But right here, surrounded by my friends, I wonder how I ever felt like I didn't belong.

CHAPTER TWO

⸜ HEATH ⸝

THE HOMECOMING FOOTBALL GAME is always one of my favorite nights, mostly because it's the only time I can convince *all* the other boys to come to a sports-themed event. But this year, I didn't even have to try to convince them. It's not hard to get Reese to attend any event with a concessions stand, but it feels different this year. Was it the months away from Gracemont that made them miss all this?

The atmosphere is electric, and it feels like the whole community of Gracemont is here. And I spend as much of the game as I can with my arm around Reese.

Yeah, I know, the future is coming at us like a freight train. But transitioning from friends to more with him has been as smooth as Reese's wool sweater, which I'm clutching. Through it all, I stay vigilant. I know the risks of being out and proud in a small town, but the four of us are unstoppable. Who would confront us? With

Gabe's passion, Sal's speaking ability, Reese's pure talent, and my ability to step in as bodyguard, no one can touch us.

I already spend three to four days a week weight training after school, keeping me in prime shape for the baseball season. Tryouts and practices don't start for a while, but for a top-tier athlete like me, the season never really stops.

"There's your dad," Reese says. "I forgot he always comes to the homecoming game."

I laugh. "He wouldn't miss it. It's like a class reunion every year."

I scan the crowd and find my dad talking to Coach Lee.

"He's talking to Coach," I say. "I better go step in before Dad signs me up for more training programs or something."

"Please!" Reese begs. "Baseball's taking up all your free time as it is, and it's not even close to baseball season."

I give him another kiss and make my way out of the bleachers, onto the gravel track that surrounds the football field, and an explosion of cheers rise up just before I can say hi. We all look over, and by the celebration on the field and the fact that the band's playing the fight song on repeat, I'm guessing we just scored.

After the commotion dies down, I shake Coach Lee's hand.

"Hi, Coach," I say.

"Heath, we were just talking about you," Dad jumps in.

"Hopefully all good things?" I say, because it sounds like one of those things you *have* to say when someone tells you they've been talking about you. Kind of like, adult speak that doesn't mean anything. But as Coach's face lights up, I can tell I responded correctly.

"Of course. I was just keeping your dad up-to-date on your progress in the off-season. I hear you've been pushing yourself hard at the batting cages, and I told your dad how you've been the only person to make it to every *single* after-school weight training session Assistant Coach Roberts has thrown. Vanderbilt's going to be lucky to have you."

I blush. "Well, that's a long way away."

Dad puts his palm on my shoulder. "Don't be so modest. You've worked hard for this, and I couldn't be prouder."

"Us too," Coach says, nodding. "Look, I'm gonna let you go. The concessions line has died down, and I need a hot dog immediately. See you all soon."

We watch him go, and Dad gives my shoulder a light squeeze. I turn to him and smile, but his sight is off toward a group of older alumni.

"Would you mind stopping by to say hi to some of my baseball friends?" Dad asks, a glimmer of hope in his eyes. He drops his voice. "I've been avoiding them, because I know they're all going to ask about your mom. But maybe, if you come along with me, you can steal the focus a bit? You know they all think Gracemont's got a future major leaguer on our hands for the first time in the school's history."

I blush. For some reason, the first thought that comes to my mind is wondering if there's ever been an openly gay active baseball player in the MLB, but before my mind can go down *that* path, Dad's already leading me toward his friends.

I know them all, of course. Some of them stayed in the area

after high school, some left and made a point to come back every year, but thanks to the shared language of baseball, I've been their key talking point for the past three years.

"Remind me, what was your batting average last year?" (.385)

"I knew you'd be huge one day. You know what they say about right-handed pitchers who bat left, right?" (Yes, batting with my nondominant hand gives me better leverage, which means I'm poised to have a better batting average.)

"Vanderbilt didn't look so good against Tennessee this last season, did they?" (They didn't.)

I deal with all their questions as well as I can, and each time I look up my dad is beaming a huge smile. He's never been too demanding as a sports parent, thankfully, but as I feel his grip squeeze a little tighter on my shoulder, I feel an anxious sweat prickle around my neck.

"How's it going?" Reese asks, and I feel my body thaw as soon as I hear his voice. "The boys are about to finish your portion of cheese fries, so I thought I'd warn you. Hi, Mr. Shepard!"

"Oh! Right, everyone, this is Reese. Heath's boyfriend." Dad turns to me and waves me back toward the stands. "You should go back before the others steal your fries."

Dad's friends laugh, so I say my goodbyes and head back.

"You looked like you needed saving," Reese says. "Too much baseball talk?"

I take a deep breath and pull him close to me as I exhale. "It's gonna be a long, long year."

CHAPTER THREE

SAL

I'VE NEVER BEEN A fan of homecoming. The football game is always full of alumni of various ages but of the exact same—very high—drunkenness level. From what I hear, the alumni association (sounds official, but it's just a boomer Facebook group) throws a keg party at a farmhouse down by where Heath used to live, where they invite all the local Gracemont High alumni.

The jewel of the weekend to the current students, though, is the homecoming dance on Saturday. I haven't been to one since freshman year, when the four of us walked into the school gymnasium, halfheartedly danced to the eight hundred Bruno Mars songs on the DJ's playlist, and swore to ourselves we'd never go again.

We replaced homecoming with our own traditions. A big bonfire at Heath's with our own playlist, a movie marathon, *anything* that got us away from the gym. We swore we'd never go back.

Unfortunately, half of us are back, out of necessity. Reese and I walk into the homecoming dance together.

"I feel like a spy," Reese says, lowering his shades.

I shrug. "We *are* spies."

Student council technically plans all our dances, but as student council president, I can't claim the homecoming dance. It has to be held in the school gym; we've used the same DJ and photographer for the past two decades; the only thing we get to choose is the theme.

We let the underclassmen take care of planning, and this year's theme is—for some unknown reason—"Born in the USA."

We walk in through the red, white, and blue balloons and streamers, and Reese takes notes on the decor, the refreshments, the music, everything. With me and Reese leading the planning for prom, we want to make sure we avoid anything too cringey. Thus, the recon mission we're on.

"I don't want to be judgmental, but this is rough," I say, which makes Reese laugh.

"You can be judgmental with me," Reese says. "But we've got to be here if we're going to throw an awesome prom this year. We need to see every decision that was made, then do the opposite, so *our* prom becomes the best this school has ever seen."

I nod. "At least it can't be the worst. Remember our freshman year when they rented that boat on Lake Erie and everyone got seasick?"

"Sure, but we can definitely do better than this." Reese gestures at the dance around us. "I mean, I went to design school in Paris and you went to all those fancy DC events for the senator."

We take our seats in the bleachers on the side of the gym. We're the only ones sitting, unless you count the two freshmen that are making out up near the top.

"Amateur move," I tell Reese, pointing toward the freshmen. "Gabe and I knew to make out *under* the bleachers, so no one saw us. Or, like, just go down the hall—they always keep the band room unlocked."

"You know, last year a sentence like that would have made me so jealous." He pats his chest. "Growth."

I shrug. "Sorry. If you'd have told us sooner about your crush on Heath, Gabe and I could have been a little stealthier about it."

"It was a me problem, not a you problem. But anyway, I get to kiss Heath whenever I want now, so it's all good. Speaking of, can we finish taking notes so we can get back to Gabriel's?"

We try out the drinks (different flavors of Hawaiian Punch that's being watched very closely by a teacher to make sure no one tries to spike it) and snacks (off-brand Oreos and pretzels) and make furious notes.

A voice calls out behind us. "Why are you two wearing sunglasses inside?"

I turn to find Lyla staring at us suspiciously, arms crossed. She slicks a strand of straight black hair behind her ear. She's a senior who's on student council with us, so I decide it's probably fine to let her in on the plan.

"We're making notes for prom. I want to come into the next meeting with a whole list of everything . . . *wrong* about this. That way, we can fix it for prom."

"You're in on this too?" she asks Reese.

"Um, yeah. Hey, Lyla."

She takes our notebooks out of our hands forcefully and tosses them on the ground by the bleachers.

"What are you doing?" I ask, blushing.

She grabs me by the wrist and pulls me toward the dance floor.

"Trying to remove the sticks from your asses," she says coolly.

Reese and I come onto the dance floor, and the flash of lights from the DJ booth hits us. The vibration of the music thumps underfoot, and I feel my body start to sway with the beat. Reese shuffles awkwardly nearby, but eventually gives in to the music.

Other people join us, mostly juniors and seniors who we know from student council. Apparently some upperclassmen *do* come to this thing. And the music is getting better. And no one else seems to care about the snacks or the decor.

So Reese and I take off our sunglasses and dance.

CHAPTER FOUR

GABRIEL

"I CAN'T BELIEVE THEY each paid twenty dollars to go to the dance for, like, fifteen minutes," Heath says, and I laugh.

"I had fun our first year," I say. "But you know I'll never say no to a bonfire."

"Same!" Heath says, slapping his knee. "I never got the big deal. Like, yeah, the Bruno Mars playlist felt like we were at a straight pride parade, but, I mean, the four of us can have fun anywhere."

I look at my phone. "Why haven't the boys texted us? I expected a play-by-play of everything bad."

"Reese texted me a little, but just, like, 'something about the Born in the USA theme feels racist and I can't put my finger on it.'"

"Fair," I say. "Sorry we're not having this at your old place, Heath. My little firepit is nothing like your bonfires, that's for sure."

Heath smiles, his face catching the firelight just right, so I can see a hint of sadness there. I mean, of course he's sad—he's stuck in a tiny apartment adjusting to life without his mom nearby. His whole thing was throwing parties and bonfires, and now he's like a smothered flame.

Still, he makes small talk with me as we sit around the fire, waiting for the other two to stop their spy mission.

"How's it going with your dad?" I ask, kind of derailing his small talk about his advanced lit project.

"Oh," he says, nervously running his bare feet through the grass. "It's going okay. Better than I thought it'd be, honestly. Obviously I miss the space, but it's starting to feel like home. Dad built me these hanging shelves for all my trophies and academic stuff; we got all these pics of the family, me and my cousin Diana, and all of us, framed and placed around the apartment."

He sighs, looking at my poor excuse for a bonfire. "It's not the same, of course, but it's something."

"Should I put another log on?" I ask, but Heath's phone rings. It's Reese, so he picks it up.

Reese does most of the talking, as evidenced by all the "uh-huh" and "hmm" and "oh wow" noises Heath's responding with. I assume he's just on his way, but if that were the case, why wouldn't he just text?

After a couple of excruciating minutes, he hangs up the phone.

"No need for another log on the fire," he says with a laugh. "I think we're going dancing."

• • •

Heath and I slip through the back door of the gym, which is being held by Sal while an anxious Reese serves as lookout. Once we're in, we breathe a sigh of relief.

"Sorry it took us so long," Heath says. "Gabriel had to steam his pants."

Reese laughs. "Literally no one will clock it, but I appreciate the effort."

We walk toward the dance floor, and I survey the crowd for any familiar faces. Of course, at this small school, *every* face is familiar. I give a quick wave to Cassie, a junior girl who's one of the only other members of the LGBTQ+ Advocacy Group I created. She asks me to save her a dance, and I give her a quick nod as she dips back toward the refreshments table.

I see Heath's and Reese's bodies pull into each other. They dance slowly, rocking back and forth, with bright smiles on their faces. It's been a couple months, but my heart still melts for them.

"Want to dance?" Sal asks, and when I turn to him with a confused look, he adds, "Normal dancing. Not . . . whatever it is they're doing."

I laugh, and we spend the next few songs shuffling back and forth. Song after song comes on, each one an absolute hit—obviously we misjudged the DJ back during our first year. The next song slowly fades in, and I recognize immediately that the tempo is noticeably slower.

Fuck, I think. I look at Sal, and I feel a hint of that familiar draw. The one that I've been sucked into for years, and the one that nearly ruined my relationship with Matt before it even officially started.

Sal smiles, though, and it gives me comfort. He takes my hand and puts his arm on my shoulder, but it's so casual and effortless.

"If it's too weird, we can stop," he says.

I shake my head. "Not weird. We need to work on this just-friends thing."

"Don't worry, I won't make a move again, I promise. I know you'd much rather have Matt here."

"Maybe he can come for prom," I say, feeling kind of excited at the idea. "I know he'd love to see you all."

"Even me?"

I smirk. "Yes. He knows you were going through a hard time."

The tempo picks up again, and it's in that awkward in-between where you have to decide whether to slow dance quickly or quick dance slowly. He lets go of my hand and my waist, but we're still shuffling back and forth close to each other.

"He's really sweet!" Sal says. "Like, too sweet. How the heck did you get someone like that?"

"*Heck*," I say, mocking his sheer inability to curse that's been instilled in him from his mom. "I don't know, honestly. I think I just followed your advice—I tried to be myself and put myself out there."

"You're going to kill it in college."

"And you're going to kill it in … whatever you end up doing."

Heath barges into our conversation. "I love this song! Reese has it on one of his party playlists."

We take that as an invitation to open up our circle to include Reese and Heath, and the four of us dance together.

"I love you guys!" Heath says.

Sal turns to me. "Has he been drinking?"

"He drove me here, so I hope not," I reply.

"Oh, come on. I don't need alcohol to enjoy a dance party." He gestures to the refreshments table. "Have you tried the punch? The pretzels? It's perfection."

"I think he's joking," Reese says. "But I can't be sure."

Heath rolls his eyes. "I'm just saying, no one gives a shit about that stuff. Look—everyone's having a blast just being with each other. Can we go to Waffle House after this?"

"Are you sure he didn't have anything to drink?" Sal repeats.

I sigh. "Just shut up and dance."

• Golden Boys •

GABRIEL + HEATH + REESE + SAL

> I feel so hungover and yet we didn't drink at all. **R**

> **G** And *that* is the power of a good dance party…

>

> **H** 😴 😴 😴 😴 😴 😴

> S— did you get the notebooks??? I think we left all our prom notes at the gym. **R**

We won't need them. If we can have that much fun at a party with half-filled balloons and Hawaiian Punch, we can throw one hell of a prom.

Hell yeah! Now we just need a theme.

CHAPTER FIVE

SAL

REESE WAS RIGHT—THERE really is something magical about Paris. The architecture is stunning, the food is incredible, and I'm surprised how well we've been able to communicate as a group of rowdy American teens spending their holiday break in Paris for a French IV class trip.

Winter break sneaked up on us. The past couple of months since homecoming were a blur of meetings, homework, and college applications . . . for the other boys, that is. I applied to one of the schools Mom wanted me to. As a backup. Otherwise, I've done a lot of *pretending* to apply to colleges, while I hold Mom off from the truth for as long as I can.

But here in Paris, those pressures are thousands of miles away.

We're approaching the dead of winter, but the weather here has been mild and perfect. (We'll chalk that one up to climate change.) I have a thin sweater on over my button-up shirt, but I haven't had to pull out my peacoat once this whole trip. The sunny days have led to some great photos, which is important for mass FOMO—Reese and I have been lighting up the group chat at every possible opportunity.

The magic of Paris fades a bit when you're here on a school trip, though. The way we're getting ushered around like cattle—from the hostel to a museum to a monument to a café and back to the hostel for the night—makes the whole trip feel juvenile compared to our summer experiences. Not to mention, it makes me feel claustrophobic.

But I've been able to steal a few moments of independence along the way. Like here, in the lobby of the hostel, I've spent the morning sipping coffee and chatting with the front desk person to practice my French.

"Today's your free day, isn't it?" the hotel clerk asks. "What will you be doing today?"

"It is," I reply in rushed French. "I'm going to see the school my friend Reese went to over the summer."

"Your accent is very good," she replies in English.

I smile, kind of wishing Reese was around to hear the compliment. This whole week—actually, the whole school year—he's talked about this city like he lived here for years, and I can't help but feel a little bitter. While I was trapped in the DC grind, Reese was fully independent, making dresses *and* friends. The closest friends I made were Josh and April, the two other interns who worked with me, but we haven't kept in touch at all since we got back. I don't think any of us have a ton of positive memories from that time, so it's not like any of us ever feel like reminiscing with one another.

We're all staying in this youth hostel in the Belleville neighborhood of Paris. The hostel is clean and nice enough, sure—but it's even more cramped than the dozens of dorm rooms at the colleges I toured with Mom. The trip so far has been good, but limited. As much as I love having a strict agenda, we haven't gotten to choose anywhere we go, anything we do.

Today, though, things change.

"How are you already so put together?" Reese asks me as he steps into the lobby. He's wearing an off-white cable-knit sweater over the tee he wore last night. "And you have a bow tie on?"

I want to tell him how I haven't slept well since before the summer. That no matter what time zone I'm in, I sometimes wake at the crack of dawn, in a cold sweat, dreaming that I've screwed up another big event for the senator.

But if I told him that, I might have to tell him how I kind of miss that rush too. Of feeling like you were waking up and doing something that *meant* something. Instead of, I don't know, calculus? Even this trip to Paris feels dull in comparison.

"Today's our adventure day," I say. "Can't have an adventure without a bow tie."

"Pretty sure I've had *plenty* of adventures without one. But on that note, we should go. We only get a few hours of free time, so I need to take you to all my favorite spots." He pats the journal in his hand. "And I can't wait to show off my designs to Professor Watts. I hope she's got some free time between classes—I really want to surprise her!"

I stand, fold the French newspaper I was mostly pretending to read, and follow him through the door. It's cold out, but the sun is blinding. We pause to throw on our shades before heading toward the Métro.

We use our phones to guide us through the maze that is the city. The mix of diagonal roads and alleys makes it easy to get lost, but there's something comforting about meandering through the city's tight streets. Each street has its own charm—twinkling Christmas lights on one, a row of vintage shops in another, a cobblestone path in a third—and the farther we get away from the hostel, the freer I feel.

"I'm starting to get it. Why you love this city so much," I tell Reese once we're finally on the train. He looks to me with a light grin.

"I love it here. But I also miss home so much right now." He sighs. "This trip is harder, for some reason."

"What could that reason be?" I say in a singsong voice before cutting a sharp look at him. "You miss Gracemont? Or maybe your parents? Or is it possibly . . . a certain person in particular?"

"Yeah," he sighs. "I miss Heath. How corny is that?"

"How many times have you texted, called, and FaceTimed each other this morning?"

"I've sent him four texts today, but it's his birthday, so we *will* be calling, FaceTiming, and using every other form of messaging possible." He rolls his eyes. "Speaking of messaging . . . If I remember correctly, last summer, *you* were the one who ghosted the chat for weeks. It was like you were on a different planet."

I pause. "I felt like I was on a different planet. A weird political planet."

"One you want to return to?" he asks, and I feel my body freeze. Do I want to go back to DC? No. But do I want to get back into the real world? The world of politics? The answer, of course, is yes.

I've been going through the motions since we got back to Gracemont. I've gotten good grades, I've done all the assignments on time, I've led the student council all year. The only thing that's brought me any kind of joy and excitement is the idea of planning prom with Reese, but we're already running into budget problems. We've been saving for years and it's *still* not enough.

"You know what I want? I want a total do-over of my time in DC. Or for anything that happens back home to feel half as important." I groan. "I'm jealous of you, Reese. You had the time of your life here, you figured out exactly what you wanted to do with your life, and when you got back, *everything* you wanted was waiting for you."

"You mean Heath?" he asks, and I nod. "Never pegged you for the romantic type. You know, I think last summer changed you."

"In a good way?"

He shrugs. "To be determined."

We stand, and he leads me off the train as I think of the many ways I am different. I'm so used to thinking ahead, but for some reason, I can't stop thinking of the summer. And thinking of the past is tripping me up as I plan my future.

Reese leads us through his old stomping grounds. The café where he'd always stop to get an espresso, the shop with the mannequin he sketched on his very first day in Paris, and finally, to Riley Design—the school Reese attended this past summer.

But once we arrive, it's clear something's off.

"I ... know this was the place," Reese says with a tremble in his voice.

"Maybe they just moved to a different building or something," I offer.

I step under the awning and look at the directory, but it's been wiped clean. The first, second, and third floors all say Vacant. Back out from under the awning, I walk up to Reese, who's staring at his phone.

"I can't believe I didn't know this," he says, showing me the list of Riley Design's international campuses. "Their website says they've closed their Paris school."

The silence stretches between us. Reese's hands, still clutched to his phone, slightly tremble, so I drape an arm around his shoulders.

"Are you okay?" I ask.

"Everything I did, it was right here. My designs were hanging in the third floor hallway. I first learned to sew in room 304. Professor Watts made me a better designer in her office. That whole summer was contained in this building, and it's like I have nothing to show for it now."

"I'm sorry, Reese." I pull him closer and say with a sigh, "I know how you feel."

CHAPTER SIX

GABRIEL

I CAN'T TELL IF my legs are shaking due to my nerves or the weather. It's *cold* today, with the high barely piercing the forties, and the winds on Lake Erie are no joke. I'm sitting on a bench, looking out over the water, but I keep turning back to see if he's here.

Even though Matt lives in central Pennsylvania, he and his family spend winter break with his cousins in Indiana. He suggested we meet up along the way, and his family agreed to a pit stop here, which means that our long-distance relationship is about to become a whole lot closer... for the next few hours, at least.

It's been four months since I've held Matt's hand. It's been four months since I've kissed those soft, gentle lips. And if I have to wait one more minute, I might just completely spiral. With the wait to hear back on my Ohio State application still three and a half months away, I've been working with my therapist on patience.

But knowing he'll be here any second? That kind of impatience can't be rationalized away.

"Oh hey!" a voice shouts from behind me, and the sense of relief is immediate. "Is that my very hot, *very long-distance* boyfriend over there on that bench?"

I jump up and turn, and Matt's grin is so wide I want to run to him. But I'm also kind of frozen in place, maybe literally. But that's okay, because he's already sprinting my way, blondish-red hair bouncing along with every step. Within seconds, his lips are on mine, his arms are wrapped around my body, and his presence thaws me completely.

"Thank god it was actually you," he says with a laugh. "Could have gotten pretty dicey if I just shouted that at a stranger."

As I rest my forehead on his, I rack my brain for a quippy reply, but ultimately just settle for the only thing my brain wants to say: "I missed you so much."

"I missed you too," he says, before pulling me into another kiss. "I love our FaceTimes, don't get me wrong. But I can't run my hands through your hair like this, I can't get all wrapped up in your hugs like this."

He squeezes me tighter, and I give him a light kiss on the neck. "I missed *your* hugs. You give exceptional hugs, and I can't believe we didn't do more of that back in Boston. How's your cross-country trip going so far?"

"Pennsylvania to Indiana isn't exactly cross-country," he says with a laugh. "I can't believe you drove all the way from Gracemont to Sandusky to meet me for the day. I'm so glad you did, but you must be tired."

"Nah, it's fun," I say as a smile comes to my lips. "I don't usually get to drive this far, and I haven't been here in a while. I can't believe my parents actually let me come on my own, but I really laid the guilt on thick. It helps that Mom and Dad dated long distance for a couple years after college."

He laughs. "Whatever you did, it worked. Because I'm here with my boyfriend in beautiful Sandusky, Ohio, and we're going to make the most out of this day."

The Erie lakefront is beautiful, and it makes me think of all the times the boys and I would make our parents take us to the amusement park out this way, Cedar Point. These minivacations always felt so special, even if they lasted just a few hours.

"You can see the rides from here," I say, gesturing at the roller coasters off in the distance. "That one is absolutely wild. Your feet are dangling, and they just kind of launch you out over the water. And that one's Millennium Force—it's so fast that once I was riding it with the boys in the rain and we had all these red dots on our arms from how hard the rain was hitting us."

"Oh wow. It sounds awesome." He sighs. "Though I should tell you now, I'm embarrassingly afraid of roller coasters. Like, the thought of going on one can make me sick."

I pull back in surprise. "Really? You seem like the type of person who's afraid of nothing."

As we walk, I feel his arm wrap around my waist and pull me closer. It's a little awkward to walk while we're joined at the hip, shuffling along to keep our steps in line with each other. His eyes are forward, but his expression looks a little sad, and I wonder if I've said something to upset him.

"There's a lot I'm afraid of," he says. "I mean, not, like, ghosts."

"Hey, ghosts are scary, I wouldn't judge." I pause. "What else are you scared of?"

"Recently? I was afraid of this, actually. All week, I was terrified that this wouldn't feel special. That seeing you wouldn't bring back the same feelings, or that it would be awkward seeing you in person after so long. But it's so totally not."

"Long distance is hard," I say, "but I, for one, think we're crushing it."

"I couldn't agree more." His hand slips down from my waist, and I catch it with my own. "Seeing you now just...makes it all worth it, you know? Just seeing you, touching you. All of it."

We're alone in this city park, so I steal another kiss. We lean into each other and sway back and forth. I don't know what thoughts are rushing through his head, but my thoughts feel so jumbled. My pulse quickens when I think about how little time we have here. My breaths shorten, and the ache in my chest returns.

I meet his eyes, and he gives me a soft smile that melts my insides.

"Everything okay?" he asks.

"Yeah, now it is." I return his smile. "One thing Dad said before I left was that back when he and my mom were long distance, they would meet up and things would feel so right. Not everything has to be physical, obviously, but just having that little bit of validation that you're in the same room, on the same page, it's something so special that no one who hasn't experienced it could possibly get it."

"I think I get that now," Matt says, pulling me in for another kiss. "So, itinerary for today: first up, there's this adorable Christmas shop in town. I was hoping we could walk around that way and, if you're up for it, maybe meet my family for lunch?"

I hesitate, just slightly, knowing that this is a big step. Sure, I've met his parents and younger sister on FaceTime, briefly, but meeting them in person, middate? This feels like a big step for us.

Just for luck, I plant one more kiss on his lips.

"That sounds perfect. I was hoping I'd get to meet them for real on this trip."

• • •

Hand in hand, we peruse the cramped aisles of the Christmas store. Decorations line the aisles, everything smells like pine, and even though it's mid-December, I really feel myself getting into the holiday spirit.

I don't plan to buy anything, but I can't help myself from looking closely at all the decorations. The corny holiday signs, the overly religious figurines, the snow globes, and everything in between.

We turn a corner, and a giant animatronic Santa starts dancing to Christmas music. Both Matt and I jump back.

"Holy shit," Matt says. "I'm sorry but animatronic toys really freak me out, and who is buying a life-sized dancing Santa?!"

"I did *not* expect something so demonic in a Christmas store." I laugh and put my arm around his waist. "Don't worry, though, I'll try to protect you from any more dancing decorations."

He fake swoons. "My knight in shining armor."

We wind through the aisles until I stop at a stand of small, bedazzled ornaments and reach out for one in the shape of sunglasses. It seems like it doesn't fit in this store, something so summery in the wintry months, but something draws me to it.

"Oh wow. Those are just like those neon-colored sunglasses you always used to wear in Boston," Matt says. "Just looking at them reminds me of those hot, sunny days where we'd have to canvass for donations on the street."

"I've had those glasses for so many summers now," I say. I think of Boston, sure, but it also reminds me of Sal, Heath, and Reese all sitting on our picnic blanket on the baseball diamond. It reminds me of all the times we'd be at Sal's aunt's for pool parties, or Heath's house for cornhole tournaments, or Reese's family's annual Fourth of July party. For a decade, summers were solely our thing, but now it feels good to have new memories to fall back on, especially when they're happy memories with Matt.

"Can I buy that for you?" he asks. "Maybe this ornament will give you something to remember me by when we're all overwhelmed at our big family holiday parties. At the very least, it will remind you of the time we got attacked by an animatronic Santa."

"You don't have to do that," I say with a chuckle, but he's already proudly marching toward the register, ornament in hand.

And even though he's only leaving me for a minute, my heart aches as he walks away.

CHAPTER SEVEN

REESE

HOW DOES A SCHOOL just disappear?

I mean, okay, the building is here. If I went through those locked doors and up that elevator in the back, and out into the third floor, I'd eventually come across Professor Watts's office. Farther back I'd hit the design workshop classroom. All the *rooms* are still there, but now they're all empty?

"The doors are open," Sal says. "The building still has a security guard in there. Do you want to ask him what happened?"

I hesitate, knowing that all I really want to do is recede into my journal or call Heath. I can't even text him right now. But...

"No, it's fine." I pull it together. "It's not a big deal."

It is *a big deal,* I remind myself.

"It is a big deal," Sal says, echoing my thoughts. "You were so excited to go back and visit your professors. You even brought your sketchbook with designs you've made this year. You'd think they would have, I don't know, let their students know they were packing up."

My phone vibrates, so I check it.

thx for the bday messages bb!

i feel old and wise now

enough about me! have so much fun seeing your school today

I groan. "I'm so embarrassed. It's like my whole summer didn't even happen."

"I wouldn't say that." Sal takes my hand and leads me down the street. "Here, let's get you to that café you liked."

While we walk, I debate what to tell Heath. He wouldn't care, of course. I mean, he would *care*. Like, he'd FaceTime me right away and try to make me feel better, but I don't want his pity, his concern. *Especially* not when I already feel bad for missing his birthday.

Shame gnaws at me, so as we approach the café, I type out a quick message:

It's been so great I forgot to take pics! Love you!

I put my phone away and ignore the buzzing in my pocket. Last summer, when I toured the city, I was truly off the grid. I didn't have an international plan and just used Wi-Fi to send my messages or calls. But my parents splurged for a weeklong international plan for this trip, which I appreciated...

Until this moment, when I really want to be by myself.

"One espresso and one cappuccino, please," Sal orders, in French, at the bar. He gives me a wink. "I've got this. Go grab a seat and leave the rest to me."

I do as he says and leave the rest to Sal.

Sal, who has better grades than me in this class.

Sal, who always gets complimented on his perfect accent.

Sal, whose summer *actually counted*.

I take a few cleansing breaths and remind myself that it's not his fault. If anything, he's trying to help. Which is why I offer a weak smile when he brings over our drinks.

"Can you show *me* your sketches?" Sal asks.

"What?" I ask before taking a sip of my espresso. "No, they're not ready yet."

"Oh, come on, you never show us anything. You couldn't wait to share them with your professor. Just show them to me."

I sigh, then pull the floppy sketchbook out of my shoulder bag. I flip back and forth to try to find one that's ready. One that's just right. But nothing jumps out to me. The silhouettes are too similar, the designs are too basic. The style is dated, but not retro enough to be cool.

Nothing feels right.

"Yoink," Sal says as he takes the sketchbook from me.

I scoff. "Did you just say 'yoink'?"

"Sound effects seemed appropriate. You weren't giving me this book anytime soon. It had to be yoinked; I don't make the rules." He flips to the middle of the book, and his fingers brush the pages. "Oh, fun."

Despite the chilly breeze that's in the air, heat rushes to my cheeks. He's silent as he takes in the rest of the looks. He inspects every design closely, yet provides none of his trademark snippy feedback. I get the very real urge to *yoink* it back from him, but I busy my hands instead with my now-empty espresso cup.

"Reese, this is nothing like what you showed me before. This isn't a sketch of a fluffy dress in the window of a shop. This is—"

"I told you it's not ready!" I interject.

"—totally original. So creative. Some of these dresses are sleek, others are so campy. Why does this one come with a telephone fascinator?"

He points to a sketch of a dress that is, admittedly, one of the stranger things I've ever created. It's a tight flapper dress, but instead of fringe, the dress has dozens of those old spiral telephone cords. The headpiece would be made of the old phone it would connect to.

"So a few weeks ago, I had to bring up decorations from my parents' basement. While I was down there, I found a couple of old phones from a box of Granny's stuff—they had these spiral cords that connected to the speaker." I laugh. "It's so weird, I know, but I saw it and was like 'how cool would it be if I made this into a dress?' It would be so hard to execute, since the slip is supposed to be really light and bouncy and those cords are a little stiff. But I think if I had enough of those cords, and I was strategic and maybe cinched my waist or something it would—"

"Wait," Sal says. "Cinched *your* waist? Reese . . . who are these dresses designed for?"

"Right." I tense up. Of all the boys, I never thought Sal would be the first one I tell this to. "I think I want to try being a drag queen."

• Golden Boys •

GABRIEL + HEATH + REESE + SAL

lol thanks for all the birthday messages guys

overwhelmed by love (H)

Shit! Sorry! I meant to text after I got to Sandusky.

(G) But happy birthday!

(S) Happy 18th birthday, Heath! Buy us some lotto tickets for when we get back?

(R) Just want to point out that I texted him separately. You guys suck.

AND reese got me a birthday cake

so yall need to step it up H

Do you want me to sing happy birthday in a voice message?

G You know I will

dear god no H

S What are you up to for the big day?

tons of stuff!

gotta get going actually but miss you guys H

CHAPTER EIGHT

HEATH

SOMEHOW, I'M ALONE IN this damn town again. Reese and Sal are gallivanting through France, Gabriel is up in Sandusky making out with his boyfriend, and normally this would make me so jealous.

But this is a new Heath. Maybe it has something to do with Reese, or Diana and Jeanie, the new family I connected with this summer in Daytona. Or, maybe it has something to do with me turning eighteen today.

Though, as I lie back in my bed, throwing a baseball toward the ceiling and catching it over and over *and over* again, I do feel a little lonely. Feeling lonely seems a little healthier than feeling jealous, but it still sucks. The pillow next to me kind of smells like Reese, though it could just be my imagination, and I wish we were back in each other's arms again.

A pang of regret thrums through my chest for lying to the

boys about my thoroughly nonexistent big plans today, but there's probably no harm in a little white lie. If Reese knew I was here, bored to death, he'd probably be worried about me. He's been so excited for this trip, I know I can't get in the way of that.

"Hey, Heath?" my dad asks just before entering my room. "How's it going?"

I throw the ball into the air again and let it fall into my palm.

"Good, just bored."

"I wanted to see if you, um, wanted to go to the batting cages again today. I just called and they have openings all afternoon."

I sit up and try to roll the dull ache out of my shoulder. "Yeah, sure. I could always use the practice."

"Right! And you don't get much of that now that we moved to this damn apartment." He wipes his brow. "I mean, I love it here, don't get me wrong. But you know, we liked having the space."

He's definitely acting weird, and I wonder if it's because he's got some birthday surprise for me. He always gets this way when he's trying to keep a secret. Or maybe with all the busyness of the school year, he just forgot to get me anything.

He steps away, so I hop out of bed and pull on one of my many Gracemont High school spirit tees.

I volunteer to drive, since my truck's already got all my baseball gear in the cab, and within a few minutes we're on the road and ready for the twenty-minute trip to the batting cages.

"This thing really does drive smoother than it did before, huh?" Dad asks, making me realize this is probably the first time he's been in the car since I left for Daytona.

"Not gonna lie, it's probably the best money I've ever spent, even if it did take up most of what I earned working in Aunt Jeanie's arcade." I break into a laugh. "You know how we're always saying they need to repave Jordan Road? There were a few times when I had Reese in the truck, and we'd hit a bump, and he'd just go flying. He even had his seat belt so tight, but it never mattered. Thankfully he doesn't have to deal with that anymore."

"One of the many ways it was a great summer for you both."

I nod. "Yet here I am again, the odd man out while everyone else is having these amazing experiences."

Shit. Okay. Maybe I'm a little jealous.

"I'm sorry, buddy," he says. "I know it was hard being away from your friends all summer, but now having to be away from them on your birthday too? *And* on your first ever birthday with a boyfriend?"

I blush. "Okay, okay, that's enough. Gabriel comes back tonight; the others will be back in a couple of days. It's no big deal. Really."

We sit in silence for a couple of minutes as we get closer to Mansfield, where the batting cages are. At a stoplight, I play some music on my phone and drop it in the cup holder to amplify the sound. When I glance up, Dad's got this sad expression on his face, and I can only guess what that's about.

"I'm sorry we—I—couldn't do anything fun like send you to Paris."

I shrug. "I'm not even in French class."

"You know what I mean. You had to pay for the new shocks

yourself. You don't even have a working radio in the car, or a way to play your music through the stereo."

"It's all busted, that'd cost hundreds. But really, don't worry about it."

We ease into the parking lot, and I pull into a spot a few lanes back from the batting cages.

"I know we don't have enough money to splurge on things too often. *However!* I do have a birthday surprise that might make up for that."

And for as much as I've tried to stay nonplussed for this whole conversation, my ears definitely prick up at the sound of a gift.

"Three hours of batting practice on me," he says, and I try not to show the disappointment in my face. I kind of assumed he'd be picking up the tab here. But as we walk toward the door, I hear a girl call my name. A girl whose voice sends me straight back to the beach.

Dad chuckles, then says, "For you *and* your cousin Diana."

• • •

After what feels like hours of gratuitous hugging and squealing, Diana and I step into the shop. It's a pretty bare studio, dimly lit with fluorescent lights. At the front is a glass case full of vintage baseball cards, signed baseballs, and other memorabilia, and behind the case sits Dave, the guy who was my first baseball coach back when I was a kid.

He gives us a wave, and Diana and I make our way to the batting cages in the back. The shop has a long rectangle interior, shaped perfectly for batting cages, but too narrow to be any other kind of store. I drop my bag on the bench outside the two cages, pull out a few bats.

"Hey, Dave! Got an extra helmet for her?" I ask. "I was going to let her use mine, but I'm guessing my head's a little bigger."

"Are you calling me dumb?" Diana asks with a fake gasp, and I blush as Dave crosses toward us with helmet in hand.

Diana gets in the cages first and stares down the barrel of the pitching machine, before timidly backing against the side of the cage.

"It's just going to . . . shoot the ball at me?" she asks in a meek voice.

I laugh. "Basically. But don't worry! It's not too fast. And it won't hit you, so scoot closer."

She does, just as the machine launches a ball at the plate. She yelps and swings wildly, somehow connecting with the ball and sending it flying.

"I hit it!" she squeals. "Wow, that hurt. Is it supposed to hurt?"

"Not usually—your grip was just a little weird." I show her how to position the bat in her hands better. "If you back up too far you won't be able to hit it right. Get a little closer, firm up your grip some, and try again."

She gets the hang of it after a while, but before we can get through the first set of twenty balls, she's ducked through the entrance.

"You're up," she says, so I put on my helmet and step inside. "So how have things been?"

"Perfect," I say before launching a baseball straight back at the machine. I roll the ache from my right shoulder.

"You and Reese still..."

A smile comes over my face. "Yeah. Never been better. I miss him like crazy."

"I'm pissed I *still* don't get to meet him, but when your dad offered to fly me up here, I wasn't going to say no."

I smack another ball, but I hook it too far to the left. Foul.

"This was Dad's idea?" I ask. "I kind of assumed you begged him."

"I was just going to buy you a cake or something, but I liked his idea way better. Our school's not out until next week—I know, what the hell?—but Jeanie let me call in sick so I can make this a long weekend."

"Well, I appreciate it, D."

My hands start to cramp, but I push through. Usually, this is when I'd zone out—totally dissociate from what I'm doing. The more I can make my baseball experience a subconscious one, the less I overthink about it on the field. The less I can worry about losing my scholarship, or—

"Aah!" Diana shouts as I twist away from a ball that slightly grazes my arm.

"I'm okay," I say quickly, ignoring the spike of anxiety in my chest.

If I'd have taken the hit directly to my arm, it would've hurt, but it probably wouldn't have caused real damage. Probably. But...

"Diana," I say as she climbs into the cages with me, pushing me back against the wall so we don't get hit by any other balls. "Only one person is allowed in here at a time."

She rolls her eyes. "You told me these things can't hit you! Are you okay? You seem really freaked out."

"I'm fine," I say. "It's nothing."

We take our places again, Diana firmly outside the "death trap" as she calls it. I nail a few more pitches, and I'm getting back in the swing of things. I don't zone out, not anymore.

Coach says I'm almost guaranteed the Vanderbilt scholarship, though I won't find out officially until mid-May, after they get my stats from the first half of the season. But regardless of my stats, the scholarship is fully dependent on me being able to use my limbs. Which means even the tiniest injury could jeopardize everything.

"Spill it, Heath, or I'm going to break in there and stand in front of the plate." She folds her arms.

I sigh and hit the big red stop button on the back wall.

"I appreciate you wanting to be a martyr, but I know you're bluffing." I smirk. "It's just a little scary. I have this tower of scholarships that all need to pull through for the exact right amount of money at the exact right time. Vanderbilt baseball has been my goal for so long... but one false move, or one broken bone, or *any-thing*. And it's all gone."

"I understand," she says, and I cherish this rare earnest moment from Diana.

I think of Sal and Reese, gallivanting through Paris as we speak. They all have backup plans on top of backup plans. But not me: I have one chance, and unlike them, I can't afford anything messing it up.

"I know you do," I say.

And though I love my friends, and Reese, I'm so glad to have someone who really understands this side of me too.

CHAPTER NINE

GABRIEL

"I CAN'T BELIEVE WE already have to say goodbye," Matt says. We both lean against my dad's car, and my heart sinks alongside his. "Glad we got to see each other, though, and I think you impressed my mom."

"Aw, really?" I ask as I curl into him.

"Definitely! When you went to the restroom, she wouldn't stop talking about that LGBTQ+ advocacy group you set up at your school. The school she teaches at is super liberal, and they still have problems getting people to coordinate these kinds of things."

I shrug. "Sal's mom—the vice principal there—has been super supportive of it. Probably couldn't have done it without her."

"Most people wouldn't even have tried." He squeezes me tighter.

We're stalling, and we both know it. If I don't get on the road soon, I'll blow past my curfew, but everything in me wants one more minute with him. One more kiss. One more hug. Even hearing his voice is different in person.

He releases me, and I open the car door as slowly as I can.

"I hate saying goodbye," I say, "but this really has been a perfect day."

"We should figure out a date for our next FaceTime date soon. It's my turn to pick the activity. What do you think about a cooking date? We could choose an easy recipe to make together on FaceTime, and then we can sit down to a nice romantic meal."

"I mean . . . I can barely bake pizza rolls without burning them, but that sounds nice. It's going to be a disaster."

"Maybe! But that's the fun of it." He places his lips on mine, lightly. "Gabe."

"What?"

He smirks, and I trace the cut of his jaw with my finger. "I just like saying your name."

And I like hearing it. To everyone, I'm still Gabriel. Inspired by the impulsive, fun person that Sal made me, I adopted his nickname for me over the summer, becoming Gabe. I still don't know how to reconcile my two lives, not yet.

"My parents are going to kill me if I don't leave *now*," I finally say. "I'm sorry."

"Hey, I don't want you to get in trouble." He gives me one last kiss. "Until next time?"

• • •

I get into Dad's car and slowly pull out of the parking spot. Within minutes, I'm on the highway again, racing the setting sun as I take this long drive. There's a part of me that feels so fulfilled. So right. I just got to see my boyfriend, and it was only a ninety-minute drive.

But the other part of me, the darker part, is growing. I feel my anxiety and my insecurity teaming up on me, and before I know it, I'm practicing the breathing techniques my therapist's given me.

Coping mechanisms.

I can't even put a finger on what I need to cope from. I had a good day. A *great* day.

"Siri, call Sal."

She responds. "Calling Sal."

And just like that, it's like I'm reaching for my security blanket again. Since everything that went down this summer—almost ruining my new relationship with Matt by falling into our old routines—we've gotten closer. But at the same time, we've respected our new boundaries.

Sal and I have a really strong friendship now. Emphasis on the *friend* part of that word.

"Bonjour," he says.

"Oh shit. I totally forgot you were in Paris. How messed up is that?"

He chuckles. "It's fine. We're back in our hostel. Reese says hi."

"Tell him I say hey. Everything go okay today?"

"We'll...chat about that later." I sense the awkwardness in his voice. "What's going on? I assume some crisis?"

"Maybe I just wanted to chat with my best friend on the drive back from seeing my boyfriend!" I say, a little defensively. "But no, you're right, I'm kind of freaking. It was really hard to say good-bye to him."

"It's the first time you've seen him since the summer," he responds plainly. "That's not surprising. You barely had any time together."

"But that's just it," I say. "When will we ever have time together? We don't even know the next time we'll see each other. He's so far away."

Sal sighs. "That's why they call it long distance, babe."

I grip the steering wheel tighter. "Don't patronize me."

I know he means well, but sometimes his blunt tone really pisses me off. Before this summer, I might not have called him on it, but not now. The power dynamics changed between us in a good way, and I think we are on an equal footing—not to mention, after being shouted at by Bostonians all summer, I'm not the coward I once was.

"Sorry, Gabe," he says softly. "I know this is hard for you both, but it's been months and you're still in it. You're both still invested in it. You two can make it work; it's just going to be a rocky start."

"Yeah, you're right. This is literally what we signed up for, and you know what? Today was perfect."

"Tell me about this perfect day," Sal says. "Let me give an AirPod to Reese; he'll want to hear all about it too."

"Gabriel!" Reese says. "It's lights out in ten, so cut straight to all the juicy details."

I laugh, and launch into a description of our day, from the

walk around Sandusky, to meeting his parents, to stealing as many kisses as I could. Eventually, they have to go, so I keep replaying the good moments, and on the way home, I put on a playlist of all our favorite songs to keep him near me, even if he's not physically here.

I know we can make this work.

iMessage

GABRIEL + MATT

> Made it back. Thanks again for everything today. 🖤 G

Hey love. Glad you made it back safely.

I know what we have is… hard, to say the least, but seeing you today made me realize just how lucky I am to go through something like this with someone like you.

M Maybe if you start begging your parents now, they'll let you come meet me in Pittsburgh someday? That's almost right in between us.

That would be awesome. I'll try, but Dad's always a little weird about me driving long distances.

Maybe next time we can see each other for longer too?

Or you could even come to Gracemont for prom?

Yes! That would be so much fun. We'll figure something out, I promise.

Love you.

CHAPTER TEN

SAL

TODAY, WE HAVE ONE last breath of free time in the city, but this one's a little more contained. We're in a touristy district of Paris, where there are plenty of shops for us to peruse and, if we want, buy souvenirs for our friends and family.

Skipping the tacky shops with ornaments and key chains, Reese and I take a look at a few boutiques in the area so he can get a little more inspiration. So much of this trip has been him taking the lead—I mean, he *did* live here, and after seeing how heartbroken he was about his school closing, I was happy to take the back seat. I mean, I'd already seen all the tourist attractions, and I've had my fill of cappuccino, so I'm content.

Just… content. Which is how I've felt about everything in my life post-DC.

"Anywhere else you want to stop?" Reese asks.

I shrug. "Not really."

He leads me to a bench, and we take a seat and get ready for some prime people-watching. It still kind of blows my mind to think that I'm thousands of miles away from home. My brain drowns in its thoughts: Should I leave the country? Should I stay in town? Should I give up on looking for other options and try to make it in DC? Like, *really* try?

There are so many choices, my brain short-circuits every time I think about it.

"Sal," Reese says, snapping a finger in my face. "Sally. Saller-son. Snap out of it!"

"Huh?"

"What's going on? I feel like both of us have been a little out of it this whole trip—I know why I have, but what about you? You're golden here. I may have lived in Paris, but you fit in way more than I ever did."

"Just because I'm better at French than you, doesn't mean I fit in more."

He glares at me, and I don't blame him for it.

"Sorry," I say. "I've been trying to be less of a jerk lately."

"You're doing a great job so far." He smirks. "But I'll give you a pass, since you're obviously going through something."

I fidget with the collar of my coat and keep my eyes on the pavement in front of me.

"I just can't stop thinking about the future," I finally confess. "And... I still haven't told my mom I don't want to go to college. At all."

"Why not? You'll feel better if you just get it off your chest."

"It's not that easy. See, I don't have an argument for this. I don't have a definite plan. I don't know what I want to do! I can't just go to my mom and say, 'Oh, hey, I'm not going to college, it's just not for me. Oh, what will I do instead? Aw, shucks, I'll just figure that out later.'"

"Aw, shucks?" Reese bumps me with his shoulder.

"You know what I mean. I just keep thinking that if I could get a plan together, maybe even make a presentation about it, then maybe my mom would—"

"You're *not* going to tell your mom about this via PowerPoint."

"That's how I came out to her, so why not?" I throw my hands up and sigh. "Then how do *you* suggest I tell her?"

"Just say you don't know what you want to do. None of us really know what we want to do. Gabriel's debating between, like, six majors; I want to go to design school even though I keep changing who I'm designing *for*; and Heath..."

"Besides baseball, what *does* he want to do?" I ask.

"I ... don't know."

We sit in silence for a bit, and I'm guessing Reese feels a little embarrassed for not knowing what his boyfriend wants to do with his life. But I feel just as bad. We're all best friends, and every time we talk about colleges, he just brings up baseball.

"Maybe he's just as confused as we are," I offer, to no response. "Anyway, you're right. I need to just tell my mom. Maybe she can help me figure it out. She's been a lot better lately, but I'm afraid telling her this might bring the old her back. The panicked helicopter mom who's always seconds away from deeming her son a failure."

Reese cups my hand with his and gives it a firm squeeze. "Just ask for her help. That's what she's there for."

Of course, Reese could tell his moms that he's decided to start a death cult and they'd probably be like, "Sure, baby, whatever you want, we're behind you one hundred percent, need to borrow our credit card?"

But that's not how Mom is. She's shown me over and over that her love is conditional, and even though she's been so much better lately, I worry this will be the thing that ruins all the progress we've made.

CHAPTER ELEVEN

REESE

WHEW. SAL IS GOING *through* it right now. I know his mom is a bit of a hard-ass, but we're in *high school*—are we really supposed to know exactly what we want to do for the literal rest of our lives?

Though, as he inches closer and closer to becoming our class valedictorian, there's got to be a lot of pressure that comes with that. Every graduation since we got into high school, our valedictorians have had these big lofty speeches about the future. They all proudly announce what college they're going to, what they're studying, and make everyone else feel like futureless weirdos.

Actually, Sal would be a fantastic valedictorian.

That said, his insecurity is tripping up my own. I mean, I haven't told anyone, except Sal, that I want to do drag. I don't even know how to start, if I'm being completely honest. Sure, I can kind of sew my own clothes, but all I've done so far is create a few shirts based on patterns of clothes I already own. I've never tried a dress. I've never really tried makeup...

I turn to Sal, and I see the brush of highlighter on his cheek. The light foundation across his face, and I remember that he has a whole vanity back at home.

"Sorry to change topics, but can we pop into one more store?"

"Sure, where?" he says.

"Can you help me pick out some makeup?" I ask, ignoring the wobble in my voice. "And don't tell the other guys. Not yet, at least."

He agrees, so we walk through the plaza to get to the nearby cosmetics shop.

One piece of feedback Professor Watts gave me last year, at my Parisian school that *very much existed*, was that some of my dress designs looked like they were made for drag queens. It's not a huge surprise, since so much of what made me want to design dresses was inspired first by *RuPaul's Drag Race*, then by following some drag queens on my alternate Instagram account that I use for all my design inspo. Over the past few months, I started following more and more—and not just the queens—some famous drag designers too, wig makers, makeup companies, and the like. And I kind of fell in love with that world.

So, yes, I want to be a fashion designer. But I want to do it for drag queens. Maybe even myself. But if I want to dabble in drag artistry at all, I'm probably going to need some makeup.

As soon as we walk in, I'm a little overwhelmed by all the items in the store. Makeup, serums, creams, and just rows and rows of tiny little canisters of various liquids. I quite literally don't know where to start.

"May I help you?" a lady asks in English, sensing (correctly) that we're tourists.

"My friend is an aspiring drag queen, and he wants to pick out some makeup," Sal replies in French. "Can you help him find the right foundation?"

She grabs my hand, and I see Sal head over toward the more colorful parts of the store. She starts by bringing out a series of liquid foundation containers of different sizes, carefully testing each on the back of her hand to show the color, then raising her hand to my face to find the right match for my complexion.

"Liquid foundation is going to be the smoothest, and it's especially good for drag—these are long lasting, which will get you through the night." She brushes it on my cheek and blends it in. She then gives me the blending brush and lets me put it on my other cheek, guiding my hand as I work.

I think about what she means by getting me through the night, and I wonder what type of drag I want to do. Could I ever walk the runway? Could I perform in a club someday? Maybe New York Reese will be able to, but Gracemont Reese doesn't have a whole lot of options.

"How does this photograph?" I ask. "I'm a little too young for the nightclub scene, at least in America."

She laughs. "Don't worry, this will be smooth and perfect for photography. It's also a more natural look," she says. "Your face can handle more, but this is a good place to start. A blank canvas."

"Thank you," I say, just as Sal comes up with a basket of colorful goodies.

"I picked out a few eye shadow color palettes you might like. This one has a lot of blues, which seems like your style."

"The darker palette would bring out his light eyes," the salesperson says. "Here, I have a sample back here."

Together, they start to paint my eyes, giving the eye shadow a soft gradient from a darker blue to a light turquoise. My eyes look bright green in this, and even without added lashes or drawn-on brows, I can feel something igniting within me. A bolder personality emerging.

The salesperson pulls out sample lipsticks and streaks them on her wrist to compare.

"Which ones are you drawn to?" she asks. "What's your aesthetic?"

"He doesn't have one yet," Sal says, but I quickly cut him off.

"A little retro. I like making mod dresses, so I'd like to carry that through with some neutrals on the lip, and—maybe with different eye makeup—a light, glossy pink. I might need darker eye makeup. Basically, I want to look like Twiggy."

She laughs, a bit vacantly. She might not have gotten my reference to the iconic sixties model, but she does what I ask, and even without a wig, I see it coming together. We make our final selections, and the cashier goes to ring it all up.

"I didn't realize how much thought you'd put into this," Sal says.

I shrug, and grab a makeup remover from the vanity. "I didn't either, really. I . . . should probably take this off before we get back. I'm not quite ready to make my drag debut on the bus to Charles de Gaulle Airport."

"That's fair," Sal says.

I pay for the makeup and stuff it into my side bag so no one can see where I've just been shopping. It's not that I'm embarrassed, but right now, this is something I'm still exploring. Something that was just between me and my alternate Instagram feed.

I say goodbye to my drag self after another long look in the mirror—the smile on my face is undeniable. It's that same sort of excitement I get when I sketch a new dress, or when I worked on my final project in fashion design school.

I pull out my phone and snap a few selfies, though I don't quite know the reason. Will I post this on my drag Instagram account? Will I share in the group chat? Maybe someday, but for now, this smile? It's just for me.

After carefully removing the makeup on my face, we walk back to the meetup spot, where a few of our classmates are already waiting. I turn to Sal.

"Thank you," I say. "For helping me out, and for keeping this a secret for a little bit longer. I guess I get what you've been saying about college—if you're not ready to talk about something, you're just not ready."

"Hey, once we get back, if you want to come hang out and use my vanity, I could help you practice." He shrugs. "You know, until you decide to tell everyone. I can also show you all the makeup tutorials I use."

I throw my arm around Sal and give him a peck on the cheek. He might be a seriously annoying person sometimes, but I feel so much better that I talked to him about this. Riley Design in Paris might be gone, but what I did over that summer wasn't for nothing.

We approach the bus, but I turn and take in the city for one last time. I might not be back here for a long time—hell, maybe I'll never come back—but I owe so much to this city.

"You know what?" I ask. "What if we themed our prom around Paris? *An Evening in Paris*, or something super cliché like that."

"I bet everyone would like that, actually. Gold and black decorations, string lights, just cosmopolitan glam." He smiles. "I have to check the budget, but if you can lead the charge on the decor, I can take care of all the event planning. We can bring it up at the next student council meeting."

I nod, and as silly as it feels, I take in every last moment as I wave goodbye to Paris.

CHAPTER TWELVE

HEATH

"I KNOW YOU SAID Gracemont was boring, but is there anything to do here that doesn't involve baseball?" Diana asks as we leave the batting cages for the second time this trip.

"Ah, sorry. You're right, this hasn't been a fun trip so far, has it?"

"Chill, Heath, it's been like twenty-four hours. But my arms are sore, and I can't spend *any* more time in that death trap." She sighs. "What other homey things do you have in this town? Like, the drive-in?"

"Closed for the season."

"What's something I can get here that I can't get in Daytona?"

I pause to think about it, and I realize there's not a ton of options. The charming parts of Ohio are ones that outsiders don't usually appreciate. The fields, the parks. We don't have a charming downtown square with cutesy shops. We have empty factories, a downtown with little more than a couple of fast-food restaurants and gas stations.

"Want to go for another drive?" I ask. It's about all I can offer.

"Boy, you Ohioans really love to drive, huh?" She laughs. "Fine. But only if you let me pick the playlist."

I smirk. "Deal."

Before I pull out of the lot for the batting cages, I shoot Gabriel a message:

hey g! gonna drive round w diana wanna join?

I pass my phone to Diana so she can let me know how Gabriel responds.

"What do you do with all that extra time?" she asks, scrolling through my text thread with Gabriel, a hint of snark in her voice.

"What do you mean?"

"I mean, you must save hours from not proofreading your texts and abbreviating everything."

I glare at her, but she just laughs. "Don't make me drive you straight back to the batting cages."

And with that, we're off. My shoulder aches from all the practice and lifting I've gotten in, so I drive with my left hand on the wheel. To think about it, I haven't given my body much of a rest since I got back from Daytona. I'm used to a pretty intense summer travel league schedule, so I can't help but feel this need to make up for it.

She starts tapping at my phone. "Can I go through your playlists?"

"I have some random taste, okay?" I hesitate. "You can look, just don't judge."

"No promises," she says, and I see her scrolling through a lit-
any of playlists. "Did Reese make all of these?"

"He makes the best playlists," I say as a smile comes across my
face. He always used to make us playlists for everything: high-
energy rap playlists to pep us up for school, low-energy singer-
songwriter lists when we're feeling emotional, top hits for our
dance parties . . .

"So he made you curated playlists for years, and you never
knew he loved you?"

"I mean, he made us all playlists."

"Half of these songs are about love, Heath. You're so dense." She
laughs. "I'm just going to play one of my own. Driving past all these
desolate farms feels a little like the end credits of the movie, so I
have this slow, all-vibes playlist for whenever I feel like I'm in a movie."

She drops her phone in the cup holder. Once Gabriel finally
responds, we go to pick him up. It's familiar, pulling in front of his
house.

"Diana!" Gabriel says as he gets into the car. "So nice to finally
meet you."

"Gabe!" Diana says in reply. "Do you still go by Gabe? I know
you kind of reinvented yourself over the summer, and I'm all about
that."

He laughs. "No, I got to be Gabe again briefly yesterday, but
I'm back to Gabriel now."

"I think I might reinvent myself after graduation," Diana says.
"I don't think I want to keep working at Mom's arcade forever, you
know?"

"You'll miss the free corn dogs," I reply.

She sighs. "I just don't know if Mom can handle it."

I turn to her, briefly, and realize that she's being serious. Over the summer, she really didn't have any other plans outside of high school, but it looks like that might be changing. I want to have a deeper conversation with her, but I'm not sure doing it with Gabriel in the back seat makes the most sense.

The others still don't know what I have planned—I mean, it's not much, really—but I do force them to stop by the gas station to get a hot beverage. I pick one of the overcaffeinated, oversweetened cappuccinos from the machine—a favorite of mine and Reese's, Diana gets a giant hot chocolate, and Gabriel gets an iced coffee. (He's been *big* into coffee since he got back from Boston—apparently Matt got him hooked on the stuff.)

"So, Gabriel—how was the trip?" I ask, and the silence that follows seems to weigh down the truck. "No good?"

"No, it was good," he says with a sigh. "I just miss him already, you know."

"And why aren't you with Sal again?" Diana asks.

I punch her lightly in the arm. "Be less blunt, please."

"I'm in love with Matt. Not Sal." He chuckles. "I was too dependent on Sal, and we've got this new, boundaries thing going on."

He pauses, and I hear the smile in his voice. "Things are finally good with us. Healthy."

"You've got to learn how to be apart before you—"

"—*Diana*," I snap. "Stop meddling!"

Gabriel just laughs, but Diana finally drops the topic.

We drive through the side roads, and I show her the many exciting parts of Gracemont, Ohio, including my old house. I take a few more turns until I'm out on Jordan Road.

"This is my favorite spot," I say, and I'm met with silence. Which is not entirely surprising, as we're flanked by two neatly plowed, empty fields. "It's perfect in the spring. Or the summer. These are huge cornfields, and when they grow in the spring, they start getting so tall you can't see any of the farmhouses in the distance. And when the sun sets? You can see every star in the sky. And it's dead quiet."

I shut off the engine. "Here, follow me."

I take some blankets from behind my seat and throw them in the truck bed. We're all bundled up, though Diana's the least prepared for this cold front, so she immediately wraps herself in the blankets. And we pile in the back of the truck, warm drinks in hand.

"I know it's not much, at least not now. It's cloudy, and it's in the middle of the day, but believe me when I say this spot is special."

"The kind of special place where you can be honest about anything," Gabriel says. "Right?"

"Sure?" I reply, as Diana buries herself farther into her blanket cocoon.

"Things with Matt are so good," he says. "I really love him. We have all these great conversations, and he creates all these elaborate FaceTime dates for us. But I miss him already.

Like, Heath, you must be missing Reese a lot right now too, right?"

"Of course," I say. "It's been awful."

"Well, imagine dating someone where it feels like that all the time. I'm trying to throw myself into school stuff, or the LGBTQ+ Advocacy Group, or *anything* to help me forget how lonely I am." He wipes a tear from his face. "But sometimes it feels like nothing's working."

"I'm sorry, Gabriel." Diana puts a gloved hand on his knee, and I curse myself for being worse at comforting my hurt friend than someone who might as well be a literal stranger. "Not everyone can do long distance, I guess. But I think you could get used to it eventually. Do you think you'll go to the same college?"

My hands start to feel numb, but it's not because of the cold. The realization I've been trying to keep at bay for so long is sinking in.

"It's possible, I guess. Matt and I both applied to Pitt, but it's neither of our top choices. My family really wants me to go to Ohio State, and I do too. But Ohio State and Pitt aren't *that* far away ... but long distance in college sounds even harder."

My heartbeat thuds, and I start to shiver. I've been avoiding this revelation for so long.

"That makes sense," Diana responds. "I still don't think I'm going to college, but my friends who went all got sucked into their campus lives, their classes, they never end up having time for anyone outside of their new world. I mean, can you blame them?"

I can't ignore it anymore, can I? After graduation, if it all works out, I'll be living in Tennessee. Reese will be in New York City. And sure, we'll try really hard to make *us* work.

But... what if we fail?

• Golden Boys •

GABRIEL + HEATH + REESE + SAL

Landed S

G WELCOME HOME

let us know when you get your bags

we're in the cell phone lot

H listening to french music

R Shit. Found my Celine playlist?

She's French Canadian though? S

H oh my god just get out here

CHAPTER THIRTEEN

SAL

OVER THE PAST WEEK, since we got back to Ohio, I've found the only thing that's cured my recent insomnia: extreme jet lag. Paris is only a few hours ahead, but I think between the exhaustion of the trip and the time difference, I've been sleeping in every day.

I haven't seen the boys since they picked us up from the airport, but that's not a surprise. With our family events, we barely see one another over winter break, except for the party we have every Christmas Eve, which just so happens to be tonight.

I've been enjoying the alone time, even if I do miss the winter days when Gabe and I would keep each other warm. But I'd rather Gabe be happy and my bed be empty than whatever it is we had . . . or whatever I thought we had, at least.

But I do need a distraction, from the boys and from my mom. Which is why I made my way to Aunt Lily's house.

My aunt's house hasn't really changed over the years, but there are little things I notice every time I come around. A few years ago, she stopped filling up the pool where the boys and I used to hang out every summer—it needed repairs, and she didn't feel like getting it repaired. Which is fair, I guess.

Last year, the siding started to come off.

Today, I'm realizing just how dingy the rest of the house is compared to Mom's.

I asked Mom about this once, and she just said, "Sal, you'll learn that people are different. People have different priorities, and that's okay. My sister has the most fabulous wardrobe you will see in this state, I promise you that. But she would let her house crumble around her." Then she smiled. "And if you look at my closet, you'd think I'm the opposite!"

If that's true, I must've gotten the best of both worlds: Everyone knows how much I care about my closet. And my room is pristine.

"What time do you have to go to Gabriel's for your annual Hanu-mas party?" Aunt Lily asks.

"Gabe calls it Christmukkah," I correct her with a laugh. "And there's no set time, but I should leave in about thirty."

"Perfect. Gives us plenty of time to gossip and exchange gifts." She narrows her eyes dramatically. "I hope you got me something good."

I laugh as she guides me into her living room, and for as much as I critique the state of her house, it's not dirty—the carpet is clean, it just looks like it came from the nineties. But it also feels cozy, especially with her big Christmas tree in front of the bay window.

"Any new 'ornaments' this year?" I ask.

"Take a look!"

I rotate slowly around the Christmas tree, taking note of the same lights and tinsel she uses every year. The 'ornaments'—if you can call them that—aren't glass spheres or angels or anything you'd see in most people's homes. In place of ornaments, she'll take printed-out photos and stick them randomly throughout the tree.

Peeking through tinsel, I see my family's past. Old Christmas parties from when Mom and Lily were kids, surrounded by cousins I've never even met. I find Mom and Dad's wedding photo—the same one Mom keeps on her bedside table—and as I go from picture to picture, I see myself age from a baby, to a toddler, to a kid, to who I am today.

Early on, Dad disappears from the photos, just like he's almost disappeared from my memory. But maybe it's better I don't remember the car accident that took his life.

"A little to the left," she says, so I break out of my trance and rotate around the tree.

I see the photo and pluck it from the tree. It's the one from this summer with me and the senator—actually, it's a screenshot of the senator's Instagram post, where he paraded me around as a shining example of his new internship program. The screenshot shows the thousands of likes this post got. I look so happy, like all my dreams were being fulfilled.

The reality could not have been more different.

"Brings back memories," I say shortly.

"From six months ago? I hope it doesn't take much effort to bring back *those* memories, otherwise you'll be a mess when you're my age."

She settles into her La-Z-Boy, and I take a seat on the couch across from her. Her sweet tabby—the most dog-acting cat in the world—jumps up onto the couch to snuggle with me.

"I want to tell you something," I say.

"Are you coming out to me *again*?" she says exaggeratedly, and we both laugh.

"No, once was enough. What I want to talk about is actually related to that picture." I sigh, long and slow. I say the words in my head, over and over, until they finally slip from my mouth. "I don't think I want to go to college."

A pause, then, "Oh?"

She does this thing, whenever I come to talk through my problems with her, where she sits comfortably in silence until I tell her the whole story. It's an old trick from her journalist days, where your interviewee feels compelled to fill the silence.

And, like a textbook interviewee, I keep talking.

"I thought I had my whole life planned out, Aunt Lily. I was going to get into a good college, get a poli-sci degree, then jet set to DC and start my life on the Hill. Going into the summer, I was already questioning college. I mean, four years of my life to get one piece of paper?"

"It's a pretty important piece of paper. To some people, at least."

"To the people on the Hill, sure. But nothing I did over the summer needed a college degree. I barely needed any on-the-job training either. My boss was obsessed with her college, but the stories she'd tell never had to do with how much she learned about politics, just the people she met and the parties she went to."

"Well, maybe for her it was a great way to network with other people in politics? Someone she networked with could have helped her get that job, even. You do get a lot from college that isn't just on that 'piece of paper.'"

"Maybe you're right." I sigh. "It's just that Mom's pressuring me so much with this and I don't know what to do. But I don't want to work on the Hill."

"Okay, let's think about it this way. You graduate from high school, you turn eighteen this summer, and you've only got *that* piece of paper in your hands. What's your next step in politics? What do you do once you're a free man?"

I say the first thing that comes to mind, semijokingly.

"I run for office."

"Oh?" she says again, crossing her legs and tilting her head slightly. Again, she's urging me to go on with a single syllable, which makes frustration bubble up within me. I came here for advice, not to talk to myself. And I was just making a joke.

Wasn't I?

"The mayoral election is coming up next year," I say. "I'd be eighteen; I could run."

"You have more experience in politics than our current mayor did when he ran, that's for sure."

"He's been mayor since I was born," I say. "No one ever challenges him. Nothing ever changes in this town."

My aunt clears her throat, and a part of me relaxes, because I know I'm finally getting advice.

"Nothing ever changes *because* no one ever challenges him."

"I could never win."

She shrugs. "Never say never. But it's also not always about winning."

My phone vibrates, and I check to see a text from Gabe. It's a selfie of him and his sister all tangled up in Christmas lights.

"I've got to go," I say. "Gabe's holiday party is about to start, and I don't want to be late."

She stands and walks me toward the door. Her supportive arm is wrapped around me, and I feel myself leaning into her. I realize, then, that I just ripped the Band-Aid off. I told a family member that I didn't want to go to college, and the world didn't end.

"Thanks for listening," I say. "And don't tell Mom. I have to soon. I just need to have a plan first. Something airtight, where she won't be disappointed."

"Oh, Sal," my aunt says, squeezing me tighter. "You don't have to have it all figured out at seventeen. And your mom's not *that* scary. She just has a plan for you, and if you tell her that plan is changing now, maybe you can work toward a new plan together. But if you wait too long…"

"I know, I know," I say, and for the first time since I can remember, I tell my aunt a lie right to her face. "I'll tell her soon."

CHAPTER FOURTEEN

GABRIEL

A COLD FRONT SWEPT in overnight, dropping temps into the twenties. A part of me loves it—the first real chill of the season hitting in late December makes it really feel like the holidays. When it comes to decorations, Mom and Dad are never big fans of putting up lights, but my sister and I are, which meant I had to wait for her to come back from Ohio State on her winter break to put them up.

"Why didn't you ask the boys to help you with this?" my sister, Katie, asks as we heave a net of lights over the bushes out front. "Heath is so tall, he could do this so much easier than us."

"Aw, I wanted to wait for my big sister," I say with a pout in my voice. "But even if it's super late this year, I'm just glad we'll have lights on outside before the boys come over for our party."

Inside the house, we have a mix of Hanukkah and Christmas decorations throughout the living room, with our menorah in the dining room and the Christmas tree in the living room. This is one of those years when Hanukkah and Christmas overlap, so from my favorite seat on the couch, I can cuddle up with my weighted blanket and watch the candles flickering and the soft lights twinkling simultaneously and think about how lucky I am to be able to celebrate both holidays with my family.

"Obligatory questions time?" Katie asks, and I laugh.

"You're not Granny. Plus, she doesn't seem to ask them anymore."

Growing up, my family all lived within a short driving distance from us, but slowly my cousins and their families started moving farther and farther away. I understand the urge to flee Gracemont more than most people, but still, holidays have felt a little less special year after year. When you have family all over the Midwest, menorah lightings and holiday parties are a little less exciting over Zoom. But it's made me closer with my sister, and Mom and Dad, at least.

I'm one of Granny's youngest grandkids, and as she gets older, she doesn't seem quite as invested in our lives as she used to be. She's still super proud of everything I've done, but it's been different lately. Specifically when it comes to her infamous "obligatory questions."

"She still asks *me* the obligatory questions," my sister explains. "Even on Zoom calls. If she's stopped asking them to you, someone's got to step in, and it might as well be me. If you're making me freeze my ass off out here I'm going to put familial pressure on you."

She clears her throat and recites Granny's questions, "Number one: How's school?"

"School is good," I reply, deadpan.

"Number two: How are your grades?"

"Still good. I think I'm getting a B in trig, which would fully knock me out of the running for valedictorian, but my GPA will still be way higher than yours was."

"Excuse me! I had a good enough GPA to get into Ohio State, and that's all that matters, thank you very much." She sighs dramatically. "No one cares about your high school GPA in the real world anyway."

I shrug, so she continues: "And finally, question three—which I know the answer to, but we must follow the rules of obligatory questions—Do you have a boyfriend?"

The third question trips me up, because I realize that Granny hasn't asked me this in a long time. In fact, Granny stopped being inquisitive about my life right around the time I came out.

"Oh my god, is *that* why I don't get any of the obligatory questions anymore?" I ask Katie. "Because she would have to acknowledge that I like boys to ask it?"

There's a thoughtful pause as Katie wraps a strand of lights around one of our front porch columns. "No, that's not it." (I don't believe her.) "She's just getting older, and I think after asking a billion times she's probably just bored of meddling in our business. I even remember back to my freshman year, when those two senior girls wanted to go to prom as a couple and the school board caused all this drama about it, I remember her saying something like, 'Oh, who cares! Let the girls dance.' I always thought that was pretty cool of her."

"Maybe it's different when the gays are in your family," I say, which makes Katie come put her arm around me.

I do remember all that prom drama, and I remember feeling a little safer at school once they let the girls go to the prom together. I remember thinking one day maybe it would be me and Sal up there, and we wouldn't have to deal with any of the drama.

A part of me still feels hurt about Granny detangling herself from my personal life, even if it is a coincidence... though I guess that's why I cling to the family I do have. My family's all been good about me being gay, at least to my face. And they love the other boys. But there are the little things, the microaggressions that I catch at family functions.

And it's not just Granny! A few uncles, aunts, cousins are a little less interested in my life, or always feel a little distant. Maybe it's just a part of growing up.

"Excuse me," my sister says with a smile in her voice. "You didn't answer the obligatory question! I repeat: *Do you have a boyfriend?*"

I plug in the lights, but even in the daytime, they look dazzling. I'm in a trance. I pause to look at them, thoughtfully, as the word slips out of my mouth: "No."

• • •

"Isn't it a little cliché to hide in the bathroom, love?"

I hear Sal's voice through the door, and it makes my heart jump. It's not that I don't want to see him, but he's probably the last person I *should* see right now. We've been doing so well lately, but that's because I've been so busy with school and enamored with Matt that I stopped seeing him as a threat—or, more accurately, a challenge—to us.

But if I open that door, I know I have to be the strong one. And I don't know if I can right now.

I wipe a tear from my face. "I'm okay."

"I'm coming in."

And he does. I'm sitting against the cabinet under the sink, knees folded up as I hold my ankles. My breaths are shallow, and I feel a little light-headed. I don't make eye contact.

He sits across from me and mirrors my body language, so I look up. I can only imagine what my bleary-eyed gaze is like, but he doesn't seem to judge. He's just sitting there, smiling softly, looking sharp in his starry blue button-up and white tie.

"No red and green this year?" I ask.

"Figured I'd go the Hanukkah route this time, get some brownie points from your mom." He smiles. "I even memorized the prayer, I think, but you'll have to test me on it later when we light the next candle."

He reaches over and gives my ankle a gentle squeeze. A small, platonic show of support, but it means so much to me.

"Can you tell me what happened? Your sister just said you ran inside and shut yourself in here, and that if anyone could get you to come out, it'd be me." He sighs. "I don't think that's true, not anymore at least. But I thought I'd try."

"Thanks," I say, before telling him what happened. I explain in detail what went through my brain before I said "No"—though, nothing really went through my mind. It was an automatic response. Because I've been feeling so down on myself lately.

"You told me your trip went well, though."

"It did," I say. "It was so great. But the whole time there was this voice in my head, reminding me that our hours were numbered. That as soon as we said hello, we'd basically be saying goodbye."

He pauses to consider this, and a part of me gets so infuriated by it. He's so methodical, considerate, and precise, while I'm the exact opposite.

"I don't know what to say," he finally says. "I'm sorry, though. I can't imagine how hard that is. But I do hope that, one day, you'll learn to live in the present a little more."

"Didn't expect cliché advice from you."

"I hate to admit this, but I don't always know the exact right thing to say. That said, I don't think you should read into it—you probably just miss him." He sighs. "You and I were so dead set on the possibility of getting boyfriends over the summer that we never stopped to think what it would actually mean if we found one."

"He and I knew what we were getting into," I say. "We talked about it in depth, and I felt so hopeful about it. But no amount of planning could make this easier. What I told Katie was simply the truth—it doesn't feel like he's my boyfriend, sometimes. Is this how every long-distance couple feels?"

"No, definitely not." He gets a little more serious. "Maybe I ruined this for you. What we had—or didn't have, I don't know— was so immediate, we were always together, always touching, always accessible. What if it's ruined your ability to be in a normal long-distance relationship?"

The doorbell rings, and I know my sister will go get it, but I don't really want the other boys to pile into the bathroom. So, with Sal's help, I get to my feet. Again, I feel the urge to pull into him. To pick the easy route.

But he just places his hand on my shoulder and smiles.

"It's not your fault," I say.

"You'll get through this," he replies, ignoring my statement. "You're stronger than you give yourself credit for. What you two have is really special."

"It is," I say.

It *is* really special. But is it too hard?

CHAPTER FIFTEEN

HEATH

AS I STEP OUT of my truck, I take in the view of Gabriel's house. A ladder still stands near a dangling strand of lights, the bushes have been hastily covered, lights blink in different cadences and with different colors and clashing whites, but it's a look so distinctly Gabriel's that it warms my heart.

I'm reminded of the various times Dad and I tried to do the same thing, but Dad being a perfectionist by nature meant every single strand had to look perfect. Every icicle light must be straightened out. It ended up looking spectacular, though.

We don't do those anymore. Not outside the apartment at least. Dad bought one of those plastic trees with the lights on them, though, and it looks pretty nice. So I guess I can't complain.

"Hello? Gabriel?" I call when I enter. When I walk upstairs, Sal and Gabriel are leaving the bathroom and Gabriel's wiping tears from his eyes.

Oof. It's going to be one of *those* parties.

"Everything okay?" I ask, pulling the others into a quick but firm hug.

"All good here," Sal says quickly. "You didn't bring Reese?"

"Nah, he's been working on a new sewing project all day." I sigh. "I haven't even seen him since I picked you guys up from the airport. But his mom's dropping him off soon."

"Ah. We all get to see the lovefest." Sal rolls his eyes, so I elbow him in the rib.

Gabriel leads us to their basement, which has become our go-to hangout ever since Dad sold the house. It's not so bad, though. His dad still calls it a "man cave" (which never fails to make us cringe), but it's actually pretty cool. He's got some old Cincinnati Reds baseball memorabilia on one wall; Ohio State flags, pennants, framed basketball jerseys, and his and Gabriel's mom's diplomas on the other. In the center they've got a pretty sweet lounge setup.

The coffee table is overflowing with snacks (Velveeta and Rotel dip, minisausages in barbecue sauce) and sweets (his mom's fantastic buckeyes, plus some grocery store cookies). Though Reese isn't here yet, he's here in spirit, because Gabriel's got his pop Christmas playlist pumping through the Bluetooth speakers.

I take a seat in the pleather rocking recliner and smile. We may never have another Christmas just like this, but I know I'll never forget how perfect this feels. I *do* have family.

"We'll do presents once Reese gets here," Gabriel says, "since Sal always gets too impatient to wait."

Sal scoffs. "Hey! Starting with Secret Santa is a sacred tradition."

I laugh. "Right, right. You know, for someone who pretends to be so even-keeled all the time, you really can't wait to open gifts."

"I'd say it's an only child thing," Gabriel ponders, "but Heath's not like that. Maybe you're just greedy?"

"Fine! I want stuff!" Sal smiles. "And if you must know, I'm excited for my gift to be opened."

The door to the basement opens, and my heart rate doubles. Gabriel and Sal both have smiles on their faces, and both of them start gesturing for me to meet him on the stairs.

I stand, even though my legs are a little wobbly. So often, it's been weird to think of Reese as my boyfriend. I've loved him for so long—first as a friend, then as more—it's hard to know when the shift happened. Sometimes we're hanging out and it's just like it was before, but other times . . .

"Heath!" Reese shouts, and starts running down the stairs as I rush toward him.

For a moment, it's cliché, it's all in slow motion. I take the stairs up as he takes them down and into my arms. He's so slight I sometimes lift him up without even meaning to, but with him coming from above, he wraps his legs around my waist and I flex my core to keep from toppling backward.

We're a puzzle, two pieces meant to entwine in one perfect way. He runs his hand through my short hair and pulls my face into his, and even though I feel the exasperated glares from the other boys, I don't care. This is my moment. *Our* moment.

"I missed you," Reese says, eyes glistening.

"I literally saw you two days ago," I say in response. "But, same."

Gabriel clears his throat, and I hear Sal say, "Can we get out of here before this turns into live action porn?"

"Sal!" Reese snaps as he drops from my embrace. "Don't ruin the moment."

I scoff. "Right, because we've *never* had to sit awkwardly by while you and Gabriel dry hump on the floor."

"That's…," Gabriel starts, then shakes his head. "We weren't that bad, were we?"

Reese and I look to each other with widened eyes.

"Maybe it just seemed like that," Reese says. "I was mostly just jealous."

We take our seats around the table, and Reese and Sal tell us more stories about the amazing time they had in Paris. Of course, we saw all the pics they sent, and we got the rundown in the truck on the way back from the airport, but hearing their stories brings on a kind of FOMO like no other. They recount zany stories, inside jokes, and it sounds like everything was perfect.

"We're going to bring it up at the next student council meeting," Reese says, "but I think we're going to make the senior prom theme *An Evening in Paris.*"

"And we'll make sure it's just like the real thing," Sal says dryly.

I laugh as we look through more photos of their trip.

"Oh, hey! You didn't show me any pictures of the school like you said you would," I say to Reese. "Was anything of yours still hanging up in the classes?"

"Right," Reese says with a cough, half choking on the sparkling water he brought with him. He shares a sharp look with Sal, then says, "Actually, yeah. Some of our designs were still hanging up in Professor Watts's classroom. It was so cool to see it all again. Really...reaffirmed why I did it, you know? I can't believe I forgot to take pictures; I just got swept up in everything."

"Yep," Sal says quickly. "I think he should have won. Those other designs were pure crap."

They laugh, and it's a little forced, and a little awkward. Reese reaches out for a buckeye while Sal takes out a compact and brushes his fingers through his hair. I notice Gabriel's studying Sal as severely as I'm studying Reese, and I pull out my phone to send a quick text.

I'm not sure what's going on. And it's probably nothing. But I'm getting the sneaking suspicion that my boyfriend just lied to my face.

iMessage

GABRIEL + HEATH

ok am i making things up or
was that weird as fuck

Sorry, trying to casually
reply without Sal seeing.

But yeah. They're being
kind of weird.

Do you think something
happened in Paris?

maybe they got into a big fight?

maybe they fell in love in paris

G That's a joke right?

obviously!!!

.... i think H

CHAPTER SIXTEEN

REESE

MY FACE IS ON *fire* right now. It's such a silly thing to lie about—I mean, schools close all the time. Probably. It doesn't mean my school was any less real. The teachers were real, my classmates were real, hell, even the alumni were real. When we toured around Paris over the summer, we met an alumna who owned her own boutique. *That* was real.

So why do I feel like my entire summer experience has been taken away from me in some way?

I've been texting with Philip, my closest friend in the program, about the school closing. He was sad, but he didn't seem fazed by it like I am. He's working on his portfolio to get "into uni," as he says, and already has his British fashion design programs all picked out. I have my American ones all picked out too, of course: FIT, Pratt, The New School. I even applied for the only program I could find in Nashville, at Lipscomb University, though I haven't told Heath about it.

I don't know if he'd push me toward it or away from it. He knows Nashville isn't my ideal location, but the program looks great! It's just not New York.

The awkwardness of the moment passes as we all catch up on winter break and hear about Heath's birthday visit from his cousin Diana, and Gabriel's trip up to see Matt. But through it all, I keep wondering: Is it normal to keep this many things from your boyfriend?

• • •

"Secret Santa time!" Gabriel eventually announces in a cheery voice, and I see Sal's eyes light up. Gabriel continues, "We'll draw names out of a hat, and whoever gets chosen has to give their gift. Sound good?"

We all nod our assent, and Gabriel pulls out the first name: Heath.

Heath stands and pulls out a poorly wrapped gift—wrapping is *not* his forte—then hands it to Gabriel. He unwraps the gift to reveal a box with a cute plushie in it. It's in the shape of a heart, and when you squeeze the TRY ME button, it glows.

"So cute!" Gabriel says, then slowly adds, "But…what is it?"

"Okay, so it's kind of cheesy, so don't make fun of me. They call it a 'long-distance hug' heart. You see how it glows? I sent one to Matt too, as part of the gift. Every time he squeezes the heart, yours glows, and vice versa. I know this long-distance thing has been hard on you, but maybe this is a cute way for you to show each other whenever you're thinking of each other."

"Oh, Heath, this is so sweet," Gabriel says, then climbs over Sal to give him a hug.

I feel tears prick at my eyes, and it reminds me of all the reasons I fell in love with Heath to begin with—his thoughtfulness, his tender heart, the way he always wants to fix things and be there for people. These months have been hard on Gabriel, so of course Heath wants to find a way to make it a little easier.

Next up is Gabriel, who gifts Sal one of those trendy portable water bottles. Over the summer, he nearly fainted from dehydration thanks to the heat, the work, and the massive amounts of iced coffee he drank, so it's a practical gift. Thankfully, Sal is a practical-gift kind of guy.

I'm next, so I give Heath my gift. My palms are sweaty as I hand it over to him, as it's something I've been working on for longer than I'd like to admit.

"It's a tie," he says warmly, like it's the best thing he's ever received. "A Vanderbilt tie."

"I, um, ordered in the fabric from a store in Tennessee. I think it turned out okay?" I say.

"You *made* this?" Heath says in genuine surprise. "I thought you got it from the Vanderbilt college store or something. Holy crap, Reese. You *did* learn a lot over the summer."

"You sound surprised," I say, and wish I could take it back.

"No, no, it's not that!"

"I know, I didn't mean it."

He sighs, smiles, and starts to tie it around his neck. Though he's just got a crew neck sweatshirt on, he keeps it on and stares at it. "You know, I hear there are going to be all kinds of formal dinners and meetings and stuff if I make it onto the team."

"If?" Sal says. "Don't you already have the scholarship?"

"Not officially. It depends how I do this season, but Coach has been talking with the admins over there and he thinks the official offer will come in this spring. But I mean, anything could happen: My grades could drop and I could get rejected from the university." His voice lowers. "I could suddenly stop playing well, injure myself, or really anything."

He looks a little dazed, but he snaps out of it to jump up and give me one of his big bear hugs. I sink into him and breathe him in. I'm relieved for two reasons: he genuinely loves it, and it shows that I really did learn something in design school.

"And finally, Sal," Gabriel says after our love fest.

Sal gets up and hands me a card. This isn't out of character for him. Sal's always been the no-nonsense type. Heath will spend hours researching the perfect heartfelt gift, but Sal will get you the most practical gift card he can find. Over the years, he's gotten them for sports equipment (Heath), donations to green organizations (Gabriel), and for me...

I open the card, and I feel three sets of eyes peering at me from over the note.

To Reese—

Save the expensive makeup we bought in Paris for special occasions. Take this MAC gift card and go nuts. I'll help you practice whenever you need, friend.

(Oh, and if you're still keeping this under wraps for now, just tell everyone it's a gift card for Michaels or wherever you buy those sketchbooks and pencils.)

Love,

Sal

"So…what is it?" Heath asks, a natural smile on his face.

I match his grin, fold the gift card up into the note and put it back into the envelope, and I lie to my boyfriend for the third time.

CHAPTER SEVENTEEN

SAL

THE BRIEF TIME BETWEEN New Year's Day and the start of school is boring. Our new classes start in a few days, our *final* set of classes, and it's really starting to sink in that in a matter of months, I'll be on my own.

"All right, Google. Let's do this," I say to my empty room.

Mom's out for the night, and most of the boys have other plans, which offers me a rare evening of silence. No responsibilities. I take a deep breath and exhale, hissing through my teeth. It's been so many months, but the idea of not being busy still makes me feel sad. Like, I have this big looming problem, but I don't have the motivation to complete it.

I *always* have the motivation to complete things.

Which is why I'm here, googling election laws for Ohio. According to the law, the only major requirement is that I'm eighteen years of age before election day. The rest of the requirements are mostly bureaucratic. Filling out the right forms will be easy enough. I have to start a petition and get signatures. Financing the campaign will be a challenge, but Gabriel could help with the grassroots stuff. Reese could help with graphics and design. And Heath's so popular in our class, he might be able to convince a lot of the seniors to vote for me.

I shut my laptop.

This is … absolutely bonkers. Sure, I can dress the part. Sure, I can lean on my DC experience. But even if this village is the size of one of the buildings in DC, no one here would vote for a teen— let alone a liberal, gay teen—to run their city.

I find myself reaching for my phone, again and again, to call Gabe. I know he'd have the right words of advice, or maybe he'd be able to snap me out of this fever dream completely. But I check one more time, and I see that our current, useless mayor has announced his run for his next term.

In the Facebook post—what a grand place to announce a political run, by the way—he explains how he is excited to serve Gracemont for four more years, and how he expects to run unopposed once more thanks to his fearless leadership.

"His leadership that turned Gracemont into the COVID capital of Ohio?" I say with a scoff. "His leadership that caused our village's only major factory to relocate to a town an hour away?"

I look at the term length again, and something feels right about it. Four years. Sure, I could go to college during that time. Maybe that's the smart thing to do. Or for once in my structured, perfect life, I could take a risk. And who knows, maybe I'll be spending those four years in town hall.

The urge to tell Gabe, or even my mom, bubbles up within me, but I tamp it down one more time and open an email to Mr. Royce, my civics teacher. Because if I'm going to try to be the mayor of Gracemont, Ohio, I have to know exactly what that entails.

CHAPTER EIGHTEEN

HEATH

BATTING PRACTICE NEVER FEELS great. It makes my hands sore, my shoulders tight, and after about a thousand smacks, an ache throbs through my entire head, piercing my temples. Ever since I almost got hit with that ball at the batting cages, I've been leery too. I don't think it'll hit me in the face or the side, or anything dramatic like that.

But it's gotten closer to me. I've dealt with my fair share of inside pitches, throws that cut so close to me I have to jump back and contort my body—but not in any way that resembles a swing, or it'll count as a strike. But when a ball comes flying at me, the knowledge that my pitching hand is *right there*. Vulnerable. And something as simple as a sprained wrist or broken finger could keep me out of commission as a pitcher for weeks. *Crucial* weeks.

But transitioning to our first real practice at the nearby indoor baseball training facility is a whole new type of fear. It's a scrimmage against the JV team, which means we have an entire fleet of new pitchers waiting to snap up a varsity spot, though there aren't many out there at my level. Grayson, a sophomore and the newest addition to the JV pitchers, comes to the mound.

"You got this, Grayson!" Assistant Coach Roberts shouts from third base. "Remember what we practiced."

He winds up, and it's suddenly very clear he doesn't *have this*. As soon as the ball leaves his hand I take a jump back. It whizzes past my face and into the netting behind the catcher.

"What's going on, Grayson?" I ask, trying not to sound too annoyed, as he furiously wipes his palms on the towel tucked into his pants. "You were way better at tryouts."

"I didn't have to pitch to *you* at tryouts," he says.

"All right, you two swap," Coach Lee says, so I take off my helmet and toss it to the side as we cross toward each other. A teammate throws me my glove from the dugout, and I lean awkwardly to catch it with my left hand.

I step up to the mound and feel the ball in my hands, while Grayson squares up against me. I take in deep breaths to get the blood flowing into my muscles. The ache in my shoulder hasn't gotten much better, but I'm still trying to work through it.

"Any day now," Coach Lee shouts from his spot behind the catcher.

I snap back into focus. I pitch, and the ache in my shoulder reverberates. It's nothing, I know. Just my body warming up; various muscles always act up for the first ten or fifteen minutes. I push through and wait for the pain to subside.

Grayson connects with the ball and drives it just over the head of our shortstop. He may be an awful pitcher, but as a batter, he's not so bad. That, or I'm slipping—I mean, that fastball could have been a lot faster. A bead of sweat runs down my back.

Each time I throw the ball, though, my shoulder ache gets less pronounced. Softer, milder, just a soft buzz. It's present, but it's not bad. I take that as a good sign.

When the next batter steps up to the plate, I throw another pitch, which curves just low enough and just close enough to be considered a strike. The spot where the magic happens. Coach Lee, acting as umpire, calls the strike, along with the two that follow it. The curveball-fastball-slider pitch series that's always been my signature knockout move.

The season officially starts in two months, and it's clear we all have a whole lot of work to do. When the next batter steps up, one of our star batters from the varsity team, I clench my grip. He's not going to make this easy.

I wind up and throw another fastball. Before my brain can fully comprehend it, his bat launches the fastball right back at me.

Gasping, I flip up my glove to protect my face in just enough time for the ball to ricochet off the tip of my glove. Behind me, the JV shortstop dashes toward the ricocheted ball and dives for it. It lands in his glove, and when he stands, he tosses the ball back to me with a smirk.

"Good catch," I say.

"That was a lucky block," he says before going back to his spot.

I laugh uncomfortably. "Yeah."

I've always thought of baseball as a sport that relied on skill, not luck. But the smallest shift can change the outcome of the game, and the outcome of my career. One home run can change everything. One injury could end it all.

A single moment can end a career. No baseball, no scholarship, no college, no future. At least, that's what I've always been told. Reese and Sal have safety nets. Gabriel's family, although I know they struggle financially, always seem to have enough to make things work out. But things don't just *work out* for me. And whether it's luck or skill, I've got this one chance and I won't let one little mistake ruin it all.

I rotate my arms to ease the pain in my shoulder, then grit my teeth and throw three fastballs, each harder than the last. Strike, strike, and strikeout.

I laugh. As it turns out, the solution is pretty easy: I just won't mess up.

CHAPTER NINETEEN

REESE

"I HOPE I WASN'T interrupting anything," I tell Sal as he lets me into his house. "I have these designs, these sketches, and I wanted to get your thoughts on what would go with them. Like, what *makeup* would go with them, specifically. I think I can make it work, but I'm still a little unsure and you're the only guy I know who really uses it and—"

"Breathe, Reese," Sal says in this unusually calm tone. "Wow, you're really nervous about this, huh?"

"I guess so. It's silly, isn't it? I don't think Heath would judge, or Gabriel, or my family or anyone, but there's this weird part of me that wants to keep this to myself until I've got it right. Like, I have to prove myself."

"I know what you mean," he says, the gravity in each word weighing down the pitch of his voice. I tilt my head in confusion, but he just waves me away. "College stuff."

I nod, remembering when he confessed to me how he didn't want to go to college, but he didn't know how to tell his mom. I feel a spike of anxiety on his behalf when I think of how that convo will go down.

"You still haven't told your mom about college?"

He shakes his head. "She's getting suspicious, though. I have to tell her soon, I just... don't know how."

Maybe that's another part of why I feel safe sharing my secret with him, and just him, for now.

"Show me your designs," he says, and I oblige.

"This is black and white, which probably doesn't help you visualize it." I draw my finger around the bodice of the dress, noting each spike that comes from the center. "This one is pretty basic, but I'm thinking white at the core with a gradient to this pale, soft blue to each peak. Cinched with a thick black belt."

"Ice queen?"

I shrug. "Something like that. It's not very original, I guess, but so many of my summer designs were of fire, I thought this might be a nice contrast. For my portfolio, that is."

"I'm not sure I'm going to be a ton of help, since I've never done drag makeup, but let's give it a shot." He laughs. "Ready?"

"Yep," I say, dumping out my bag of makeup.

He guides me by first instructing me how to put on tinted moisturizer and a light layer of foundation, which he smudges across my face with soft dabs of a fresh blending sponge.

"I'm going to be honest, I'm not really sure how to contour your nose and cheekbones," Sal says. "Should we pull up some tutorials?"

This leads us down a rabbit hole, after which I feel simultaneously empowered to do this and absolutely confident I can't even come close. I glance at Sal, whose eyes are wide. He shuts his laptop.

"Maybe you can practice that on your own?" he suggests.

I nod. "Let's play with the eye makeup, then."

I bring out the eye shadow palette I recently bought from MAC, which has the biggest variety of colors I could find. From metallics to bright colors to pastels to what seems like six shades of black, anything I need for this look should be on here.

Sal guides me through the motions, but when I start, I realize how this is just another art style. Graphic design, illustrations, sketches, line art—drag makeup is the same idea, just a different format.

"It's kind of like when I work with charcoal," I say as I bring a soft blue into the crease of my eyes.

"Try the darker shade there," Sal instructs, "then fade into the light blue. Make it kind of a smoky eye."

I do, then I spend more time than I'd like to admit trying to make the shape of each eye even.

"This looks bad," I say, which makes Sal laugh.

"Here," he says, taking a smaller brush to my face. He dusts it with the gold metallic color and brushes it against the lower portion of my lid. "You need something to break it up. Also, you should probably figure out how those queens make the whites of their eyes look bigger. The proportions look weird."

"Thanks."

He chuckles. "Just being honest."

He dusts my face with some blush and dots my cheekbones with some highlighter.

"Do you have lashes?" he asks.

"Was I supposed to buy them?"

He sighs. "Let's try the mascara."

I point to the bottle. "It's supposed to be volumizing."

"Volumizing for someone who wears makeup to work, not a drag queen who wears it to the club." He bites his tongue as he applies it. Despite what he says, it *does* do something.

"I look like...," I start, but trail off.

"Like you need a wig?"

"And a miracle."

Sal puts his arm on my shoulder and eyes me closely, and I can't help but smirk. I feel so vulnerable in this moment, but I'm glad I chose him to guide me through this.

And that's when it hits me: I feel more comfortable revealing this part of myself to Sal than I do my own boyfriend. As I stare into my own reflection, I see the color start to drain from my face, even with the blush, even with the foundation. A weird feeling of shame creeps into me, like I'm betraying Heath.

I know he would be supportive. He's always been supportive of my art, plus he loves all the drag shows we watch together. Sure, he's a little more masculine, a little less flamboyant than the rest of us. But he's still not judgmental.

"What's going on?" Sal says sharply. "Something changed."

"Nothing," I reply, a little too quickly to be convincing. "It's just... nothing."

"You look good, especially for a first try."

"It's not that," I snap.

There's an awkward moment of silence as we both just stare at each other. I want to say something, but I don't even know how to explain it. *It shouldn't be you*, is all I can think.

I riffle through my bag to grab the pack of makeup remover wipes and start going to town on my face, a blur of gold and black and blue smearing all over the cloth. As I rub my face so clean it turns red, Sal quietly places my makeup and brushes back in my bag.

"Do you want to talk about it?" Sal asks.

"No. I don't even know what to say." I sigh. "Sorry, I've got to go. Thanks for your help."

Sal keeps quiet as I pack the rest of my stuff up and head out his door. I get in Mamma's car and slam the door too hard. It's freezing in here, but I still can't bring myself to put the key in the ignition. I just put my warm head against the cool steering wheel and sigh.

My brain refuses to process my emotions, but one question keeps echoing in my mind: Why have I suddenly stopped telling the boy I love the truth?

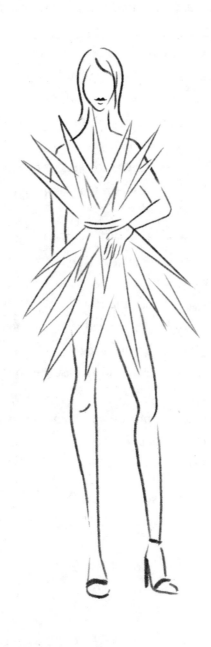

CHAPTER TWENTY

GABRIEL

"ARE YOU SQUEEZING YOURS now?" I ask Matt on our FaceTime call. "I'm not sure why this isn't working."

"Well, I downloaded the app, connected it to Wi-Fi, and I'm squeezing it. That's all there is to it, right? Should we read the instructions again?"

"We'll figure it out later," I say.

I take the phone off the shelf by my bathroom mirror, where I've just finished brushing my teeth and washing my face. The Sunday scaries are on another level right now, but I'm focusing on what my therapist tells me to do: acknowledge the emotion and play it through to the end.

What's the worst that can happen? she would say. *If that's your fear, play it through to the end.*

I play it through to the end as I walk back to bed, thinking of starting my final semester of school.

"I'm afraid of tomorrow," I tell Matt. "The first day after winter break is bad enough, but I have a meeting with Sal's mom to talk about the LGBTQ+ Advocacy Group at school. Did I ever tell you that five years ago, the school wouldn't let this girl go to prom with her girlfriend? And I might be going crazy here, but I think some books have started disappearing from the library."

"Maybe they're just being checked out?" Matt offers.

I shrug. "Maybe. They've been showing up as available when I go into our school checkout system, but before break, I could only find a couple of the books I wanted to check out over the holiday."

"Let me guess, the only ones you could find were straight?"

"*And* white." I sigh. "It's the new librarian, I think. Miss Orly. The last one would order books specifically for me, and she would have these diverse book displays. But now? It's nothing."

"Well, thankfully you have an in with the vice principal this time. Maybe you can talk to her?"

I shrug. "We're not that close."

"But weren't you and Sal *very* close?" I check his expression for any sign of jealousy, or the hurt I caused him last year. Thankfully, I find none.

"That was mostly behind her back. But she never seemed to like me, until this year, I guess. She made a big display of affection toward us all once Sal finally snapped, but she's slowly getting back into her old habits."

There's a pause, and again, I sigh.

"Or maybe I'm reading into nothing."

What's the worst that can happen? I play it through. She disbands the LGBTQ+ group, all my classes are ten times harder than I expected, and, I don't know, the librarian holds an old-fashioned Back-To-School Book Burning.

Usually when I play it through, the anxiety-inducing scenario in my brain is either too outlandish to count or totally manageable. This time, it's definitely outlandish, but either way, it usually makes me feel better.

"I miss you," I tell him. "I wish you went to school here. Maybe *you'd* actually join my club."

"I miss you too." He sighs. "Still just Heath?"

"No, we have a couple others. But out of the four of us? Yeah, just me and Heath. But Sal and Reese are always busy with student council."

"Heath's busy with practice, but he still shows up." He bites his lip. "Sorry, that's probably not helpful."

"It's fine. You're not wrong. I just want to make an impact this year, you know? To do something half as special as what we did this summer, as annoying as it was sometimes."

"I, for one, don't miss being yelled at by businesspeople on the street. I miss Art and Tiffany, though. We should do a group Face-Time soon and catch up. Think we'll ever be in the same room together again?"

I shake my head. "Probably not. But it was special while it lasted, right?"

"If it ended up with me and you together, then it was absolutely special." He winks at me, and I feel my whole body blush.

"I'm going to read some before bed to try to unwind a bit," I say. "Good luck at school tomorrow."

"You too! Love you, babe."

"Love you too," I say, ending the call just as a tear falls from my eye and down my cheek.

When I grab my book, I barely crack it open before I close it again. I lie back and stare at my ceiling, thinking of school, of Matt, of why my first love is so fucking far away from me.

And just as I start to wonder how much longer he and I can last, a bright light glows in my periphery. The heart, on my bed-side table, is glowing softly. And as I touch it, I swear I feel Matt's warmth.

"You finally figured it out, I guess," I say to the plushie like it's Matt.

Even though it's only nine thirty, I turn off the lights and hold the heart close to mine. I squeeze it, sending the warm light to his in Pennsylvania. He squeezes his, and it sends the light back to me.

And for once, it really is enough.

CHAPTER TWENTY-ONE

GABRIEL

THE FIRST DAY BACK to school after winter break wasn't a bust, but it wasn't anything exciting either. A lot of "Happy New Year" and "How was your break?" from semi–checked out teachers. My classes all seem manageable for the semester, but I'm not really excited about anything that isn't my pending OSU application. But I've been waiting for so long, I can wait until the decision comes in just under three months.

Right?

Anyway, as all my classmates start pouring out of classrooms and off to their cars, bikes, or to the buses, I wait in my English teacher's classroom. All our school's clubs have to have a teacher or faculty member signed on as the adviser, and like every good gay kid on the planet, I went directly to my English teacher for help.

"You need me to stick around?" Miss H asks, and I shake my head. Technically, she's supposed to hang around, but she's got plenty to do and hanging around a handful of awkward gay kids is probably not at the top of her priority list.

Sal pops in, and I feel my heart swell.

"I can't stay," he says, and my chest deflates. "But I wanted to say hey. Reese and I are going to work on our Advanced English homework."

"Shit, they gave you homework on your first day back?"

"I guess that's why they call it Advanced English. Mr. Marsh is a total sadist; you choosing the regular English class was the right call." He shrugs. "Oh, Mom wanted me to tell you that she can't meet with you guys today."

"Wait, what? When did she tell you that?" I start pacing the room to hide my anger. "She couldn't even tell me herself? I've been anxious about this all day."

"It's first day stuff, she just told me. I'm sorry. She's getting better, really. She just needs to push it a few weeks."

"A few *weeks*?" I sigh. "Okay, fine. Well, there goes my first agenda."

He comes over and pulls me into a hug, and I feel myself relax into it. We don't get to hug much, to be honest. We haven't really talked about why, but it's obvious. Whatever we had is over, and that's okay.

But I miss hugging him. As a friend. So I wrap my arms around him. It's quick, but it's enough. He releases me and steps back with a smile, and I feel the familiar pull to him again—this would normally be the time when he leans in for a kiss, but for obvious reasons, he doesn't do that anymore. Thank god we're both stronger than we once were.

As he leaves, Cassie pops into the classroom with Heath right behind her.

Cassie drops her book bag onto one of the free desks with a huff. She's a junior, but she moves with the sort of confidence I never had. Her freshman year, she founded the school's first advocacy group for students of color. Though our school and our village aren't very diverse, she was able to push the needle—she even coordinated a full-school assembly with an antiracist lecturer, which was no small feat for a fifteen-year-old Black girl amid a sea of mostly white rural Ohioans.

"Thank *god* this day is over." She smiles widely. "Well, not totally over, I guess. We've still got to meet with Mrs. Camilleri."

I sigh. "She pushed our meeting. For weeks."

"Really?" Heath asks. "Well, maybe that's good. Doesn't look like a lot of people are coming today, so maybe we can get more numbers by then."

"Reese and Sal are already playing the homework card," I say. "And there aren't many other openly queer people here."

Heath gives me a concerned look, but Cassie cuts in before he speaks.

"We might be able to get a few allies in the club," she says. "It's what I did for the PoC group, but sometimes they tend to center themselves and make the whole thing about them. So I'd watch out, especially if we're going to cover some big topics with her."

I blush, thinking of the many times I've spoken up in her group.

"Not you, Gabriel." She tilts her head. "Well, sometimes you."

"Sorry," I say, but she just waves me away.

"Let's get allies on board, but not for the meeting with Mrs. Camilleri—what was on our agenda anyway?"

"First, we were going to ask if there was a budget to get a queer speaker for one of our upcoming assemblies. Then I wanted to know if the school was ready to push back if there was any prom drama with, uh"—I look to Heath—"any queer couples who choose to attend."

"I've got to go," Heath says suddenly. "Sorry, Gabe. I'll explain later."

He rushes through the door, and Cassie gives me an awkward look.

"Should you not have mentioned prom?"

"Maybe not." I shake my head. "I didn't know he was worried the school would try to stop him."

"No, not that. I can't think of a single person who dislikes Heath enough to make it a big deal." She swallows hard. "Maybe something's just up with him and Reese. Some drama there, perhaps?"

She could be right. Thinking back, I realize his demeanor shifted as soon as I mentioned Reese and Sal doing homework. He can't think . . .

"I'll figure out what's going on later," I finally say. "Anyway, the third thing was about the missing books from the library."

After a bit of discussion, we work together to catalog all the books that seem to have disappeared, and we come out of it with a list of almost all queer, diverse books.

"How do we know someone's not stealing them?" Cassie says.

"Maybe a closeted person? Since they implemented that new program that alerts your parents every time you check out a book, that might have people freaked out."

"Or they could be stealing because they secretly hate these kinds of books," I offer.

"I don't know. You'd think all they'd have to do is cry to their mommy about how the library is forcing them to realize diverse people exist or something, and then they'd shut the whole library down."

I laugh. "I hate that you're only slightly exaggerating."

"People like that, they love to make the news, they love to make a big splash. I don't know, this is … quieter."

"Should we pop into the library right now? Just take a little look around?"

She smiles. "I thought you'd never ask."

CHAPTER TWENTY-TWO

HEATH

"PUT ME DOWN FOR two hours, if you have the space," I tell Dave after walking into the batting cages. My shoulder aches just from holding my bag of equipment, but I push the pain out of my mind. The only thing that'll relieve it is practice. Just like fitness training, just like endurance training. I'll take it slow, I'll stay consistent, and it'll ease.

It *has* to ease.

"Two hours?" he responds. "Shouldn't you be resting?"

"Need to improve my swing," I say shortly. "Our JV pitchers struggled a bit at our scrimmage with them, so I feel a little out of practice."

He just nods and allows me back. He loads the balls into the machine, and I warm up my neck, my shoulders, my arms. I take a few slow practice swings, and things feel okay. I pull on my batting gloves, my helmet, and grab a bat. Everything's okay.

Physically, at least.

I hit the big red button behind me, which basically tells the machine to go ahead and start assailing me with baseballs, but as I square my body to the machine, I'm not scared this time.

"So, let's review," I say to the machine. "In our last class of the day, the only one Reese and I share, I tell him how I'm glad I didn't have any homework on day one."

I swing. Miss. That's fine.

"He says, 'Same here! Maybe they're taking it easy on us this semester.' We laugh at that."

I swing. The bat connects, but my swing is too fast and the ball launches to the side. Foul.

"He tells me he's going to Sal's after to work out the budget for prom, since Reese is the treasurer and Sal is the class president. It makes perfect sense. Of course, I don't question it—" Swing. Miss. "—because why *would I?*"

Another ball is launched toward me. My bat connects with it, and it sails into the net above the machine. Home run. After a few more swings, I go and hit the button to stop the machine. I grab my phone out of my gym bag and start a FaceTime call with Reese.

As it tries to connect, I curse myself for jumping to conclusions and not just talking to him in the first place. There's probably a normal reason for it, and there's no reason that a simple miscommunication should turn me into some jealous, untrusting monster.

My breaths slow, the tension in my shoulder eases.

Until he rejects the request and follows it up with a bold-faced lie.

• iMessage •

HEATH + REESE

Sorry! Just trying to finish up this homework.

I'll call on the way home.

i thought you were doing student council stuff

· · ·

we just talked about it

Yeah I mean this student council stuff just feels like homework.

I'm doing a whole budget for prom to figure out ticket prices. It's basically math homework.

R

H

CHAPTER TWENTY-THREE

REESE

I'M NOT SURE HOW much makeup is actually on my cheeks, but it's enough that I don't see them turn bright red. In retrospect, telling Sal he could use my phone to give Heath our excuse while I evened out my eye makeup was an awful idea. Mostly because he thought our excuse was homework, when I distinctly told him our excuse was student council.

"My boyfriend now thinks I'm a liar," I say. "So thanks for that."

"You *are* a liar."

"I've been thinking about that. About why I don't feel comfortable telling him or Gabriel about this. About what we've been doing." I sigh. "But then I realized I'm not even comfortable with *you* knowing. I mean, why do you think I got flustered and stormed out last time? I wanted to keep this to myself, but I felt like I needed your help since you were the only one with the technical knowledge to help, but more and more I'm realizing I might be screwing things up with Heath."

"Then tell him," Sal says.

"I will. I have to, thanks to you. He probably thinks we're cheating or something."

"Ew," Sal says. "No offense."

I shrug. "You're not exactly my type either. But damn, you know your way around a makeup brush."

Sal once told me that his obsession with makeup started when he was a preteen; once he started getting acne, he would play around with ways to cover up pimples and ended up on this deep dive all about face care. I mean, this kid had a skin care routine at age thirteen.

But I should have gone to Heath first. Or at least clued him in earlier.

I text Heath. **Sorry. I can explain. Can you come pick me up from Sal's?**

I don't hear from him for a while. As we finalize my first drag look—or something close to it—I find myself glancing at the phone, wondering if I've gone too far, or let this go on for too long.

After twenty excruciating minutes, he finally texts me. But it's not what I want to see.

Can't. Practicing, he texts.

And I feel like I've seriously screwed up.

CHAPTER TWENTY-FOUR

SAL

AFTER YET ANOTHER SUCCESSFUL drag session, Reese's mom picks him up from the house. Mom got in a while ago, and I can already hear her banging around in the kitchen.

The first day of the semester has always been sacred to us. When I was a young kid, way before I understood the concept of semesters, Dad always made a huge deal out of first days of school, and Mom has carried the tradition along nicely. The older I get, the more I appreciate it, because I know how crappy first days back are for the vice principal. So to toss all that stress aside and help me celebrate starting a new set of classes is really special.

I come down the stairs to the smell of flank steak, and my stomach immediately starts growling. Making my way into the kitchen, I grab a soda and give my mom a kiss on the cheek.

"How was your day?" she asks, her voice sounding only half as tired as she looks.

"It was good, actually. My classes seem challenging, but I think I'll manage." I laugh. "I've got to keep this up if I'm going to be valedictorian."

That makes her smile. "That's exactly right. I know you'll get into plenty of colleges before we find that out, but that doesn't mean it's meaningless. You're at the top of the class right now, but anything can happen this last semester."

"I'll do my best."

"I know you will," she says. "Thankfully, I know that your best will be enough to keep you at the top. You know, your father would be so proud."

"Really?" I ask.

Not because I don't believe it, but academics never seemed like his thing. I have this idealized picture of him in my mind where he thinks I can do no wrong, where he's my biggest supporter and sticks right by my side when I say I don't want to go to college. But I know I'm just… fantasizing. I don't remember him well enough to know what he'd think about any of this.

I set the table as Mom puts the finishing touches on dinner, and by the time we sit down, my stomach is roaring. Mom opens a bottle of wine and pours herself a small glass, and pauses before putting it back in the fridge.

"What should we cheers to?" Mom says. "It's your special day, and you can wish for anything you'd like. Last January, you said you wanted to get chosen for that internship with Senator Wright, and that's exactly what happened. Maybe this time, you should wish to get into your top college."

"That's right," I say, a little uneasily. "And yeah, I should do that."

I think for a minute about what I really want. Honestly, I want to know what I'm doing with my life, or at least be fine figuring it out as I go. I want to stop dreading every email that pops up in my inbox, wondering if it'll be yet *another* reminder from a university I toured explaining that my time to apply is rapidly disappearing.

"I'm going to keep my wish secret this year," I say.

She eyes me suspiciously, then shakes her head.

"That goes against tradition, but I'll be honest, I'm starving and dinner is getting cold, so you do whatever makes you happy."

It's a small win, but I relish it anyway. She's never usually like this, she's usually stuck in tradition, stuck in whatever expectations she's laid out, but this shows some flexibility.

I make my wish:

I want my mom to understand me.

We cheers, my soda with her wine, and we're quiet for almost the entire dinner. I think it's silly Reese won't tell Heath that he wants to do drag, but my secrets? I keep them for a reason. I know how she's going to react, how with so few words I can reduce this charming, smiling woman in front of me to a caricature of a helicopter mom.

But at the end of the day, I know what I want to do, and even if it breaks her heart, I'll need her to accept that and accept me. I just don't think she can.

• Golden Boys •

GABRIEL + HEATH + REESE + SAL

> Did you see the mayor's latest Facebook post? **S**

> **G** ... none of us even have Facebook

> **R** Even if we did, we wouldn't be following him.

> The Columbus Dispatch did this feature on all the new Pride parades and festivals that popped up last year. They talked to all these small town mayors who were already planning for June.

He was angry they didn't ask him for "his side" of the story... aka the homophobic side.

Asshole. What are people saying?

The comments are a mess. All the boomers are fighting, and the superintendent of the school is very much in agreement. Gross.

God we need a new mayor

I couldn't agree more.

CHAPTER TWENTY-FIVE

HEATH

OVER THE PAST FEW weeks, Reese was all I thought about, no matter how much I tried to cover it up with practice, or school-work, or *anything*. I even went from being the loudest one in the group chat to the one who rarely pops in.

Regardless of what might happen to us after graduation, I thought Reese and I would at least have this year. I thought we'd have so many more months of the pure joy I felt when he met me in Orlando and we confessed our love for each other for the first time, until the real world finally tore us apart.

But here we are, in late January, and it's like the end of us is staring me in the face. I know he's hiding something. And staying laser focused on practice is the only thing keeping me going.

At lunch on Friday, I walk through the halls slowly, not feeling hungry. I peek into the main office and ask Sal's mom if I can grab a book from my car, which she agrees to with a nod and a light flick of her hand.

Technically speaking, we're not allowed off property. Some schools let you off school property for lunch, but…not good ol' Gracemont High. It would be fine if any of the other boys were in my lunch period, but they're not. I'm all alone, and though I'd normally sit with a few baseball friends, I feel like being alone today.

As I head to the front doors, I hear a voice behind me shout, "Hey, let me come with you!"

It's James Amani, our team's new relief pitcher. Though he's only a sophomore, he made the varsity team as a catcher last year thanks to his insane batting average, and precision when it comes to throwing runners out at second base. This year, he's only gotten better.

I'm close with him, since we practice together so often, but I was hoping to take this moment to be alone. But one thing about James is that if he sees anything interesting happening, he's going to weasel his way in.

"I'm just going to my car to hang out for a bit," I say.

"Sounds great. Ella's taken your spot at the baseball table and keeps making out with Daniel. It's not appetizing."

I laugh, and gesture for him to come along. Our boots crunch through the snow as we get to my truck, which is parked in the very back, and as soon as we shut the door we sigh so loud it starts to fog up the windows.

"This week's been brutal," James says. "How did you get through Mrs. McCartney's class? We've had homework every single day. Thankfully it's short enough for me to do on the bus on the way to school. Still, damn."

"Honestly that class was a blur. All of them are now."

He laughs. "Now that you're about to be a big Vanderbilt star?"

I blush. "That's the hope."

We both tear into our bagged lunches. After having bologna, mustard, and American cheese on white bread every day for five days, I consider not finishing it. But then my stomach grumbles, and I know I'm not going to let food go to waste, so I power through.

"No offense, but I'm excited for you to go to college," James says. "I think tryouts went really well for me, and I'm excited to be a relief pitcher, but after watching I wonder if I'll even get some play time."

"Hey, you never know—they might even bring you in as a starter," I offer. "I don't think any of the pitchers are up for replacing Blake since he graduated last year."

"No offense, but they only brought Blake in to start when they knew we could afford the loss. They barely took you off the mound last year." He gasps. "But maybe they will want to keep you in prime shape for Vanderbilt. They know we won't win any championships, but having a star pitcher come from Gracemont High, they'd do anything for that."

"I kind of wanted alone time so I didn't have to think about this kind of stuff." I sigh. "My grades, my pitching, my boyfriend . . . there's just so much pressure that it's easy to want to give up."

James and I make eye contact, and I see a confused look come over his face. We're close teammates, but we've *never* been the share-our-feelings type. I always had the boys for that.

I expect him to flip out—sports-obsessed straight bros tend to not be the best at dealing with emotions, let's be honest—but he just puts a hand on my shoulder and squeezes it tightly.

"Man, I am not looking forward to senior year. You're, like, the most unflappable person I know, and if it's making you freak out, there's *no* hope for me."

We laugh, and finish our sandwiches, making sure to keep the rest of the conversation light and free of baseball or drama.

Once we come back in, I breathe a quick sigh of relief that none of the admins seemed to notice that I went out for much longer than it takes to grab a book, and that a friend tagged along. James and I walk into our next class side by side, and I feel this immense relief that there's someone here who can put a smile on my face even when I'm feeling down and overwhelmed.

On the way, Reese passes by me. He flashes a quick smile, and I try to mirror that smile, but I feel like gravity's just tripled for me with how hard it is to smile for him. I know we'll talk about what's going on, and maybe we'll be fine, but maybe it won't be. Maybe I *don't* want to know what's going on.

All I know so far is that he and Sal were working on a "secret project" that he couldn't tell me about. I have no idea what that means, and I'm not sure I even want to know.

I didn't think he'd ever cheat on me, and I still don't think he would—Sal is cute, but they'd never do that to me. Not to mention, he and Reese aren't exactly compatible. Anytime they're in the same room together for too long, they start getting snippy and competitive.

But I guess that has changed. I just don't know if it's for better or for worse.

CHAPTER TWENTY-SIX

GABRIEL

IN THE HALLS BETWEEN classes, I spot Cassie and sprint to catch up with her. She's carrying her flute in her left hand, and a big folder of sheet music in her right hand. Ending the day with concert band sounds ideal, honestly. I know it's not easy, but I haven't done anything musical since I dropped out of choir back in my sophomore year, and I kind of miss it.

"Band practice?" I ask.

"No, chemistry," she jokes. "This flute case is actually filled with beakers."

I chuckle. "Okay, fine, I'll get just right to it: I have a list of fifteen books that were listed as available to check out, but none of them are on the shelves."

"I have seventeen on my list, so we should reconcile that before going to Mrs. Camilleri in our meeting on Monday. Also, I tried to check one out online, and I got an email reply saying that the title was no longer available. Something's up."

"We'll get it figured out," I tell Cassie. "Miss Orly won't know what hit her when we come to Sal's mom with *facts*. We're going to start some trouble."

"Good trouble," she says with a laugh. "And I can't wait."

• • •

I sprint to English and make it just before the bell rings. Miss H is still at her computer, and she gestures for us all to take our seats and talk amongst ourselves.

When I pull out my phone, I see a text from Matt. He's sent me all the ingredients for our romantic FaceTime dinner date tonight. We're making Cacio e Pepe, one of my favorite pasta dishes, and I feel this rush of excitement.

As it turns out, Matt's a pretty good cook, and I'm ... well, I'm getting by. We've done this a few times, and each time I find myself wishing I was having a bit of his meal instead of mine, but having that kind of shared experience is good for us.

Do I miss him? Yes.

Would I rather he be here where I can touch him? Absolutely.

But lately, I've been thinking about how if we can get through this school year, we can get through anything.

All right, groceries have been ordered to your house—my treat this time. Also, I may have slipped in a package of Oreos in there. 😉

I send back a few kissy face emojis, and I can't stop the smile from taking over my face. Then my phone vibrates with a new message from Sal:

Want to go to Melody's after school and crash H+R's date? I could go for some onion rings, and I think we all need to chat ASAP.

I type **Sure. I can only go for a bit though . . . it's FaceTime date night with M.** in response, and sit through the rest of class wondering just what he wants to talk about. Is it how Heath and Reese have been super weird lately? Does he have some sort of announcement? Or does he just really want onion rings?

My mind races, but I can't help but feel like I've been left out of a *lot* here.

Oh well, at least I'll get some free onion rings out of it.

CHAPTER TWENTY-SEVEN

REESE

AFTER HEATH CAUGHT ME in a lie last month, the vibes have definitely been off. I gave him the briefest answer I could. He's not pushing me for answers, and I...I'm not ready to give them. Not to mention, I barely see him anymore—he basically runs to practice every time I try to talk to him. He's still kind to me at school. Like lending me a pen when mine runs out of ink, or carrying my bag in between physics and history every day, things like that. And we do talk between classes, but when he speaks to me, it's like that glimmer's gone from his eyes. Or maybe I'm reading too much into it.

Thankfully, it's Friday. To separate from the group, we always make a point to go to Melody's Diner right after school for a little date, before meeting up with the rest of the boys. He's skipped the past few ones to go to the batting cages, but he agreed to go today, which means there will be some progress. And, finally, some alone time.

We walk side by side to his truck in silence. I keep looking to him, and I see him massaging his shoulder, gritting his teeth. I might be keeping a secret from him, but he's keeping something inside too.

He opens the passenger side car door for me, and I drop my bag on the seat and pull him into a light kiss. We're not big on PDA unless we're around the boys, so this is unusual, but he doesn't pull away. He leans in and sweeps me up with his arm.

"What was that for?" Heath asks, a little dazed, once we part.

"Loving me," I say. "We just haven't had much time to be together since winter break, with baseball and student council and all that."

Once the hormones die down and I can breathe and think a little easier, I start planning how I'm going to reveal this to him. Should I just tell him at Melody's, over our usual mozzarella sticks?

But what if he's weirded out by it, and it ruins mozzarella sticks forever? I think, then giggle to myself at how absurd I sounded.

"What?" Heath asks with a cheeky smile.

"Oh, nothing."

Once we arrive at Melody's, we grab our normal booth, put in our order, and hold hands across the table, pausing only so we can take sips of our sodas. My chest aches with the joy of being with him in this familiar environment. This tradition we have, where everything feels right. I want to speak, but something unspoken is happening between us, and I wonder if words will ruin the feeling.

"So you've been practicing a lot," I say finally. "I thought you usually took it easy in January."

He shrugs. "You know, it's been weird. I think it's getting to my head, all the Vanderbilt pressure. I keep feeling like I'm not good enough, no matter how much I practice. It could be just because my shoulder's been acting up, though."

"Why don't you see a doctor?" I ask; then he avoids eye contact.

"I ... don't think it's that bad yet. Plus, it's the new year, and Dad hasn't hit his deductible, so that means he has to pay for all the doctor bills in full until he does."

I look at him oddly. "What does that even mean?"

"Insurance." He sighs. "Every year, you have to spend a certain amount of money before you hit your deductible. When you hit that, then insurance pays, like, eighty-five percent of your bill, until you hit your out-of-pocket max. Then—"

"How the hell do you know all this?" I blurt out. "Did you pick up a job in human resources or something?"

His face darkens. "Reese, it's like this every year. If I need physical therapy, or if this shoulder is bad, then we'll have to drop thousands before insurance even kicks in. Or if I go and they say 'nothing's wrong, just ice it,' Dad *still* has to pay that entire bill, and I don't want to waste his money."

I've never had to think about these things, so I stay silent.

"It's fine, it ... really is," he continues. "It's just not something you and the other boys have to think about."

My face burns red. Here I am, tiptoeing around and playing with expensive Parisian makeup with Sal, while Heath's trying to heal an injury through sheer force of will.

"I'm not trying to shame you or anything." He sighs. "It's good that you don't have to think about this."

"But what if you got hurt, like really hurt? Or what if your dad did? You'd just not go to the emergency room?"

He grips my hands tighter. "I...the ambulance alone costs hundreds of dollars. A hospital stay would be...I mean, look. If Dad collapsed and gripped his chest, I'm not going to sit around and say 'oops, we're poor.' I'd call 911 immediately, and we would figure it out. But it's just that unless we were *absolutely sure* that it's a big problem, I can't waste money like that. I can't put us into debt for possibly nothing."

I pull my hand away slowly. "Is the pain really bad? Do you think it's becoming a big problem?"

He looks away, which gives me enough of an answer, even though he confidently says, "No."

"Can you talk to your dad about it?" I ask, but he shakes his head.

"I shouldn't have even told you. I don't want anyone to worry; it's really not a big deal."

I nod. "Okay, I believe you."

Our mozzarella sticks come, but I'm not very hungry anymore. He confessed something to me, so it's only natural that I do the same in return. It feels, oddly, like I'm coming out *again*. Which I know is an unfair thing to think. It's just drag.

But if I really do this, what would he think? What would his teammates think? What would his family think? It's no longer just me and my own choices; I just don't want to screw things up with him. But if I don't tell him soon, I really will screw things up with him.

"Okay," I say. Heat floods my cheeks, and my hands are instantly clammy. "Well. I wanted to tell you about something that's been going on with me."

"Does it have to do with Sal?" Heath asks, not jealously, and I nod.

I take in a breath to speak, but out of the corner of my eye, I spot Sal and Gabriel bounding toward us. My chest deflates as they take their seats next to us, and Heath bristles uncomfortably when Sal sidles up next to him.

Sal puffs out his chest and takes over the conversation.

"All right, boys. I've got an announcement."

Of course you do, I think.

CHAPTER TWENTY-EIGHT

SAL

IF I'M GOING TO be able to command a room as mayor, I know I have to bring that presence with me wherever I go. Whenever Senator Wright or Congresswoman Caudill stepped into the room, all eyes would go to them. I'm not very confident right now, but I'm tired of meandering through life without a plan.

I have a plan, but first, I need buy-in from my three best friends.

"I am not going to college," I say. "You all know that now. But for months I've been trying to figure out what I want to do. 'What's my next step in life?' I would ask myself. And I've found a very particular four-year program that's going to get me where I want to go way faster than college."

Across the table, Gabe's and Reese's faces give off their confusion, so I figure I should cut this campaign speech short and get right to the point.

"I've decided that I want to run for mayor. I want to beat Mayor

Green, who thinks he's running unopposed. If you three help me, I think we can do it."

They look at one another in quasi-stunned silence, and a rare feeling of vulnerability hits me in the chest. Is this just a wild fantasy? Am I throwing my life away just to get destroyed in a local election?

But I steel my core and exude confidence. That's what a politician would do, so that's what I do.

"I know how this sounds," I say.

"Do you?" Heath asks. "Green has been the mayor for forever. The whole village apparently loves him."

"Well, we don't," I say, "and for good reason."

Reese chooses his words carefully. "I . . . it's just, you're seventeen—"

"Eighteen by election day, which is all that matters."

"—fine, eighteen. That's still really young for a mayor, right? Especially to challenge someone like Mayor Green," Reese says.

Heath clears his throat. "Do you even know how to run a town?"

"I'll learn," I say. "I know how the village council is structured, I know how town council meetings work, I know what the mayor has control over and what's outside his jurisdiction. And I will keep learning as I go."

"Why don't you try to work *for* a local politician?" Reese asks. "There must be a state senator or state houseperson who's hiring around here, right?"

"I know that's the logical thing to do. But I spent all summer drowning in bureaucracy, barely making a difference. I know I can do this." I turn to Gabe. "Think of what we can do."

"We?" Gabe says, a hint of red brushing his face.

"All those protests you organized, all the drives you've organized, you've done because the mayor couldn't provide support for the people who needed it."

"But...I...we'll all be gone in a few months, and the election's not until November."

"You won't be far," I say, "if you go to Ohio State."

He blushes. "I'm not set on a school. I don't even know if they'll accept me."

"Everyone in your family went to Ohio State. You're going to go, just like your sister, just like your dad. You've been in OSU attire since we were kids."

"But that's just my dad," he says, then drops his gaze. "Okay, it's not just him. I guess they're not actually pressuring me to go. I've always wanted to go. I love it there so much. But it's not one of the schools Matt's applying to, and I know I shouldn't pick a school because of him, but I have to keep my options open."

"Okay, I get that." I look to each of my friends. "But let me put it this way. I'm doing this with or without your support, but I really want you there by my side. At least, until we graduate, and you all leave me forever."

There are a few moments of uncomfortable silence, but I clench my core and sit through them, waiting for my friends to join me.

"I'll make you a logo," Reese says, and he gives me a firm nod.

Thankfully, I can count on him the same way he counts on me.

"I can . . . lift stuff?" Heath says.

I laugh. "I need you to use your popularity. Our civics teacher is already trying to get everyone registered to vote. Since you're already eighteen, I want you to be vocal about registering to vote. And I'll need your help getting a whole lot of signatures to even get *on* the ballot."

"I can do that," Heath says with a cheeky smile. "And if the need arises, I can also lift stuff. Oh, and I can reach tall shelves, but I'm not sure how helpful that is."

"Gabe?" I say, and I see the unease on his face.

"Will you come to the LGBTQ+ Advocacy Group meetings? And Cassie's PoC Resource Group meetings? I believe you can win if you get enough of the young people to turn out for a vote. But I won't help you if you're just running for attention."

His words pierce me like an arrow.

"Gabe," I say.

"I'm not trying to be mean, but I need to know you're doing this for the right reasons. Convince me first, and I'll help you convince everyone else. Deal?"

Without thinking, a smile comes to my face. This isn't the Gabriel who left for Boston, weak and scared and dependent and spineless. This is Gabe, the fierce boy I knew was in there all along.

"Deal."

"All right, then," he says. "I don't know how this works, but let me figure out if fundraising is even allowed for local elections.

I'm not sure we can post anything around school, but maybe we can just focus on getting everyone who'll be eighteen by November registered to vote. And then I'll see about getting a booth at any of the spring festivals in town."

"You just thought of all that off the top of your head?" Heath asks.

Gabe shrugs. "Just brainstorming."

"You really are something," I say, which earns me a rare wink from Gabe.

iMessage

DIANA + HEATH

Omg you know how I follow everyone and everything on IG?

yeah it's kind of creepy

like you even followed Vanderbilt's baseball account before me

They'll eventually be posting about you so why not

Anyway not important. But I didn't realize Reese's school in Paris closed?

wait what?????

he's gonna be so sad

i wonder when it happened

It closed like, right after the summer

Check their page, it says the Paris branch permanently closed

That can't be right tho, didn't Reese visit when he was in Paris?

well

that's what he said, at least......

CHAPTER TWENTY-NINE

HEATH

WHEN I GO TO look at the Instagram post by Riley Design, the blood drains from my face. This school closed in August. Reese and Sal visited in December. That means they've both been lying to me.

It's a Sunday night, and though I'm already in bed, I shoot off a text to Reese. He's usually more of a night owl, so I know he'll be up.

We need to talk. Can I come see you?

I wait for a response as I start to put on my clothes. I should wait to see if he says no, but I'm full of this anxious energy and I need to do *something* to occupy my mind.

"Hey, Dad," I say, "I've got to go see Reese for something. It'll be quick. That okay?"

"Oh," he says. "Sure, just don't be long."

In a matter of minutes, I'm out the door and in my truck. I haven't left the parking spot outside our apartment, because Reese still hasn't responded. But I start the truck anyway. It's freezing in here, and it takes a while for the car to warm up.

Dad cautiously peeks out at me from the blinds, and I give him a wave to show that everything's okay. Somehow, last summer, the role of Dad got turned into more of the role of roommate, and I don't think either of us know what to do about it. There's no way he and Mom would have let me drive away with barely an excuse to see my boyfriend on a school night.

Dad closes the blinds just as Reese responds:

Yeah, sure!

He's not usually one for exclamation points in his texts, so I'm guessing he feels the seriousness of my text. Though, in retrospect, *We need to talk* is possibly the most dramatic thing to text someone.

I ease out of my parking spot, but before I pull out into the road, he sends a second text, and my heart hits the floor.

Pick me up at Sal's, if that's okay?

REESE

"Well, it's official, we're breaking up." I say this to Sal, and he sighs so loud I feel it on my cheek.

He's brushing out this cheap wig I bought on Amazon, trying to make it do anything but look flat. When I first put it on, it looked like a man with clown makeup wearing a wig. But as he styles the hair, even though he's basically guessing how to do it, it's starting to look real.

"You're looking good," Sal says. "And you and Heath are *not* breaking up. He just probably thinks you're cheating on him with me, which is totally understandable, as I'm obviously the hunk of the friend group."

I laugh at that, despite the nerves and the anxiety bubbling up in my chest.

"All right, he'll be here soon, so I need to wash all of this off," I say.

Sal pauses for a second, then says, "Why don't you keep it on? You're going to have to tell him anyway—I can't keep going through life thinking Heath is going to deck me for seducing you, so it's time you came clean."

"I am going to come clean, but I don't need to show him."

"Why not? You look good. It's only been a few weeks, but you're really getting the hang of this. Once you have a finished dress to go with this look, you're going to be set."

I look in the mirror and see the art in my drag. I first confessed this to Sal only a few weeks ago, and here I am, looking *okay.* I mean, it's not going to get me cast on *RuPaul's Drag Race*, but I actually look pretty, and I finally get to marry my love for art and fashion design in a way that feels right to me.

Headlights filter in through Sal's front window, which tells me Heath is here to pick me up. I text Mamma saying I'm getting a ride back, so she doesn't come pick me up like she planned.

"Okay, I'm going for it," I say, standing. "Your mom's not going to see me, is she?"

"She knows what we're doing."

"Sure, but I don't need your mom to be the second human to ever see me in drag."

He laughs. "Fair. No, she's probably in bed reading by now."

I give Sal a hug. We're not the touchy-feely type, usually, but I really do appreciate all his help and his confidence over the past few weeks. I pack up my backpack and throw it over my shoulder, and I head down the stairs and out into the night.

I walk more confidently, on the balls of my feet, feeling this transformation, feeling this moment.

I open the door, and when Heath looks up from his phone, his jaw drops.

I shrug. "Hey, stud. Can I get a ride?"

HEATH

Reese looks... really pretty. I know that shouldn't be my first reaction, as I just spent this whole drive rehearsing my *Why do you keep lying to me? Are you hooking up with Sal?* speech, but my brain pretty much shuts off when I see him like this.

It's dim, but I can still make out most of his features. Warm cheeks, slim nose, a shiny lip, and a dark cat-eye all covered in the shuffle of light blond hair. It's the hair that feels odd—his hair's always been so dark.

But wait, I guess his suddenly being in drag is the odd part.

"You're not saying anything. Of course, why would you?" Reese laughs nervously. "It's... well, I need to tell you something."

I swallow hard. "I think I can guess what it is, ma'am."

He laughs. "No, seriously. Let me tell you."

Reese tells the story to me, and I listen as well as I can—though it's a lot of information. Over the summer, his professor pointed out that so many of his designs seemed inspired by drag, and that planted a seed in him that blossomed over the next few months.

"In school, I kept getting asked who these dress designs were for," he says, looking down. "But it wasn't until I got back that I realized they were for me. At least, I think they are. Or maybe I just want to design dresses for drag queens—there are so many of them, I might be able to carve out my niche. Or maybe I can just post my drag on social media? I know enough about photo editing that I can probably make all of this look flawless."

He gestures to his face, which I take lightly in my hand and turn toward me.

"It's a little surprising," I say, "but wow, you're beautiful."

"Sal helped me."

"Yeah, I pieced that together." I laugh. "Do you have any clothes? Like, did you make any dresses?"

"Not yet." He shakes his head. "I have a few works in progress. But it's been hard to focus."

After we're both buckled in, I back my truck up and out of Sal's driveway. I feel a little embarrassed about the jealousy—there was a moment I thought there *might* be something with those two.

Though I feel a little silly, the hurt doesn't fully go away. I take a deep breath as we ease onto Main Street and in the direction of Reese's house. We only have a couple of minutes to talk about it, but we have to.

"Reese, I don't know why you didn't tell me."

"I wasn't ready to talk about it, I guess."

I sigh. "That wasn't the only lie you told, though. Your school *closed*. How could you have visited it?"

"How'd you find that out?" he asks with a start.

"When you're related to a digital investigator, it's pretty easy."

He sighs and pulls off his wig. I turn to him as we come to a stop sign, and I want to laugh. His sweaty black hair fans out over his forehead, but his makeup still looks so polished and neat.

"Would it kill Diana to not follow every social media account connected to any of us?" he says. "*I* didn't even follow the school on Instagram."

I shrug. "She likes to stay connected. But thank god she did— how much longer were you going to go with this? How many other lies would you have said?"

He places his cool hand on my leg, an assuring gesture that calms me down enough to think clearly.

"I just didn't want your opinion of me to change."

"Just because of drag?" I ask.

"Because I don't know what the hell I'm doing with my life," he says abruptly. "I go to Paris to study graphic design, but then I change my course of study on a whim. My school *closes* mere weeks after I come back. I apply to all these fashion design schools, but then I start playing around with the idea of doing drag."

"I mean, you could do drag *and* fashion design, Reese," I say. "They go hand in hand."

He pulls out a makeup remover wipe and uses the truck visor's mirror to see as he takes off as much as he can. Streaks of black appear, and I can't tell if they're from the wipe or from him crying.

"You don't get it," he says.

"Babe, that's because you're not explaining it."

At the next stoplight I lean over and plant a kiss on his still-shiny lips. We hold the kiss for a few seconds, too long to be just a kiss but too stoic to be a make out.

"Let me in," I say.

He stays silent as I pull the truck into his driveway and put it in park. We both stare straight forward, our breaths slowly fogging up the windows.

He clears his throat. "What if I decided not to go to school, like Sal. I could come with you and maybe I could find my way into Nashville's drag scene, or something? Or I could do drag videos and monetize them. Or I could take virtual classes—"

"Reesey." I get the very real urge to cry, but I will *not*. Not now. Not when he needs to hear this. "If you sacrificed even a single dream to come be with me, I would never forgive myself. You can't do that—"

"But—"

"And I think you know it," I say. "I'm not going to be your biggest regret. We'll figure it out, I promise, but you have to stop lying to me. I'm a big boy, I can take it."

He leans his head on my shoulder, and I just rest my face onto the top of his head. The smell of his shampoo hits my nose, and it comforts me, just enough to feel okay.

"I'm sorry for lying," he says. "I was going to tell you at the diner, but then Sal came in and made such a big deal about his mayoral campaign. But there were plenty of other times I could have told you, so that's not much of an excuse."

"I'm still mad at you," I say. "But I get why you did it. Kind of."

"Will we really get through this?" he asks.

My mind swims as I try to think of a response. I want so much to say "yes," but I don't really want to lie to him either. I thought this was something we'd have to deal with in April, or May, once all our plans were finally locked in and we couldn't avoid it anymore. I didn't think we'd be feeling the pressure of what's to come so soon.

"I want us to get through it," I say. It's not a lie, but it's also not very hopeful.

He opens the car door and sighs.

"I want that too, Heath."

CHAPTER THIRTY

SAL

DUE TO A FEW scheduling conflicts, I made the executive decision to move the student council meetings to Monday mornings, before school. Not everyone was thrilled about that, but it frees me up to go to the LGBTQ+ Advocacy Group meetings on Mondays, after school, and fulfill my promise to Gabe.

Personally, I've never minded having meetings before school. With Mom's schedule, and my crappy sleep schedule, I'm up anyway. Before I could drive, she used to take me to school every morning and I'd sit in an empty classroom or her office and finish up any homework I hadn't done yet, waiting for the guys to come in on the bus.

And even though the entire student council is a little groggy, we're making good progress planning our *An Evening in Paris*–themed prom. We have a tight budget, but if we get the venue we're hoping for—an old art gallery outside of Mansfield—we'll have just enough to plan everything else. And *then* we have to sell tickets, but that's something I can delegate to a few other eager student council members.

Though it's only February, I'm already checked out when it comes to school. My teachers call it "senioritis," and maybe that's a part of it, but my classes aren't fun and I've been spending more time researching mayoral campaigns and planning my run, so I haven't had quite as much time to care about school. I've turned in a couple of assignments late, which I've never been known to do.

So maybe my grades will dip a little. Maybe I won't be valedictorian after all. But I feel more relaxed.

Once I get downstairs, Mom greets me with a smile, "'Morning, Sal. Can you ride with me today and have one of your friends take you back? I want to run some things by you before your student council meeting."

I shrug. "Sure, Reese can probably drop me off."

We get in the car, and Mom takes the long way around to stop by the gas station to pick up her daily coffee. I go in with her and make my own. Once we're back in the car, we take tentative sips, and I wonder why she hasn't started the car yet.

"Do you know if Gabriel's going to give me any trouble today?" she asks. A sinking feeling settles in my gut. "I want to know what to expect in our meeting, and he and Cassie always seem to be up to something. It seems like you've joined their club lately, so I would appreciate a preview of what I'm dealing with today."

I choose my words carefully.

"I've only shown up for one meeting so far, so I don't really know what they're going to talk to you about. But whatever it is, it's probably for a good cause."

"That's true. I just worry sometimes. Gabriel can be dramatic, he wants to make everything big and showy, and you know I hate making a spectacle out of everything."

I do. Which is why I could hardly believe it when Reese showed me that news article, over the summer, when Mom actually spoke to the local news about creating an LGBTQ+ advocacy group and making antibullying training mandatory for all teachers.

"Sometimes spectacles are needed, Mom." I tack the "Mom" on there to garner a little bit of sympathy.

She sighs, then turns to me. "Your friends are all good kids, but I don't want you to start acting like them. *Sal* is who I love and respect, and *Sal* is who I want you to stay."

I turn away, control my breathing, and watch as the light fog brushes the window in a slow cadence. There's a part of me—a growing part of me—that knows she loves and respects the vision of Sal who's in her head. And though it seemed like she grew so much over this summer, I wonder just how much of that was sincere.

So often when the guys are dealing with drama like this—like Reese and his drag panic—I just want to shake them and say, "Tell them! Be honest! It's *fine*." Because for them, it usually is.

But it's different for me. How do I tell my mom that the Sal she loves and respects doesn't even exist? That he was created specifically to seek approval from her? That he wishes his dad were still here because, who knows, maybe Dad would have loved him unconditionally?

"Sal, do I have to worry about your friend today?"

I grit my teeth, take another breath, and turn to her. "No more than you need to worry about me."

She puts the car in reverse and pulls back on to Main Street, heading toward the school.

"And what, exactly, does that mean?" she asks. It's her vice principal voice, not her mom voice, and I smirk at the shift. "If those boys are being a bad influence on you, I will not hesitate to keep you from them."

"*Those boys?* You mean my best friends? Heath, the second-best student at this school? Reese, whose greatest vice is sketching and journaling? Gabriel, who's racked up the most community service hours of any Gracemont student of probably all time? Okay, yeah, I'll try not to be like them."

We pull up to a stoplight, and she puts her face in her palms.

"This is exactly what I'm talking about, Sal. You didn't use to talk back to me. You didn't use to spend your nights putting makeup on your friends instead of studying or doing homework." She pauses. "I don't have a problem with *that*, I mean. But you used to put academics first, your career first, and *college* first."

We have two country blocks until we get to the school. Is this the moment? Is this when I can tell her my plans? It would be so easy to tell her, jump out of the car, and never look back.

But even if she's being a little annoying right now, that wouldn't get me any points.

"We haven't had one of our 'college takeout' nights in a while," I say. "Why don't we do that—on Thursday?"

Her face visibly relaxes, and I see her sigh. "That's a good idea. You know, you only ever sent me the application confirmation for Michigan. Can you forward all the others over before we talk? I know you always say you'll take care of it, and I trust you, but I like to keep my own records."

"Sure," I say, even though I absolutely don't have the emails to send. I only applied to one school, U of M, because it had the lowest application cost of the ones on our list. Mom made it very clear that she didn't care which ones I applied to, and she trusted me with her credit card for it, but I'm still not going to waste her money just because I'm scared to tell her the truth.

Before I get out of the car, she gives me a quick peck on the cheek. I know we won't talk too much before Thursday, but I feel confident for once—I set a date, and I know exactly when I'm going to tell her my plans.

CHAPTER THIRTY-ONE

GABRIEL

CASSIE AND I WAIT in Miss H's classroom until it's time for our meeting with Sal's mom. There's this vibration running through me, one I haven't felt in a while. Over the summer, there was this moment when everything clicked. When I got that first donation, and it all started to make sense. One part vulnerability, two parts excitement, and four parts anxiety.

Because we have a mission. On behalf of the LGBTQ+ Advocacy Group (which is basically just us two plus Sal and Heath anyway) we're going to do what we can to stop discrimination from happening at prom since there will be at least one queer couple in attendance. And we have CVS-length receipts about diverse books being removed from the library.

My phone vibrates. Matt's sent an audio message, so I put in an AirPod and listen:

Gabe! I'm running to my trumpet lesson, but I wanted to say "Good luck!" I know confrontation makes you anxious, but remember what they taught us at Save the Trees: focus on the message. You can be flustered, or the reaction might be different than you expected, but as long as you get the message out, you can connect with people.

He follows it up with a second, shorter message:

Whoa, that was cheesy. Please disregard. Unless it was inspiring! Um . . . okay. Now I've really got to go. If I'm not warmed up in five minutes, my tutor will lose it. You got this, babe! Love you.

I chuckle, and Cassie shoots me a look.

"What?" I ask innocently.

"Don't flaunt your love like that."

I roll my eyes. "I just laughed!"

"You *giggled*! That's totally different!" She shakes her head. "How's it going with you two?"

"Good!" I say, maybe too quickly. "I miss him, but we're working it out. FaceTime dates, phone calls, voice messages, whatever it takes. We've both been super busy lately, so it hasn't been easy."

It's been hard, actually.

"We're hoping to get into nearby colleges so we can see each other more often. But, you know, that's up to the college gods."

"God, I can't wait to get out of here," she says. "I'm going to *thrive* in college."

"I think you're going to thrive wherever you go. Where do you want to go to college?"

"California!" She smirks. "The gayest school I can find. Also the hottest—temperaturewise, that is. If I never have to wear these snow boots again it'll be too soon."

"That sounds nice," I say, then I look at my phone. "I kind of want to stay in Ohio. My whole family went to Ohio State, and I think it would be cool to be at school with my sister—and the campus is big enough that it's not like we'd be forced to see each other, but I don't think I'm fully ready to say goodbye to Ohio. Not yet, at least."

She grunts. "Don't take this the wrong way, but maybe I'd feel that way if I had a group like you do. I keep trying to create my own groups. It's just not the same. It's like you all met in the womb or something."

"You have friends, though."

"I do, but I still need to leave and find somewhere I'm more accepted. And I feel so guilty thinking like that, but as much as my friends are there for me, I want them to *get* me. Even you and Heath in this group can, like, communicate telepathically, it's so bizarre. I've never had someone get me like that."

"You will," I say.

She waves her hand. "All right, it's time. You ready?"

I nod. "Let's do this."

The walk to the main office from English feels suspiciously long. Am I subconsciously taking smaller steps, or is time slowing down? All said, it's still a high school of only a couple hundred students, so we make it to the end of the hall before I can get too dramatic about it.

"Gabriel, Cassandra," Sal's mom says with a genuine smile. "Come in, sit down. It's nice to see you."

I look to Cassie, and she gives me a shrug as we take our seats.

The vice principal's desk takes up most of the space. From where she sits, the wall behind her is made of windows, and the closed blinds can't do enough to keep out the light, or the heat.

"It's always a hundred degrees in here," she says with a laugh. "That dang sun."

"Wow, it must be hard to work in here all day," Cassie says with a smile. I note the slight changes in her voice since we walked in—joyful, light—which tells me that she's still slightly on the defense.

But I remind myself that this is the mother of my literal best friend. The boy I spend so many of my days with. The boy who I used to spend so many nights with too, but she never knew that.

Ultimately, I know I can trust her with this. To listen to me and treat me like a concerned friend. I practice controlling my breathing to keep my heart rate down. My therapist once told me that fear is excitement without breathing, and neither of us fully believed that corny phrase, but it always sticks in my mind in times like these.

"All right," she says, "how can I help?"

"First, we wanted to talk to you about prom," I say. "I know that the student council has already started discussing the event— fundraising, venue sourcing, things like that—but we wanted to talk to you about the steps the school can take to mitigate discrimination."

"Mitigate" is a word that got thrown around a lot back in my volunteer experience, and yes I feel a little smug sneaking an SAT word into the conversation so smoothly.

Cassie jumps in. "I brought in a printout of the ACLU's guidance on LGBTQ+ students' prom night rights that I think will be useful as a guide—"

"I understand your concern," Mrs. Camilleri cuts in, "but I assure you there will be no discrimination to the LGBTQ students at prom. We recently had a few teachers go through this virtual training on stopping bullying, and I think that will be very helpful."

"It's not just about bullying, though," I say. "Five years ago, there were—"

"I'm very aware of that situation, and it won't happen again. It was due to a few concerned parents, and it would have been fine if two girls hadn't flaunted themselves for attention like they did, but what's in the past is in the past."

I feel the tension pulling at my muscles, and my breathing tactic has just flown out the window. *Flaunted themselves?* They were just vocal about their relationship, like every straight couple has done here in the history of ever.

"I don't think you can blame the girls for other people's homophobia," I say with a wobbly voice.

"Now, Gabriel, don't put words in my mouth." Her cool, smooth, condescending tone makes me flinch. "I know you're very worried about your two friends now that they're together, but we're not going to have any problems, not unless Reese decides to come in a dress!" she says with a laugh.

"In a what?" I ask, and my mind goes blank for a second.

"No, it's fine, I know all about it. I don't care what he and Sal are doing, as long as they keep it in the bedroom."

"That's not what's happening. And you shouldn't be telling people about Reese's—"

Cassie cuts me off and passes the ACLU papers to her. "Actually, you couldn't stop Reese from wearing a dress. It's right here; there was this lesbian couple in Mississippi back in 2009 where one of the girls wasn't allowed to wear a tuxedo, and the state ruled that stopping her from wearing a tux was a violation of her First Amendment rights."

"Oh boy. First Amendment rights." Mrs. Camilleri sighs. "I don't know why you're being so combative, both of you. I know it will go fine, and I need you to trust me."

"We just want to know what you're doing," I say. "You said you were going to protect LGBTQ+ students this summer, so why wouldn't you want to—at the bare minimum—know the laws so you can fight for us, at least. There are still homophobic parents here, and regardless of what any of us wear, it's your responsibility to protect them."

The look she gives me borders on a glare, but then she just scoffs. "I knew this was going to happen. You can try to be as kind and open as possible, but your group is always going to find a problem. If you see an 'act of discrimination'"—she says with air quotes—"then you tell me about it and I will handle it."

I feel Cassie tense up next to me, so I put a hand on her knee.

"Should we just go?" I ask, but she shakes her head.

"Speaking of discrimination," she says, "we've noticed that eighteen titles are missing from the library. Every single one of them is a book by a queer author or an author of color. We think that *someone* might be taking them from the library, and we want to figure out why."

We both agreed not to blame Miss Orly directly, since we have no proof that it was her. I mean, who else could it be? But we thought it was best to let Sal's mom come to the conclusion herself.

"Are you accusing me of removing those titles?" she asks.

"What?" I ask. "No, but someone obviously is."

"Someone. Right." She barks out a laugh, though I can tell that this conversation has her flustered. "My son is gay, Gabriel, or did you forget that? I want to be open to the problems of the school, but I will not sit here and be accused of all of this."

Like she's done throughout the meeting, Cassie scribbles down notes. Sal's mom notices.

"I will take your notes, Cassandra." Sal's mom sighs. "You kids only care about going viral and making a big deal about things."

I see Cassie write down '*VP Camilleri tried to take our notes from the meeting.*'

"Cassandra, unless you hand them over now, you will serve detention."

I see Cassie write down '*VP Camilleri threatened retaliation for taking notes during our meeting.*'

Taking the ACLU handout back from her desk, I grab a pen from her desk and circle a section where the ACLU suggests that students document everything—conversations, dates, witnesses, and so on—in case a problem arises.

"Cassie, let's go." She stands, and I turn to Sal's mom. "Give us both detention, I don't care, but if you don't look into the disappearing books issue, we'll investigate it ourselves."

As we walk out, she calls to me to come back into the office. I see her stand from her seat, so I fling the door backward. Without speaking, Cassie and I jog out of the office and into the parking lot.

"I drove my sister's car today," I say. "Want a ride home?"

"Only if we can stop and get a milkshake on the way back, because I need to cool the fuck down."

"Ditto," I say.

The anxiety in my chest slowly releases the farther we get away from the school, so much so that I start to chuckle at the absurdity of it all. Cassie joins me, and before long, we're at a stoplight laughing so hard we can't breathe.

"I don't know why I'm laughing," I say. "It's not funny."

"Not at all," she says after another laughing fit. "But don't you feel *alive* right now? Did you see how freaked out Mrs. Camilleri was? Fuck that school. I think I should wear a gay-ass tuxedo to prom."

I nod. "Only if I get a dress to match."

• Golden Boys •

GABRIEL + HEATH + REESE + SAL

> Sending a pic of my room so you can see the exact chaos I'm living in right now
>
> **R**

S Whoa. Is this a cry for help?

each time I see your room you get like 3 more rolls of fabric

and your desk has fully become a makeup stand

H are these all going to become dresses??

That's the hope. I've been so slammed with classes and prom planning with S that I only get to practice my drag like, a couple hours a night.

Can you all follow my drag alt? I just DMed it

Ⓡ

Ⓖ Followed. Obsessed. Liking every post you've ever made.

Ⓢ Wait your eye makeup is getting so good. Last month you looked like Moira Rose as a crow

Thanks . . . I think. Ⓡ

CHAPTER THIRTY-TWO

HEATH

I'M USUALLY THE ONE who plans my and Reese's dates. It's a role I kind of naturally stepped into, though it's nothing we ever spoke about or decided. I like it, usually. Growing up he and his family rarely did outdoors things for fun—he often stayed in playing video games and drawing—but I was never like that with my parents.

Dad and I always used to take our bikes on the local trail, and we'd bike miles and miles without even stopping, and it wasn't until I was much older that I realized that he so greatly preferred outdoor activities like sports and hiking over indoor ones like bowling and movies because outdoor things cost much less money.

But today, Reese is picking me up for a date, and he's got it all planned out. All he said was to wear a button-up shirt. I'm not sure if that means a casual one, or the crisp white ones I save for special occasions, so I pull out something in between. Its black-and-yellow-plaid design pops out in the mirror, when I give myself one last look-over for surprise zits, spots I missed while shaving, and things like that.

It's been harder to look in the mirror lately. And I don't know why.

I've lost some definition in my chest, and now my upper arms are so big the shirt struggles to fully contain them. I feel lopsided and wonky, with my aching shoulder and the hint of fatigue sprawled across my face.

It's my face, really, that bothers me. The dark circles under my eyes are noticeable, and I wonder if I should get tips from Sal or Reese about how to cover them up. But then again, I don't really want to cover it up. I'm not embarrassed that I *look* tired, I'm embarrassed that I *am* tired. All the time.

My hands shake lightly as I button the top button, but I breathe slowly and it gets better. Anyway, today's about Reese. Me and Reese.

My phone buzzes. It's Diana:

Ready for your big date?

I roll my eyes. How does she know everything that's going on in my life? But when I check Instagram, I see that I was tagged in a story from Reese. It's just him in sunglasses in his car with the text **I've got a hot date tonight with this guy.**

This must mean he's on the way, so I finish getting ready, pull on my nice sneakers, grab my keys, and sprint to the door.

"Well, don't you look dapper," Dad says. I turn to see him and Reese sitting in our living room recliners, a smirk on their faces.

"I saw Reese pull up outside the apartment and invited him in, I hope that's okay."

"Oh," I say. "Totally fine. Ready to go, Reesey?"

He stands and gives my dad a quick handshake before following me out the door.

"Sorry about my dad," I say, but he cuts me off quickly.

"No, I'm glad he did, though he definitely caught me taking a selfie in the car, which was a little mortifying."

We get in Reese's car—rather, his mamma's car—and we head south, out of town, while he catches me up on his conversation with Dad.

"He seems worried about you," Reese eventually says. "He didn't say anything specific, but he said you've not been yourself lately, and that he was glad you had a date to take your mind off things."

"Oh, um, right."

"Do you want to talk about anything?" he says. His words are free of judgment, but also free of expectation.

"Let's talk about your drag! Sal was right, your eye makeup looks so good in those pics."

He sighs. "That's because I'm good at Photoshop. Don't change the topic."

I sigh, wishing my misdirect would've worked.

"I'm just feeling the pressure," I finally admit.

"What pressure, exactly?" he asks.

"Everything. How is it already February? Every time I write the date, I have to double-check the year, and I start to panic a little bit. Like, it's our *graduation year* already. One last season to prove myself in baseball, one last year to prove myself in school. You know, I actually have a shot at valedictorian? It's all been leading up to this."

"You're starting to sound like Sal," Reese says. "No offense. I know you didn't talk to him much over the summer, but I did. Some. Just enough to really get how much stress he put himself under that whole time. I know it wasn't his fault, and this isn't yours either, but you can't keep pushing yourself this hard."

I hesitate. Usually, I'm the one driving, so I can ground myself by gripping the steering wheel, adjusting the mirrors, something that connects me to what I'm doing, so I don't have to sit with all these thoughts.

"I do, Reese." I sigh. "This scholarship is so complicated. I have to find out how much federal aid I'm getting, then I will get a merit award as long as my grades stay the same, and *then* the biggest chunk is covered by the athletic scholarship—*if* I get it. I'm working with, like, three different offices, and if a single one of these pieces falls through, I'd have no prospects."

"It's going to work out, though. It has to."

"Last year, when I first started really getting the attention of scouts, I felt so special. Like, I've worked so hard for this and finally knew what I wanted to do with my life."

Reese hesitates. "What *do* you want to do with your life, outside of baseball?"

He asks it awkwardly, and I realize that for years I've gotten by with talking about baseball, dodging all the questions that I'm even asking myself: What will I study? What do I even want to *do* after college?

"I don't know. I'll be starting undecided, I think." I laugh. "I mean, of course there's a little part of me that wants to follow this baseball thing through to the very end. Could you imagine me touring with a minor league team or something?"

"The concessions stands would be so much better," Reese says with a laugh.

"So you'd still come?"

He smirks. "To as many as I could. I don't care where your games are."

"I like to hear that. But otherwise, no, I don't know what I want to do. Maybe something in science? I'm not huge on physics this year, but I thought bio and chem were really fun."

As we approach a strip mall about thirty miles outside Gracemont, Reese pulls into the nearest parking lot and turns off the car. I look out the window.

"You're taking me to Steak 'n Shake?" I ask, and he laughs.

"No, I'm just not used to talking to you and driving. I keep wanting to look at you, or, like, put my hand on your knee, or something, but I also don't want to kill us."

"I appreciate that," I say as Reese turns to me.

"Maybe the answer to this isn't putting all your hopes into one thing, then? If you're not looking at Vanderbilt for any program, maybe you could apply to a few more backup schools? I'm sure there are still a few whose deadlines haven't passed."

I've done that, of course, but my only backup is our local

community college. Which would be fine. And maybe I could even transfer into Vanderbilt after a year.

"I don't think you get how much I need this *one thing* to work out," I say. "I want the four-year, away-from-home college experience. I know it's not for everyone, but I know it's for me. It's for people like Gabriel too—I'm pretty sure he was born wearing an Ohio State hoodie."

"Believe me, I know how much you need this to work out, Heath." He sighs. "I don't know how scholarships work, but there must be something out there that can help."

"It's not as straightforward as it sounds. I've talked to our credit union about taking out a student loan, but then Dad would have to cosign, and I don't know if we'd even get approved for the full amount. And then, what, I spend the rest of my life paying it off?" I sigh. "Sorry. This isn't exactly date night conversation, is it?"

"I asked," he says. "And I think when your date night is just a few months from your high school graduation, it probably is." He pauses. "Just... know I'm here for you, if you need to talk. I know I'm coming off of a few mistakes, and a whole lot is up in the air now, but I love you and I want to be there for you."

I shake my head. "I know. I love you too."

He leans over and kisses me, and I instinctively put my hand on the back of his head and pull him in to me. Our kisses were once hesitant, full of awkward passion but a completely blank knowledge of where to put our hands, our lips, our tongues, but as my comfort with him has grown, our kisses have become less restrained.

We break apart, just enough to catch our breaths, and I rub the side of his nose with my own. The khakis I put on are tight, and I'm fully regretting the lack of space in them, but I can't exactly adjust myself right now, so I rest my forehead against his and settle into the discomfort.

"I really love you, you know," Reese says.

I lick my lips, and a hint of his vanilla lip balm hits my tongue.

"Yeah, I can tell," I say with a smile.

CHAPTER THIRTY-THREE

REESE

HEATH COMES BACK INTO the car holding two large shakes, and I greedily grab my chocolate-strawberry swirl one from his hands. I really did pull into this parking lot to give us a place to talk where I didn't have to concentrate on driving, but when you're in the parking lot of a Steak 'n Shake, you can't really justify leaving without getting one for the road.

Once we're back on the highway, I put on a new playlist. This one's titled *For Heath*, and it features all the pop and country artists that I know put a smile on his face: Cam, The Chicks, and early Taylor Swift, along with a few recommended songs that I liked.

"Oh, by the way, my cousin is having a party for the whole family in a couple of weeks. It's her daughter's christening, which is…not as exciting as a normal party, but she wanted to make sure you got the invite."

"As long as it's on a Sunday I'm in the clear." Heath sighs. "We start Saturday practices next week."

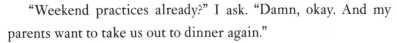

"Weekend practices already?" I ask. "Damn, okay. And my parents want to take us out to dinner again."

"Sure," he says coolly. "Anytime."

"Anytime that isn't a weekday or a Saturday?"

He shakes his head. "I'm sorry. I hate it too."

Mom actually asked me to ask him about this a few weeks ago, but with how awkward things were between us while I lied about my drag, I never asked. And now that I have, I wonder how smart it is to have him so integrated in my family—when he was my friend, it was perfect. But now that we're more, there's a part of me that's starting to wonder whether it's a good idea, considering graduation could very well be the end of us.

But no matter what, I remind myself, he *is* family. He's always been. And even if things don't work out like that, he'll always be a part of me.

And maybe that's why I hesitate.

Before I know it, half the playlist is done and we're coming up on Upper Arlington, a neighborhood of Columbus that happens to house our destination. I follow the signs for Buckeye Art Center and park in a spot.

"On all our dates, you always get to share with me some part of you. Whether we're hiking a trail you loved, or you're trying to teach me how to ride a bike, I love experiencing things that excite you."

He looks out the window, and a wide-eyed expression covers his face.

"You're going to make me do *art?*" he says dramatically.

I laugh. "Come on."

He pretends to resist as I drag him into the art studio. It's empty, save for a few canvases. A fairly young but gray-haired woman comes out from the back and gives us a big wave.

"Hello, hello! You must be my five-thirty private lesson." She checks the journal behind the front desk. "Reese, right?"

"That's me," I say.

"I'm not an artist," Heath jumps in. "I mean, I can't do art. He can."

The artist looks at me, and I shake my head. She gives me a wink and waves us along. Into the studio, I see the setup, so I guide Heath to it.

"I know that forcing you to 'do art' would not be your ideal date night. And maybe this won't be either." I smile. "But I've been working on my charcoal portraits, and I think I'm finally ready to do one for real. With Estelle's help, that is."

"I'm simply here to guide you, Reese. I'm sure you'll barely need me," she says.

"You're going to draw my portrait?" he asks. "Wait, that's so cool. And I don't have to do any art?"

"No, you just have to sit on that stool and look hot." I roll my eyes.

"I can do that," he says smugly.

I place the drawing board and drawing paper on a wooden easel, and I take a seat on a stool with the perfect view of Heath, who looks so cute I want to steal a kiss. On the table next to me are various charcoal tools—pencils, powders, a couple of erasers, and a compressed charcoal stick—it's more than I've got in the kit at home, but with Estelle's guidance, I'll be able to figure out what I'm doing.

I look at his face and study it before I take a palette knife and dip it into the black pen pastel. I use this tool and start with the eyes, to give the impression of his face. I ignore the details and try to capture the shape of his face, the angle of his eyes, the proportions of his face.

"How am I looking?" Heath calls out after about five minutes have passed.

I look at the blurred sketch in front of me, a mess of shadows and lights without a detail in sight. But I have a vision for it, and even in this form, I recognize something about Heath in there when I squint.

"Looking good," I say with a laugh. "Now, stop moving."

"Yessir," he says, giving a quick salute.

After a short consultation with Estelle, she helps me add structure to the start. She explains how I need to focus even more on impressions before I go into detail work, so I stop focusing on the sharp line of his nose, the flare of his nostril, and add more layers of shadow and light to the piece.

It's almost haunting, this ghost of Heath on the paper in front of me. The shadows gather deeply under his eyes, and I don't know how not to show it. I use the kneaded eraser to smooth it out, to bring out the highlights—what's inside him.

I push and pull the piece with the flat brush, slowly adding details to Heath's face. I etch out his soft chin, highlight the cheekbones, and find myself working on his eyes for minutes at a time until I get every impression right.

Estelle puts a hand on my shoulder, her way of telling me to move on, to stop fixating on it. So I grab the charcoal pencil and fill in even more detail.

Within minutes, his face comes fully into view. Details of his eyes are lost in the shadow, so I use one of the detailing erasers to bring out the sparkle in his eyes. I cheat here, and I feel like Estelle knows it, but she must understand it.

Heath runs to the bathroom, and Estelle takes his spot.

"We all want to show what's inside, don't we?" She laughs. "If he's sad, let the portrait reflect that, Reese."

"I can't," I say. "It has to send the right message; it has to be perfect."

She stares at me. "Sadness can be perfection too."

Heath comes back and greets me with a smile, so I tell him that I only need about ten more minutes to finish up the final details, and then we can go get some dinner. His stomach grumbles in response.

I darken the eyes, again, and draw what I see. What Heath is feeling. Not who I want him to be right now, but who he is, and I realize that even if he looks a little sad in this, he's just as beautiful as he's ever been. And maybe one day, when things get less stressful for him, I can draw him that way too.

"Ready to see?" I ask.

"The only other drawing of me I've ever gotten was by a caricaturist at Cedar Point, so I want you to know my expectations are sky high."

I laugh as he comes around. "Well, I can't beat that, but maybe I can come close."

There's a pause, a moment of silence where I think I might have done the wrong thing, that I should take that eraser and start the eyes over again. But he wraps me into a hug and stares.

"I've never...," he starts, and I hear him get choked up. "I've never had someone see me like you do, Reesey."

CHAPTER THIRTY-FOUR

GABRIEL

I SINK INTO SAL'S pillow, and a warm, nostalgic feeling takes over me. It's an odd feeling—we haven't been together since that one mistake of a week back in Boston, but something about the smell of him on this pillow reminds me that, for better or worse, he's always going to take up a whole lot of my heart.

"Can you at least take off your shoes if you're going to lie on my bed?" he asks, swiveling around in his desk chair.

"Fine," I say, and I do. "I forgot how comfy this was. My mattress is so freaking hard."

I look to him, but he just rolls his eyes. "Can we finally debrief? How did your meeting with Mom go?"

"Let's just say I'm very glad she's out for the night, because it was *not good*. Sal, it was like she was before the summer, but twice as annoying."

"I figured," he says, rubbing his face with his hands. "She was weird this morning. I'm not sure what's gotten into her."

"It's good we went in with all the ACLU 'know your rights' shit in our hands. I thought Cassie was just being paranoid, but we actually needed to use it." I think back to the conversation, wondering where exactly it went wrong. "Oh, your mom also said something about Reese coming to prom in a dress. Do you think she's going to go around and tell people about it?"

"Crap. She must have seen him leaving one night." His cheeks turn red. "She actually *said* that to you?"

"Yeah. I mean, he told me about it briefly, and I obviously followed his drag alt, but what's this all about?" I ask with a coy pleading voice.

"Basically, Reese wanted to do drag, and he needed help. He came to me about it in Paris, since I'm the only one who knows how to apply makeup, but he's really picked it up better than I could. It's, like, his art now."

I stare at Sal's ceiling, taking in everything he's saying. I think of how each post showed something new: colorful eye art, drag tributes to his favorite queens, and he's started posting videos detailing his design and production process. It's like he came back from Paris the first time with a new skill, and he's already looking like a pro at it.

"Hmm," I say.

"Do you think the whole drag thing is weird?"

"No, it kind of makes sense for him. I think it's weird he kept it a secret for so long, even from Heath."

It's not like Reese to keep a secret from us. Especially something he should know we'd be all in on.

"I think…I think he just wanted to figure it out on his own, before he started actually doing it. He's always the type to measure twice and cut once." Sal shrugs. "I think that's a woodworking term, but it applies to fashion design too."

"You're that way too, though. Maybe that's part of why he came to you about it?"

"Maybe." He shrugs. "It's not important. I'm sure he'll give us all a real show when he's ready."

"Not sure I can picture him on a stage," I laugh. "But I'll get my dollar bills ready, just in case."

But once the laughter dies down, an awkward silence replaces it. As much as I tried to breeze past this thing with his mom, it's obvious it's something bigger for Sal.

"I don't think your mom's a bad person," I say quietly.

He drums his fingers on his desk, which is the only sound that breaks up the silence that follows. My heart hurts for him. Sure, I've had my own spats with my parents, but overall I can say they support me. I can say that about Reese's moms. Heath's dad.

"The only thing appealing about going to college is that I'd be able to leave my mom here," he says.

"You don't mean that."

"I do." The tapping on his desk grows louder. "How can you just dismiss her after what she said to you? During the school year it's like everything she does is just one big microaggression. I really thought she was going to change."

"I'm not dismissing her, or what she said. But if I spent time being this angry at everyone who disagreed with me or pushed back on what I wanted to do, I would lose my fucking mind."

I sit up, and we make eye contact. And it reminds me of the summer—me, confident and sure; him, small and shaken.

"You know you have to tell her, right?" I say. "I know you have a little bit of time before this campaign gets off the ground, but if we actually want to give the mayor a run for his money in November, we have to start soon. It'll be March before we know it."

"Okay," he says. "You're right. I keep setting dates where I think I'll tell her, then I chicken out and pretend I'm sick. I can't keep this up, or she's going to put the pieces together on her own."

"Call a meeting of the boys this weekend, and let's get planning started."

He nods. I smile.

"You can do this, you know," I say.

He shakes his head. "We'll see."

• • •

On my way home, I give Matt a call. It rings a few times, then goes straight to voice mail. At a stop sign, I check our texts to make sure he said he'd be free tonight, and confirm it. But he hasn't responded to a text all day, and he hasn't responded to my call.

There's a weird insecurity that starts to eat me up. It's not the first time I've felt a little jealous or paranoid—I mean, that's bound to happen when your boyfriend's a few states away from you—but it's the first time I've felt . . . ignored.

He knew I had that big talk today with Sal's mom, but he never even checked in on me. For all he knows, I could've been expelled!

"Okay, drama queen, that's enough," I say aloud to myself, in hopes of keeping myself in check.

I need to keep my mind busy, so I call my sister instead. She picks up on the first ring.

"Bro!"

"...Sis?"

"You're right, that was awkward," she says. "Want to call and we can try this again?"

I laugh. "No, we're good. I'm just driving home, and I think I'm losing my mind."

"That's no good," she says. "Anything happen?"

"Yes and no. I had a meeting with Sal's mom to talk about some LGBTQ+ Advocacy Group issues. I wanted to bring up what we talked about—the whole prom issue—and she dismissed me entirely. Then when Cassie brought up this ACLU resource about our rights she became unhinged."

"Oof," she grunts. "That's hard. She always was impossible. But whenever I dealt with her it was like, we did that senior prank with the silly string everywhere and she went ballistic, even though we were going to clean it up."

"This is a little different."

"Okay fine, that didn't infringe on my human rights. But she's still annoying. How'd Sal take it?"

"Hard, actually. He's starting to become a little closed off again. Which I guess he did a lot, but *I* could always get him to open up."

"And you're not sure how to get him to open up without, you know, whatever you two did." She adds quickly, "I'm not asking for details."

"I'm not going to give them," I say. "But you're right. He's only been truly vulnerable with me a couple of times, and I miss that side of him. He should be able to show emotion all the time, not just when he's midbreakdown or if we were mid—"

"Again, don't need the details." She sighs. "Look, maybe you need to just…I don't know. Find a way to be intimate with him, without being *that kind* of intimate."

"Right," I say. "Can I also complain about my boyfriend?"

I pull into our driveway and shut off the car. I don't really want to face my parents right now, as they'll want to know how my conversation with the vice principal went too. I sit in the car and keep talking to Katie.

"What did he do wrong?" she asks.

"Literally nothing," I say, and my breath starts to fog up the car window. "He's just not here, and I wish he was. I haven't talked to him much today, and my mind is already trying to turn this into some huge offense—but he's busy! And so am I!"

"We're all busy," she says, "but are you making time for each other? My roommate is in a long-distance thing, and they are so structured with their time it's kind of exhausting. She's on one of her scheduled weekly calls with her girlfriend right now."

"I don't want schedules," I say.

"Well, what *do* you want from him? A schedule could help, even if it changes every week. Or! You could—"

"Stop," I say. "I don't think that's it. It's too hard. I miss him all the time. Even when I got to see him, I was just counting down the minutes until we'd be apart again. The phone calls aren't enough. The FaceTimes just show me something I can't touch."

"Long-distance relationships are totally doable."

"I know they are," I sigh. "I worry they're not for me, though."
There's a silence on the other end.

"Talk to him when you can. I'm not sure what's going on, but
maybe he's having the same feelings and you two can figure out
what works for you. Just don't do that thing you did this summer,
when you got overwhelmed and just... disappeared."

"I know. I won't."

• • •

When I get home, I warm up the leftovers from Dad's dinner and
take it up to my room, escaping an awkward conversation with my
parents. My phone vibrates in my pocket, and when I pull it out, I
see it's a message from Matt.

**Hey, love. Sorry, I just saw your calls. I have some time to
chat tonight if you want to FaceTime.**

I walk into my room, and the heart Heath bought me starts
glowing. Another text:

I miss you.

I drop the plate of food on my desk and go to FaceTime Matt.
Sure, Katie's right. I need to talk to him. I *know* this. But when his
face appears and his voice hits my ears, all my anxieties wash away
for a second. I don't want to mess up what we have, not just yet.

CHAPTER THIRTY-FIVE

SAL

"YOU SHOULD REALLY GET the pool fixed," I tell my aunt when she opens the door.

She laughs. "You want to go swimming? At nine at night? In late February?"

"I mean generally," I say, shaking my head. "We had fun. Things were so easy, those summers. I really had no idea."

"Does your mom know you're here, or is this another one of your secret-keeping things?" She waves me in. "You need to stop putting me in this position—I hate keeping things from your mom."

I give her a quick hug, which melts her defenses.

"Oh, fine," she says. "Make it quick, I've got a show coming on in thirty minutes."

"Thanks, Aunt Lily."

I come into the living room and chuckle at the giant Christmas tree, which is still fully decorated, despite it being weeks past Christmas.

"Don't laugh, it keeps me merry," she says.

We take our seats—her in her giant La-Z-Boy, me on her plush sofa. The energy in her house is warmer, in a way, than what I'm used to. Maybe it's the messy room, or the soft lighting, or the fact that it's perpetually Christmas.

Or, maybe, it's just an aunt thing.

"I'm hoping to make my mayoral run official," I say. "But to do that, I have to first convince Mom that it's a good idea."

"And let me guess, your mom still has no idea you don't want to go to college."

I shift nervously on her sofa. "I'm waiting for the right time."

"If you keep waiting, she's going to find out on her own, and it's going to be *bad*. For all of us." She sighs. "Here, let's role-play this—"

"What do you mean?" I interrupt, but she shushes me.

She pulls her hair back in a tight bun and gives off a prudish look. "Pretend I'm Rachel. Tell me."

"Fine," I say, rolling my eyes. "Mom, I don't want to go to college."

"Why not?" she says.

"I just don't feel like college is for everyone."

"That's true, but we've always felt like college is for *you*."

"No, Mom, you don't get it," I say.

"Tell me why you don't want to go to college."

"It's a waste of money," I say.

"We have the money."

"It's a waste of time!" I shout. "This summer, I thought I needed to escape, to leave our small town behind to make a real difference, but I found out that all college did and all that work did for people on the Hill was waste people's time. I don't want to be in politics like that. I want to help on a local level. I want to make this town better, this county better, and maybe one day I'll want to make Ohio better."

"Now we're getting somewhere," my aunt says. "Elaborate."

"I want to run for mayor. I want to push back on Mayor Green's lazy agenda. I actually want to *attend* town council meetings and listen to people in this town, no matter how much I don't agree with them personally, so I can make sure we move forward as a community. I want to—"

"Stop," my aunt says. "Take this feeling, write it down, rehearse it, and deliver it to your mother. I don't need to hear the whole spiel, but she does."

I smile. "You think it'll work?"

"Not at first, but I think you'll get your point across. And when she eventually calls me, I can pretend it's the best idea in the world."

"You really think it is?" I ask.

She sighs. "No, of course not. But it's not the worst. And you'd have my vote—someone needs to knock that racist homophobe on his ass, and it might as well be someone like you. But I also want you to be prepared for the reality of this. I don't even know if our mayor gets paid, and if he does, it's not much. It's not a full-time job."

"Oh, I never thought about that."

"How am I, an adult, supposed to trust a teenager to run my town?"

I sigh. "I don't have a good answer for that either."

"This is where your mom will break you: the specifics. How will you pay for this career? Will you be living at home? No judgment, plenty of teens do for a while. But more importantly, what happens if you lose?"

I look away, gazing into the bright Christmas tree. I don't know what happens if I lose. Would I try to start college in second semester? Would I take some community college courses? Or would I be able to find a career in politics—local politics?

"I'm going to tell Mom soon, I promise. But first, I think I should talk to Congresswoman Caudill."

"Sal, you can't keep telling everyone but your mom. You're making excuses."

I shake my head and stand to leave. Before I go, I give my aunt a big hug. "Thanks for listening to me."

"I'm always here if you need me," she says. "But so is your mom."

I shake my head. "We'll see."

• Golden Boys •

GABRIEL + HEATH + REESE + SAL

SNOW DAYYYYYYYYY

after our group hang today
can we go sledding??

or a snowball fight? i just
got done with pitching
practice but i think I still
have a few good snowball
throws left in me

come on guysssss H

S No.

G No, sorry.

R — Also a no from me. 🖤

S — We have a strict agenda.

you guys seriously have no whimsy you know that? — H

CHAPTER THIRTY-SIX

REESE

SNOW. AGAIN.

It's the first week of March, which is right around the time when I get fully sick of snow. And the cold. I've heard the winters in New York aren't much better than the ones here, even though I have fantasies of myself all bundled up and walking through a secluded part of Central Park, the snow dusting the trees, and everything feeling right.

In those daydreams, I'm distinctly alone. Because I know if I choose this path, if I get into design school and move to New York City, I'll have to say goodbye to Heath.

The rattling of Heath's truck wakes me out of my reverie, and I smile and give him a wave from my porch. I climb into the truck and drop a duffel bag under my legs in the front seat.

"Want to throw that in the back?" he asks, but I shake my head.

"Priceless cargo in here. The first dress I've ever fully designed and executed."

He laughs. "I can't believe you finally did it. *And* I can't believe you're actually going to model it for us."

"Too weird?" I say.

I'm used to feeling vulnerable. Maybe that's an artist thing, but whenever I share my designs or drawings, or like when I presented the boys with their own designed charm bracelets, I feel like I'm showing off a part of me. This, though, is so far outside my comfort zone that the pressure is building.

I feel like I need to prove something with this look. Sure, I still don't know what I want to do with my life, but I'm having fun. That's all that really matters, right?

"Not that weird," Heath says. "I'm excited to see the full look. I assume there's a lip-sync performance to match?"

I roll my eyes. "One thing at a time. I'd really just like to get one good Instagram post out of it, maybe a couple of TikToks that show off the look."

"Need me to take videos?" Heath asks.

I hesitate. "I already asked Sal to, since he's, um—"

"He's way better at taking pictures than I am—I'm not offended." He laughs. "If we do your show early enough, we might be able to get pics out in Gabe's back yard."

"One, I'm not showing off my drag to all of Gracemont. Two, since when do *you* call him Gabe?"

He shrugs. "It's something I've been trying out. I think he likes it better. And he really did change over the summer. That boy is not Gabriel—he's Gabe."

Once we get to *Gabriel's*, we go right into the rec room in the basement. Gabriel and Sal sit on opposite ends of the sofa, sharing a long knitted blanket between them to keep their legs warm.

"Hey, guys," Gabriel says. "I have to go put some appetizers into the oven. Drag show, then snacks, then the first meeting of the Sal Camilleri for Mayor committee?"

"Big agenda today," I say with a chuckle. "All right, I'll go ahead and get ready."

I go to the basement bathroom and unpack all my items. I pull out the makeup I bought in Paris—it's finally time—and hang the dress over the towel rack. I hear Gabriel take the stairs up to the kitchen, and as I look into the mirror, I see Sal come up behind me.

"Need any help?" he asks.

I pull out the tinted moisturizer and rub it evenly over my face, then take a glue stick and press upward on my brows. Once it dries, I'll be able to cover the brows with foundation and draw entirely new ones on. It's the latest technique I've been working on, as my boy brows started to get really distracting in drag.

"I think I'm good, but you can supervise."

"I'm on it," he says, taking a seat on the toilet.

I work in silence, ignoring the light shake in my hand as I detail my eye with liquid eyeliner. I bring my eye shadow palette to the dress, picking a gradient that goes with the whole look.

"Are you nervous?" Sal asks as he gently brushes the double-stacked blonde wig I brought.

"Yes and no." I sigh. "I know it's good; I've watched hundreds of instructional videos, and I've become a lot more confident in treating this work as art. But it doesn't mean that, I don't know, it'll be *too much* for Heath, or if people will think I have no idea what I want to do with my life."

"It's not too much for Heath," Sal says. "And obviously we're all cool with it. You've dabbled in all kinds of art over the years, from digital fan art to oil paintings to sketches. I'm not surprised that you're turning yourself into the canvas, in a way."

I chuckle. "Yeah, I guess that's right."

"You should know, though. Mom said something to Gabriel about not wanting you to wear a dress to prom," he says, gritting his teeth.

"Whoa, that's not good." I set down my brush. "I was really hoping to fly under the radar with prom, considering what happened a few years ago."

"Well, Gabe and the whole LGBTQ+ Advocacy Group is on it—they're all reading up on laws and stuff." He pauses. "And I didn't catch the final verdict, but I think you could wear a dress, if you wanted to."

"I don't want to wear a dress," I say. "I want to show up in a tux, with a boutonniere that matches Heath's, and dance with him without anyone giving us a second look."

"Right."

"I just want to be with him. I don't want drama or attention."

"I know," Sal says. "And for what it's worth, Gabe's group is trying to take care of things behind the scenes so we can all have the prom we deserve."

"Okay," I say. "Now, get out! I've got to change and get ready for the show."

"Break a leg," Sal says as he closes the door.

CHAPTER THIRTY-SEVEN

HEATH

ONCE GABRIEL COMES BACK from the kitchen, we catch up on how our March has been going so far. Mine's a pretty easy recap: practice, studying, practice, hanging out with Reese, practice. His has been varied, but he seems to be spending a lot of his time on some extracurricular business for our LGBTQ+ group.

"Have you asked Reese to prom yet?" he asks. "Like, officially?"

"I'm keeping my options open," I joke. "I haven't, though. You don't think he expects a big promposal thing, right?"

Gabriel shrugs. "I don't think you have to worry about that. But you should ask him, before someone else nabs him."

"I'll get on that," I say. "What about you? Think you'll ask Matt?"

"I don't know," he admits. "We haven't gotten to talk much lately, and I'm afraid to know the answer."

"You know he would if he could. Or, hey, maybe you can go to his?"

He shrugs. "Heath, it's so hard—we keep missing each other's calls, and I feel like my relationship is now fully made up of voice messages that we pass back and forth in iMessage."

"Ah, I'm sorry," I say, placing my hand on his knee.

I've been watching his relationship develop closely over the past few months. I wanted to pick up what worked for them, maybe learn from things that didn't, so that if... *when* Reese and I try the whole long-distance thing, we can do it right.

But they're doing it right. It's just not enough for Gabriel. And I think that's okay—sometimes it's hard to hold on to relationships like that, but watching them drift apart, watching their priorities change, and seeing Gabriel how he is now: sullen, distracted, and in pain, it makes me wonder whether trying long distance would be worth it at all.

"Love you, Gabe," I ultimately say. "You'll get through it."

"Hey, you never call me Gabe!"

"Thought I'd try it out." I give him a wink. "You do seem like a new person after this summer."

"Thanks," he says. "I like the name."

Sal comes back and joins us on the couch. Without thinking, I scoot to the edge of the couch, while Sal and Gabe snuggle closer to each other. This is the time when I'd make wide eyes with Reese, so I find my eyes aimlessly drifting to the two coffee tables in the rec room.

"We should move the tables together," I say. "Like a runway toward the couch."

"Oh my god," Gabe says. "Yes, absolutely."

We jump up and start rearranging the furniture, and I'm surprised at how heavy these antique coffee tables are. I'm struggling less than Gabe, but as we move along, I feel the strain on my shoulder. Once I drop the first table and put it in line with the second, I instinctively rub my upper arm.

"You okay?" Sal asks.

"We're fine, but thanks for offering to help," Gabriel responds sarcastically.

Anxiety creeps into my mind, as it's becoming clearer that my shoulder is getting worse. It's taking longer to warm up, and it's hurting almost all the time, and my range of motion has been greatly reduced.

If I don't have full motion, I don't pitch.

If I don't pitch, I don't go to school.

Sweat prickles on my forehead, and as Gabe chatters on about something I take the time to collect myself and breathe through the pain. Breathe through it. *Breathe through it.*

"Y'all ready for a show?" Reese says after busting through the bathroom door. The light obscures his details, but all I can see is a flowy dress and the silhouette of some big ol' hair. "Oh god, wait, did you guys really make a catwalk? I don't even have heels."

"My sister might have left some here," Gabe says. "She's got huge feet."

"I'm not making my first time in heels on top of two coffee tables from the 1920s," he replies.

"Fair," I chime in. "Okay, let's see you!"

Reese takes slow steps toward the "stage" and hikes up his

dress to step barefoot onto the table. Sal whips out his phone, but Gabe and I take in the show. Reese struts on the pretend catwalk— I'd never have pegged him as a strutter, but I'm not sure I imagined him to ever be in a dress—and I can see the detail in his dress as he walks.

It's a short, icy-blue dress constructed around a tight-fitting bodice with geometric shapes coming out from all angles. It looks haphazard, but I know every white-blue triangle was placed onto the dress with intention, to give off this sharp, powerful ice queen look.

His makeup is also impeccable—a smoky eye with varying blues, a cat eye that looks like it was drawn on by paint, and actually flawless skin. It's like a leveled-up version of what I saw in the car.

The wig has also improved greatly from the one I saw in the truck. It's got a lot more volume now, which makes the rest of the proportions of his body look just right. As he walks, he takes steps on the balls of his bare feet—like he's already pretending he's in heels. He moves with a kind of confidence I don't see from him often, and I start to understand what drag queens mean when they say that they have an entirely different drag persona.

"What, no tips?" Reese says to break up the silence, which makes Gabe and I laugh.

Sal keeps taking photos and video from his phone, and I have no doubt that they'll all turn out fierce.

Reese takes another walk down the "catwalk" and pivots a bit too quickly at the end. I see him start to lose his balance, so I jump up to catch him. Thankfully, most of his weight falls into the arm that isn't throbbing, so I'm able to slowly guide him down to the floor. I give him a peck on the lips, careful not to mess up the lipstick.

"What do you think?" he finally asks.

"It's really good, babe."

When I see him like this, I think of his life in New York and all the wonderful things that'll be coming his way. I have no idea whether he wants to use drag to try to become some sort of social media influencer, or if he wants to find his way into the drag circles in the artsy eighteen-and-up NYC drag scene, but no matter what he does, I know he's going to fucking crush it.

I do *not* think about how I'm not going to be there to enjoy it.

GABRIEL + MATT

> Have you followed Reese's drag account yet?

> Sal just took these incredible photos of him, and it's already getting a little bit of attention on there. He looks so freaking good. Ⓖ

> Out with friends now but I'll check ASAP!

> Ⓜ I wish our friend groups could meet someday. I feel like they'd all get along.

> Yeah, I guess you've only met Sal. And *that* was a mess. Ⓖ

That was a bit of a mess, yes.
But he was in love with you,
and I can't blame him for that.

That's not love, that was this
weird codependence we
had. Believe me. It was toxic.

Oh. Okay.

Didn't seem very toxic to me.
Just seemed like your friend
was hurting, and he turned to
you for help.

It felt like love to me. But hey,
you know him better than me.

CHAPTER THIRTY-EIGHT

GABRIEL

AFTER OUR IMPROMPTU DRAG show, Reese puts on one of his chill playlists, Heath and Sal move the tables back, and I go upstairs to load up a platter with every frozen appetizer my oven could handle and grab every condiment I can carry.

I try not to think about what Matt said. What Sal and I had wasn't love, I know that. At least, it wasn't from my end. I've always loved him, but not like *that*. Can you really love someone who's stopping you from becoming your true self?

When I come back down, Sal's pulling out an easel with a pad of sticky paper on it. We have a couple of them in school, so I wouldn't be surprised if he was able to borrow one from there.

"Thanks for the food," Sal says as he leans in to grab a mozzarella stick.

The others thank me and dig in, and as soon as I take a seat, the first meeting of the Sal for Mayor campaign comes to a start.

"All right, thanks for helping me out, everyone." He flips through pages on the easel, until he hits one that says *Grassroots Efforts*. "Gabe, first brainstorming session goes to you. How do we get the word out about this?"

"Oh," I say, not realizing I was going to be put on the spot. "Well, have you told your mom? That seems like step one."

"Gabe—"

"Sorry," I say. "I know. But I can't do anything publicly without your mom knowing. And we all know that if anyone can help with the communications campaign, it'd be her. Didn't she manage Congresswoman Caudill's communications when she ran for office?"

"I know, I know. In our next college check-in I'm going to tell her. It's supposed to be tomorrow. I'm still working up the courage here."

His face looks pale, and I see a bit of that vulnerability we *never* see anymore. He must be feeling really messed up about this. So I jump in and start brainstorming a plan.

"It's okay. Let's see, I would create a Facebook page for your campaign."

"*Facebook*," Heath says. "Is anyone even on there?"

Sal jumps in. "Gabe's got a point. I might get the younger vote just because people in school know me, but it's going to be harder to get people our parents' age and older on board, and that's where Facebook comes in. That's also where Mayor Green has the biggest reach. If I start getting in debates with him in comments, maybe that'll pull more people to my side."

"Exactly," I say. "Next, we'll want to get you into the two

parades we have this year: the Gracemont Founders' Day Parade this summer and the Homecoming Parade this fall. We can raise money to make a float, or just rent one of those fancy cars without the tops."

"Unless that's too elitist," Reese interjects. "I think you'd get more of the vote if you were just in the back of Heath's truck."

"The *opposite* of elitist," Heath says with a laugh. "You're more than welcome to it, though. First years aren't allowed to have cars on campus anyway, so even if I won't be here my truck would love the attention."

Reese and Heath look at each other for a beat, and a sad silence takes over.

I cut through the awkwardness. "We'll think about it, but I'll figure out how people even do that."

"And this isn't really flashy or anything, but you should really be going to the town council meetings," I say. "Start by listening to the people, hear their concerns and see if there's anything you could do that the mayor's not. And outside of that, I'm not sure— I could try to start a GoFundMe or something, but there might be laws and stuff about raising money for a political campaign."

Sal finishes writing out my suggestions, then turns to me and gives me a sweet smile.

"Thanks, Gabe." He flips to the next page. "All right, Reese— designs?"

"Present!" Reese says, then corrects with, "This isn't roll call, sorry."

Reese digs around in his bag for his sketchbook. He opens to the page on the first try and passes over the page of sketches to Sal.

"I had a look at... way too many campaign slogans and designs. The ideas I have there are pretty basic, but I like the idea of dropping your last name on some of these. Make the website SalForMayor .com: it's punchy and will look good and be easily readable on a sign."

"These are all great, Reese," Sal says. "I think we'll go with this one. What do you guys think?"

We debate on the logo for a few minutes, before Reese finishes up his report with what he'll need to design a website for Sal.

"I can have it up in a month," Reese says, "but I'm not doing anything until you tell your mom. You know how sneaky she is; I'm afraid if I open a website she'll get some alert on her phone or something."

"Noted." Sal laughs. "All right, that just leaves Heath."

"I didn't prepare anything," Heath says.

Sal shakes his head. "No, that's fine. I really just need you to try to get the word out around school once this is announced. Get people to go to the website, ride the float with me, and basically make me cooler by association. I'll also need to get a petition signed by a lot of voting residents. Could you help me get people in school to sign the petition so I can get on the ballot?"

"It'd be my honor," Heath says.

"Oh, and Gabe—can we do a newsletter and link to it on Reese's website? I feel like that's something people still use."

"Sure thing," I say. "I could help you come up with content for

CHAPTER THIRTY-NINE

SAL

HEATH MOVES THE EASEL out of the way of the TV, as Reese cuts the music and starts streaming the latest episode of the show we've been binging. Gabe and I watch the show, inches apart, acting like everything's normal, acting like nothing happened— I mean, nothing did happen!

Something about Gabe will never stop pulling me into him, I know that. Over the summer, during a moment of weakness, I was drawn to him so much that I got on a bus to Boston to see him.

But he was with someone else. And *I* was ruining it. He's still with someone else. And I can't ruin it again, no matter how much he means to me.

After the show, Reese and Heath head out.

"Look, back there, I—" I start, as Gabe says, "I can't believe I put my arm around—"

We stop. We look at each other.

it. I have like eighty-thousand emails in my promotions folder from different social justice orgs, and I'm sure you get a ton of political ones, so maybe we can plan it out."

After about thirty more minutes of brainstorming and planning, Sal sets down his marker and sighs. He comes around and snags the last mozzarella stick before sinking into the couch next to me. Instinctively, I put my arm around him and he leans into me.

I pull my hand away just as he lifts his head from my shoulder. *Right. We don't do that.*

Sal scoots over, and I can't help but think we were just sharing a brain cell in that moment. My cheeks flush with heat, and I pull my knees up to my chest, as casually as I can. Love or not, whatever we had *was* real. And thank god neither of us wants to start that up again.

"Old habits die hard, Gabe."

He nods. "It didn't mean anything, right?"

"Maybe we're just drawn to each other when we're stressed, or something." I laugh. "I bet that's all it is."

"I'm not stressed," he says.

"Well, that makes one of us. I've been rehearsing my speech to Mom all week. Every night before bed, every morning in the shower, and I can't even convince myself that it's a smart idea, what I'm doing."

He puts his hand on my arm and squeezes it, with a kind smile on his face.

"To be fair, I don't think what you're doing is smart. I don't think that's the case you have to make to your mom." He lets my arm slide through his hand until he's able to grip my hand. "Logic isn't going to win here, because this isn't a logical choice. This is an emotional one—it's something you care about. It's something you want to do—and it's something you *can* do. You can make this town better."

"I haven't been attending the town hall meetings because I didn't want someone to mention to Mom that I was there. But I've been downloading all the minutes from the town website, and they log every single complaint—and the mayor's doing nothing. Our parks are overgrown, there's got to be a stack of fifty permits on his desk that he won't sign, and the village's website has his most recent state-of-the-town address . . . which was right after his 2012 election."

Gabe smirks. "You really care about this, huh? Like, it's not just a stepping stone to you becoming a state rep or something?"

"Maybe someday," he says. "Who knows. But all summer, I just kept thinking about all the people who called Senator Wright, and how many people we had to tell that they were being heard, and that their voice mattered, but really? Nothing ever mattered. He voted in his own interests, or the interests of his party. Every vote was positioned so that he could make himself look great if he ran for president someday. His goals were so far outside of Ohio that he never consulted the calls we were getting. Not once. And I know not everyone's like that—Congresswoman Caudill would even jump on the phone with her constituents from time to time!—but that's around when I realized that I wanted to help people in Ohio. And this seems like the best way to start."

"Wow," Gabe says, finally dropping my hand. "You know, I believe you."

I shrug. "You think my mom will be cool about it, then?"

"Oh, not at all. Not at first, at least." He sighs. "She'll come around, though."

"But what if she doesn't?"

When I feel the tears come to my eyes, I start packing my things up, and eventually pull Gabe in for a hug before I leave. I linger midhug, just a little longer than normal. Of the many things that are mine, he is not one of them. Not anymore. Not like he ever was.

But he'll always be my number one.

I throw the easel in the trunk and my backpack in the back of the car and drive the short trip back home. Sweat prickles my body, making the steering wheel slippery and my pits sweaty. If

I'm being completely honest, I might be catching feelings for Gabe. Again. For *real* this time.

But there's nothing I can do about it. No, I have to be *extra* supportive of him and Matt, because I already almost messed it up once. I need to be better—no reflexive leaning, no hand holding, no sharing blankets.

I can't mess this up.

After parking, I turn off the car and take the steps to my front door. When I open it, the house is mostly dark, except for a light in the office. I lock the door behind me and walk quickly toward the stairs, but freeze in my tracks when I hear Mom's voice.

"We need to talk." She emerges from the study with a bill in her hands. "Where did you apply for college?"

"What do you mean?" I say, then blurt out, "University of Michigan."

"And where else?"

As she comes closer, I see that the bill she's holding is her credit card statement. The statement that probably showed her all the colleges that I did not apply to. I get the very real urge to sprint away and never look back, but I can't keep running, I can't keep lying.

"Nowhere else. Can we sit down or something?"

"I'm fine standing," she says quickly. "Explain."

I set down my bag and we stand face-to-face. I'm feeling a little sick, and a little faint, so I clench my fists to bring life back into them. I think of everything I told my aunt, of all the many reasons why I've done this and kept it a secret, but nothing sounds right.

"I don't want to go to college," I say, my voice high-pitched and soft. Scared. "I know this has been in our—*your*—plan for me for a long time, but I don't want to. I can't spend four years away when I've found what I'm passionate about."

She stares at me, impassive.

"How long have we been working toward this, Sal? The years of testing prep, the dozens of tours I took you on. The one thing your dad and I would talk about, back when you were just a baby, is making sure you had every opportunity when it came to college." The papers clench in her fist. "And you've just ruined it all!"

"It's *my* future," I say. "I'm not wasting four years of my life for that piece of paper. Over the summer, I saw the life it could give me, and I . . . I don't want it."

"You can't have a future without that 'piece of paper,' Sal," she snaps. "I don't care what you want to do, unless you want to go be a drag queen with Reese, you need school. Actually, Reese is doing all this and, last I checked, he *still* plans to attend college. What's not clicking for you? What don't you get?"

I clear my throat. "I have a plan."

"I don't want to hear your plan," she says. "I can't even look at you. I can't even deal with you. You've really screwed this all up. I'm going to talk to the school's guidance counselor to see how we can salvage this, and you'd better be prepared to apply to any school that could possibly accept you on our next college check-in."

"But—"

"But nothing." She throws the balled-up credit card statement to the floor. "You're grounded for lying to me. No friends, nothing. I suggest you do some research on your own because we will be fixing this problem."

She storms off, and I feel the tears start to prick at my eyes. I'd been thinking the problem was Mom all along, but maybe she's right. Maybe the problem is me. Maybe I can't do this.

• Voice Message •

GABRIEL + SAL

S)) Well, it's over. Mom knows I didn't apply to all the colleges I was supposed to. She said we were going to have a big talk on our college check-in on Tuesday because she "couldn't even deal with me" right now. Maybe I should give it all up . . . I don't know. I really want this, I know I'd be good at it, but how can I even pretend I have a shot at being mayor if I'll never even have my mom's vote?

G)) Oh, Sal, I'm so sorry. I don't know what to say, since I don't really think anything I say can actually help right now, but I guess . . . just know that at the end of the day, she can't make you do anything you don't want to do, right? You're about to be eighteen, and we're all going to work so hard for

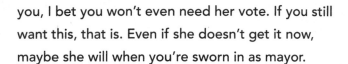

you, I bet you won't even need her vote. If you still want this, that is. Even if she doesn't get it now, maybe she will when you're sworn in as mayor.

S)) Thanks, Gabe. I really want this, and I know I can do it. But I can't do it without her. She wants me to look into schools and come prepared on Tuesday.

G)) So come prepared. If you can make a powerpoint presentation to come out of the closet as an eleven-year-old, you can probably give a convincing presentation to convince her you want to run for local office.

CHAPTER FORTY

SAL

SINCE EVERYTHING WENT DOWN Saturday night, I've been bored out of my mind. Even though I'm grounded—I can only go to school and home, no pit stops, no seeing the boys, nothing—I have a feeling Mom wishes I was anywhere but here. She's all but stopped making dinner, which is something she always really loves to do, and instead we have cleared through all the takeout options Gracemont has to offer in the past couple of days.

When we are in the same room, she avoids eye contact. Not enough to seem immature, but still enough to be noticeable. That's what burns the most, I think. I haven't apologized, because I know it won't sound sincere, so we're in this weird stubborn holding pattern. One that will hopefully end tonight, during our scheduled meeting.

I have no idea why she didn't just rip off the Band-Aid and confront me earlier, but now that everything's out in the open, having some time to cool off isn't bad. But she's flipped from angry to this weird state of depression that I don't really know how to handle.

So I hide in my room. Today, just like every other day.

We're getting pizza tonight, and I know that we'll be forced to talk once it arrives, so for now I just spin around in my desk chair, idly waiting until I hear the delivery person pull into the driveway.

The boys have texted me some, but I don't feel like replying. I'll give them an update tonight, but there's not much to say. I know I should have told her sooner, but it's also not like it's an easy thing to bring up—we've been collecting college brochures since I was in kindergarten!

I sigh and hope the ache in my chest goes away soon.

A few minutes pass, but then I hear the familiar *thunk* of a car pulling into our driveway, and know I can't avoid it any longer. I look into the mirror and adjust my bow tie—I started tying this one to pass the time as a nervous habit, but I figured I'd keep it on. If I want my mom to take this seriously, I might as well look the part.

I come downstairs just in time for the doorbell to ring. I don't hear Mom around, so I open the door.

"Sal, my boy!"

I pull back in surprise. "Betty—er, Congresswoman Caudill?"

"Surely we can drop the formalities after everything we went through this summer," she says with a satisfied chuckle.

I take her jacket from her and hang it on the hook behind the door.

"The weather is *finally* breaking, isn't it? Feels like spring is coming any day now."

"Sure," I say. "I mean, yes. Very mild."

She eyes me oddly and guides me into the house toward the dining room.

"Your mom didn't tell you I was coming?" she says.

"Honestly, I thought you were delivering pizza."

She barks a laugh. "I'll have you know I used to do that way back, before I even met your mom in college. I had this rundown junker of a car, but I always thought I had the best high school job of all my friends: I just got to drive around and listen to music all night."

"I never knew that about you," I say.

I haven't seen Betty in a few months, not since I said goodbye to her office in DC. After Senator Wright completely flopped on his responsibilities in leading an internship program, Cong— Betty stepped in to make sure I actually got something out of the experience. And I did.

That's when I realized that, regardless of how much my mom wanted me to leave Ohio for what she called "bigger and better things," I could take that energy and put it somewhere where I could make a bigger impact.

"Oh, Rachel!" Betty exclaims when Mom steps into the dining room to join us. "How are you doing, dear?"

Mom shrugs. For anyone else, she'd have put on her strongest, bravest face and hidden her angst from the world. But not for the congresswoman, who happens to be her closest friend of years. *Decades.*

"I'm doing about as well as can be expected," she says, not sounding unlike someone who's just gone through a deep personal loss.

"Should I put out the good plates?" I ask, but my mom just waves me away.

"I think we have some paper plates up in that cupboard above the oven," she says.

When Betty and I make eye contact, she gives me a startled look. When she last came over for dinner, just before I left for DC, Mom cooked a feast fit for royalty, topped off with a homemade pavlova for dessert. *That* is how Mom hosts.

Obviously, there's nothing wrong with eating pizza off paper plates—hell, when we have it at Gabe's, his family will sometimes grab the slices so quickly they don't even need plates. But this is a cry for help, and I'm not sure either of us are equipped to answer it.

I busy myself in the kitchen grabbing paper plates, pint glasses for the local beer Betty brought, and a stack of napkins. I listen hard to see if I can eavesdrop on their conversation, but it doesn't sound like they're even speaking. It's all silence.

After the pizza comes, the tension thaws a bit. Until, that is, my mom clears her throat.

"Sal, I think it's time to talk." She makes eye contact with me for the first time in three days. "I invited Betty over for moral support for both of us, but since she's someone you look up to and someone who obviously went to college, I figured she could talk some sense into you. I was also able to talk to the guidance counselor at school, and she says there's still time for some schools, so all is not lost. It's a momentary hiccup, but we need to get going now if we're going to rectify the situation."

"Ah," I say. Both of them are looking at me, so I take the floor while I can. "Before we get into that, I have something to tell you. Mom, Congresswoman—I mean Betty, sorry—I don't want to go to college. At least, not right now. I've been creating a different plan for myself, one that I'm quite a bit more excited about."

"And who else knows about this *plan*?" Mom asks.

"Who do you think?" I snap, but when Mom's fiery gaze lands on me I look away. "The boys know. I'm sure that will feed into whatever weird complex you have about them leading me astray or whatever, but it's true. I didn't feel comfortable telling you, so I told them."

Mom starts to speak, but Betty cuts in. "Well, first, let's hear this plan."

"I could go to college, study political science and history and communications or whatever else, but last summer showed me that I'm not fit for a career in DC. At least, not right now."

"First," Betty says, "I'd have to disagree. You did splendidly this summer, and I think you're a wonderful fit for that career path. But you do have to want to pursue politics to really make it there."

"And I do want to pursue politics," I say, then turn to my mom. "But not like that. The only parts of it that I loved from that experience—outside of getting to cosplay as a young professional in DC—were the parts where I was connecting with people here, in Ohio."

For the first time since I can remember, Mom doesn't interject.

Maybe she's too tired, or too over this, but maybe... maybe she'll listen to me.

"Betty, one thing you said last summer stuck in my head. It was something about how you truly believe your district has some of the best people in the whole country."

She laughs. "I say that a lot. *And* I truly mean it."

"Mom, you've always pushed me to leave Gracemont. You wanted me to go to college and never look back, and I think that's totally valid, but for now, I want to stay." I sigh. "I want to run for mayor in Gracemont. I want to show Mayor Green that there's strong support for a new, progressive voice in the community. I can't let him run unopposed. I know this town is small, but with a little help, I know I'd put up a good fight."

And... silence. Great.

"I'm not sure how to process this," Mom finally says. "Who got this idea in your head? Was it Gabriel?"

"No, Mom. This may surprise you, but I have my own thoughts and ideas."

Her nostrils flare, but I don't back down. I've spent too much time living my life by her rule book.

Before I can say anything, Betty jumps in to smooth things over.

"It's not the *worst* idea," she says, in a way that makes me feel like she doesn't fully believe herself, but it's clear that Mom's still furious. Betty grabs her hand. "It's not like he's running for governor, Rachel. You've got to admit, Gracemont hasn't had a mayor who's actually cared about the town since you moved here."

"That's true," Mom says, before tears come rushing to her eyes. "But it's so outlandish. *Mayor?* What does a teenager know about running a town?"

Gotta love that feeling when two people are talking about you like you're not in the room. I clear my throat.

"I actually know quite a lot now. I've attended the past few town council meetings, and it's clear that our current mayor is phoning it all in. In Gracemont, I would deal with all the formal grievances of the village, I'd do a ton of paperwork—permits, licenses, things like that, overseeing every meeting, and I'd select my own town officials for the government. Where Mayor Green's just given the roles to his other old, white, straight male friends, I can highlight our town's diversity while actually fixing problems."

"This is all nice, but it feels like all the planning we've done was for nothing, Sal. All the college visits. All the future planning. You've had the same goals since you were ten, and you've obviously done a marvelous job googling how a mayor does his job, but it sounds more to me like you're just throwing your career ambitions away."

"Why would I do that?" I ask.

"Because you're scared? Because you don't want to leave your friends? Because DC was harder than you expected it to be?" Her lips quiver. "Because you want to hurt me?"

Mom puts her face in her hand, and when I look to Betty in confusion she just shrugs.

"Hold on," I say, then dart out of the dining room and upstairs to grab the Post-it easel with all my notes from my meeting with the boys.

Once I'm back, Mom seems to have composed herself a little more. She sips from her pint glass and stares off into space.

"I've been meeting with the boys to plan it all out." I flip a few pages. "Here are a few of Reese's designs we can use for the logo, here's a plan from Gabe about getting grassroots support, and we already have a plan to activate as many high school seniors as we can, plus the juniors with early birthdays."

I set the easel down and look to my mom, who, for once, holds my gaze.

"I know you don't agree with it, but it's what I want to do. If I lose the election, fine—I will figure something else out. You know me. I'll have plan B, C, D, and E—and one of those will probably be college!" I sigh. "I've even come around to the idea of community college, where I can take some classes and continue my education part time while continuing to pursue a job in local government. But I really need your help with this. You know communications. You know all the local reporters, you know how to run a campaign. Betty showed me your massive communications campaign from back when she was running for House representative, and it was incredible."

Nothing.

"I need you, Mom."

"You don't have the experience," Mom says. "You're seventeen. People are going to think this is a complete joke."

"Maybe," Betty says, "but let's think about this: He's had an internship in DC. He's been attending town meetings and learning how local government works. And let's not forget, he's student council president. I know it sounds silly, but this is a rural village and being mayor is a part-time gig. Gracemont doesn't need someone with an impressive resume, they need someone who cares—someone who will do the work—and from watching Sal work with me for the summer, I know he can do this."

Betty looks to both of us, until Mom downs the rest of her half-full beer in one gulp.

"Fine," she says. "I don't agree with this, but I'm not going to let you look like a fool out there. I hope you're ready for this, Sal."

"I hope you are too," says Betty. "While I think you can do it, just know... politics—real politics—is extremely harsh, especially at the local level. You thought having Rachel watch your every move was bad? Try having an entire community watching, waiting for a single misstep, or even creating their own."

I nod, but before I can respond, Mom chimes in.

"He can handle it," she says. "In a way, we've been training for this all along."

• Golden Boys •

GABRIEL + HEATH + REESE + SAL

Operation SalForMayor is a go.

Not an easy conversation, but it was a necessary one.

S

R
Proud of you! I'll have some website design proofs for you ASAP

G
I'm starting the Facebook page now. Still got some research to do on fundraising.

H
give me the clipboard and I'll get you the signatures you need! we're with you bud!!
📣📣📣

G **Proud of you, friend.** 🖤

Thanks. S

CHAPTER FORTY-ONE

REESE

AFTER SCHOOL ON THURSDAY, Heath drives me back to his dad's apartment.

"I know baseball's kind of your thing," I say, "but I really wish you didn't have so many practices this year."

He laughs. "It's putting me through college, so I don't have a choice. Oddly enough, they don't let you skip practices in college either."

"Hmm. Seems unfair."

The drive from the high school to the apartments on Main Street only takes a couple of minutes, not long enough for us to even start a playlist, but once he pulls into the driveway and we step inside, he gives me full Bluetooth access to the speakers in his room.

Though we usually spend time at my house, we'll sometimes stop by Heath's instead. His dad doesn't get off for another thirty minutes, so we always try to use our alone time to our advantage.

I put on Heath's playlist and throw myself onto the bed. He joins me, and within minutes, his lips are on mine. I'm still cold from the short drive, but he pulls the covers over us and presses my body into him, and warmth floods my body.

Our bodies fit together like puzzle pieces, his arm around my neck, our legs intertwined. And for a moment, time just stops. Our lips are barely separate, but I feel his breath on me—in and out—and when his nose grazes mine, my body goes into a full shiver. Which makes him hold me tighter and press his lips into mine again.

In between kisses, I reach to pull his shirt off, but as I get it up to his shoulder, he grabs my arm to stop me.

"Oh, sorry," I say. "We don't have to—"

"It's not that," he says, and after my initial embarrassment subsides, I notice he's wincing with pain.

He slowly strips off his shirt, sliding it carefully down his right arm. The way he does it makes him seem wounded, somehow. Like every movement his right arm makes is just pummeling him with pain.

"Heath, what's wrong with your shoulder?"

He shakes his head, though he's still gritting his teeth. "Nothing, it's just sore from practice."

"Let me see," and I inch closer to him. I feel his hot breath on my neck, as I check his upper arm and shoulder for any bruising—though I have no idea what I'm looking for.

Slowly, I place my hand on his upper arm and softly massage up to his shoulder. He groans slightly, then sucks in a breath when

I get up to the joint where his arm and shoulder meet. I try again from the top of his neck down, but as soon as I get to the joint, he grabs my hand.

"Please," he says.

"Have you been to the doctor?" I ask.

He sighs and looks away from me. I know why he and his dad avoid the doctor, but this seems too serious to ignore.

"What if you're hurt? Like, really hurt. Don't you think it'll get worse if you don't do something about it?"

"I know my body, it's totally normal. I mean, this hasn't ever happened to me, I guess. But I've had similar injuries. Really, it's nothing to worry about, Reese." He puts his hand on my cheek. "So, where were we?"

I roll my eyes. "We were at the part where you were going to tell your dad you need a doctor's appointment."

He thinks about it for a while.

"Reese, I can't... it can't be something serious."

"I know," I say. "It probably isn't. But you can barely put your arm above your head."

He pivots his body and reaches for his phone, which is on the nightstand by his bed. Every action he does is with his left arm, the one that isn't hurt. I feel panic creep into me, because what if this *is* something serious, and how long has he been in this much pain?

I lightly scratch his back while he types out a message.

"Oh shit." His body goes rigid. "*Shit.*"

"What?" I ask. "Is it your arm? Can I get you something?"

He shakes his head. "No, no, it's not—oh god, gross."

"What is?"

He turns to me, and with wide eyes, he says, "Dad's not coming home after work. He has a *date*."

As it turns out, nothing puts a damper on sexy time quite like finding out your dad's about to have his own. So we move into the living room, and I put the least sexy playlist I can find on his living room speakers, then go busy myself in the kitchen.

"Kraft Mac & Cheese okay?" I ask. "Do you want dino nuggets too?"

"I don't care," he says dramatically. "Nothing matters anymore."

I roll my eyes. "Heath."

"Yes, I need dino nuggets, do you see the state I'm in?"

I laugh before coming around to the couch to bring him a soda and give him a kiss. I give him another kiss, because while I'm trying to be sensitive here, it's kind of impossible *not* to kiss your hot boyfriend when he's still shirtless.

"I know this is a lot for you, babe, but it's got to be a good sign. Your dad was so upset when we came back from the summer, it was like someone had died. I know he tried his best, and he really put on a great attitude when he gave me the grand tour of the apartment, but still—this is really good for him." I pause. "Even if it's a little icky for you."

"Is it completely unfair for me to just want him to be single until I go off to college? Once I'm at Vanderbilt he can do whatever he wants, but I don't think I should have to be here to witness it."

I laugh. "That is completely unfair, yes."

"You're already taking her side." He scoffs. "*Sandra*, from *work*. Gag me."

I ignore him and put a pot of water on the stove to boil. After I put the dino nuggets into the air fryer, my phone buzzes, so I check it.

The subject line sends my heart rate flying.

THE NEW SCHOOL—DECISION ON YOUR EARLY APPLICATION

"God, this day can't get any worse, can it?" Heath says, still a little jokingly. "The nuggets will help, though. Gotta keep focusing on the positives."

I think I respond with some form of affirmative grunt, but I can't be sure, because I'm positive this is a dream.

I can't open this email now. If it's a yes, then that would make Heath's day even worse. If it's a no, then Heath would have to comfort *me*, and I'm not trying to take attention away from the spectacle that's happening in the living room.

But I can't not check.

So I open the email, and within a millisecond, my eyes have scanned enough words to know what it says:

Congratulations from The New School! You've been accepted for early entry into the Parsons School of Design Fashion Design BFA program!

I look into the living room, where my cute, funny, sweet, goofy, annoying, perfect boyfriend is spread out on the couch. Then I look to my phone, the email that holds my entire future in it. My ticket to New York City. My dreams of pursuing fashion design. This fantastic, perfect, wonderful life is paved and waiting for me...

But my heart breaks, because I know that life will always be a thousand miles away from him.

CHAPTER FORTY-TWO

GABRIEL

FOR ME, LATE MARCH only means one thing: I only have a week left before I hear back from Ohio State. And though my hopes are high, I have to keep working on my patience. Thankfully I have other things to occupy my time.

For everyone else, March is when our school hits its peak sports obsession. With baseball season starting and basketball season coming to a close, there's a little something for any sports fan. Like how, today, our last class of the day is canceled for a mandatory pep rally for . . . some sports reasons. Apparently, it's meant to be a pass-the-torch kind of moment: as we approach our basketball team's final game, the varsity and junior varsity baseball and softball teams have just been selected.

As much as I'd like to be there to support Heath, Cassie and I have other plans.

The library is silent when we walk in: the lights are dimmed, and we didn't see another human on our way here. Which is good. We're kind of breaking the rules right now.

"I wish Miss Orly would have just confessed," Cassie says. "I feel so weird sneaking around like this."

"I know," I say. "But there's something going on here. All we have is circumstantial evidence—we need something real. And if something real exists, it'll be in her office."

Cassie and I walk through the stacks of books toward the front desk. There's the very real possibility that we'll get in trouble for this. *Anyone* can come by and see. The librarian could come back from the rally early. A custodian could come by. Or they can just check any of the security cameras that are on us right now.

"You don't think they monitor the cameras full time, right?" I ask Cassie.

"If I know this school, and I think I do, they probably don't have the funds for full-time security. But if they think something's up and check the tape...yeah, we're screwed."

"They won't check it," I say with a confidence I don't actually have. "Unless we knock over a bookshelf or something."

Cassie chuckles as she steps behind Miss Orly's desk. "I wouldn't put it past you."

Behind the desk is the main office of the library, and that's our goal. If the books aren't on the shelves, and they're not in the hands of other students, where else could they be?

The light's on here, so it feels like much less of a heist, but I'm still on guard. There are a ton of books back here next to a laminator.

"Great, more copies of *To Kill a Mockingbird*," Cassie says with a sarcastic tone. "That will make up for all the stories by Black authors that were ripped from the shelves."

I groan. "You know, I showed my dad the suggested reading list for this district and he said he had nearly the exact same syllabus when he went to school here? And that was in like 1999."

"Oh, how the times have . . . *n't* changed."

There are stacks of books everywhere, and we're careful not to move them. If there's any sign that someone else was here, they'd definitely check the security cameras, and one's staring me right in the face.

"Hang on," Cassie says. "Come here."

I cross to the other side of the narrow office, behind a desk, where a stack of books lie on the floor. From their spines alone, I can tell that this is what we've been looking for.

"Jason Reynolds, Nic Stone," Cassie reads.

"Adam Silvera, Juno Dawson," I echo, but the list goes on and on.

"Well, we've found 'em."

I sigh. "Looks like it. Now, can we figure out any reason why?"

I investigate the stack, and see a slip of paper underneath them all. I've been careful not to touch anything so far, but at this point, we're running out of time and we need answers.

I unfold the paper after getting it out from under the books, and what I'm looking at is just a spreadsheet of titles. *So many* books are on this list, and from a quick glance, all of them are diverse.

"Look at the header," Cassie says. "*List of books to pull for investigation.*"

"Where did this even come from?" I ask, but a noise catches our attention.

My anxiety spikes, and my heart rate doubles. An ache thrums through my body, but my senses are alert. I fold the paper quickly and stuff it in my back pocket—there's no time to sneak it back under this stack of books, and we need to get out *now*.

Cassie snaps a few pictures of the book stacks with her phone, and I take one last look to make sure nothing looks touched. If they notice the missing book list, they might check the cameras, but that's a risk we'll have to take. I grab Cassie's arm and pull her toward the exit.

When we approach the library proper, the lights are back on. We don't have time to think.

"*Go*," I whisper to Cassie, pointing at a long row of books that could separate us from the office and the desk.

We step quickly into the book stacks as I hold my breath for dear life. When we're partially hidden, I hear the clack of Miss Orly's heels on the tile, and I've never been more thankful to be wearing sneakers.

We freeze, taking shallow breaths as the librarian walks around to her desk. If she takes a seat, we're stuck here until she leaves. But if she doesn't . . .

She drops an envelope off at her desk, then walks briskly to the back room where we just were. Now's our chance.

We quickly sneak out the library door and into the hallway.

"Okay, that was enough excitement for me. Are all the other teachers coming back?"

"No, looks like it was just her. All the classrooms are empty, and no one's in the halls."

She sighs. "Good, let's hide in Miss H's class until the pep rally is over."

Once we're safe and sound in the classroom, I take a seat on the floor and lean against the wall.

"Jesus, I don't think I took one breath that whole time," I say.

"Tell me about it." Cassie shudders. "But it's okay, we made it. Now, show me that list again."

We scan the list, but there's nothing indicating where it came from. *Who is leading this investigation,* I wonder.

"I think I need to talk to Sal's mom about this," I say, but Cassie shakes her head.

"If you confront her with the list, then she'll know we *took* the list." She sighs. "Let's think, let's think."

"Is it the superintendent? Obviously the librarian was just told to find any of these books on the shelves and take them down if we have them. All the ones she snagged are circled, and I don't think we have any others on this list. Not like we had a huge selection of diverse books to begin with."

"To say the least," she adds. "I guess it could be the superintendent. Or maybe Miss Orly found this list online and pulled it herself? But you're right, it looks like she was checking them all off so she could report back. And what exactly does 'investigation' mean? They were just sitting off in a corner."

Our eyes meet, and I shake my head slowly. "I think it means that, whatever this is, this is bigger than just our school."

CHAPTER FORTY-THREE

HEATH

AFTER THE PEP RALLY, the baseball team has to get on the bus for yet another away game. I pack my equipment bag, sling it around my good shoulder, and make my way to the bus.

James, who's settling into his new role as varsity relief pitcher a little too easily, slides into the seat behind me.

"Time for the showdown with the Barton Springs Bulldogs," he shouts to the rest of the bus. "They'll be lucky to get one hit off of us."

I roll my eyes. "Sit down, James."

"Ah, you're no fun." He pats me hard on the shoulder before sitting down. "We've been on such a roll lately."

I wince. "Y-yeah, I know."

Since Dad was distracted with his date yesterday, and I was distracted with Reese, I never got around to telling him about my shoulder. I'm still hoping it all kinda resolves itself somehow, but my range of motion is slowly closing up, and it's hurting all the time now. The games are getting harder, and my numbers are slipping—just slightly.

Briefly, I picture James taking my place *this* year instead of next. I see Vanderbilt giving their athletic scholarship to someone else, and without that big chunk I could never pay for it myself. I don't even know if me and Dad could get approved for a loan that big.

So I'll just push through it, like I always do.

Over the twenty-minute drive to Barton Springs, I stare out the window watching the fields go by. Between our two towns, there's no main highway, just country road after country road. Each house I pass reminds me of my old one.

The bus hits a bump, and my shoulder hits the window. I gasp.

"Hey, you okay?" James asks.

I straighten up. "Yeah, fine. Just, uh, hit my head on the window when we hit that bump."

I turn back toward the window, but he comes up and sits next to me. "Something's wrong."

"Everything's *fine*."

Despite my *please go away* tone, James stays and waits for me to turn to him. Slowly, I do, and when our eyes meet, I sense a great deal of concern behind his expression.

"I . . ." My defenses are lowered, and I trust him. "It's my shoulder."

"Have you told Coach?" he asks.

I shake my head. "Can we drop it?"

Usually, when I tell the boys to drop a topic I'm sensitive about, they'll refuse. They'll prod, they'll pry, and eventually they'll get their way. But my friendship with James is different. He returns to his seat and passes over a travel bottle of Tylenol.

"Thanks," I say, quickly swallowing two pills.

"Just talk to Coach, okay?"

We get off the bus in Barton Springs. After a quick stop at the locker rooms, we're out on the field warming up in no time. Despite the chill outside, my body feels so overheated right now it's like I'm in a hot tub. My adrenaline has kicked in, so between that and the Tylenol, my pain has numbed a bit. I'm very aware that I'm about to hurt—*bad*—after this game.

Coach eyes me wearily, and I wonder if it's because my cheeks are flushed, or if he can just tell that I'm in pain. I do a few quick warm-ups, clenching my teeth as I stretch my right arm. After a few rotations, some of the range of movement comes back, and it feels a little less tight.

"James," Coach Lee says, "you go warm up with Arvin."

James pouts. "Aw, but I wanted to pitch with Heath!"

"You'll have all season to do that," Coach says. "Go!"

James listens and leaves the two of us alone, only sulking a little bit.

After he leaves, Coach takes a catcher's mitt from the bag and tosses me a ball.

"Warm up?" he asks, though it's not much of a suggestion.

It's unusual for me to warm up with Coach Lee before a game. Maybe Assistant Coach Roberts, if there's a specific thing I'm working on, but even that's usually at practice.

I take a few paces away from him, estimating the distance from pitcher's mound to the catcher. As I look around, spectators all over start to join the stands. Even though I know no one at this rival school is looking my way, it feels like every eye is on me. I try to ease the tension in my face, but it won't let go. Not when I know how much this is about to hurt.

But Coach is waiting, glove open and extended, and once our eyes meet, I know I can't delay it anymore.

Gripping the ball, I wind up and use as much of my range as I can to launch a fastball at Coach. Two problems: One, it's not fast. Two, it hits the ground just before it reaches him. He smothers it with his glove and tosses it back to me.

"Again," he says.

"Right," I reply. "Um, sorry."

I take a deep breath. I need to learn how to work *with* my injury, not against it. I aim higher this time and whip it at him sidearm. A flare of pain surrounds my arm, but it's noticeably less than the last throw.

And I'm right on target.

"Trying out a new pitching style?" Coach asks with this dead-pan voice, so I can't tell if that's a good or bad thing.

"I've pitched sidearm before," I say.

He just nods. "Again!"

I do, again. This one's supposed to be a slider, but it doesn't slide like I expect it to. Coach catches it around his face, but he doesn't throw it back to me.

"Sidearm slider?" he asks. "That's a bit old-fashioned, don't you think? Here, let's take a walk."

He takes off his glove and rests it on the baseball, and I follow him down the foul line toward the fence in left field. Along the way, he passes a few supportive comments to our third baseman and shortstop as they warm up together.

"I'm not surprised you can pitch sidearm, obviously." He sighs. "You did it in the last game, and I said nothing. But it's pretty hard for me to track where it's at, and that makes me worry our new catcher is going to have some problems with it."

"Oh," I say. "Is it really that different?"

"There's a reason it's not used much anymore. There are only two benefits to it that I see: It's hard for the batter to track it, so you're likely to throw off a few batters with it, like you did in our last home game. Also, it's easier on the shoulder."

My cheeks flush. "Gotcha. So no sidearm, then."

Coach turns to me, and I make sure to meet his eyes and find a confidence I don't honestly have. He puts a hand on my left shoulder and gives me a sincere look.

"I need you to tell me what's wrong with your arm," he says.

And there it is. I grit my teeth, but I try to keep a calm expression on my face.

"It's a little sore," I say, but then I feel my lip quivering.

"I've known you since you were ten. I've coached you for seven years, making the jump to varsity high school the same year you did." Coach Lee looks at me with a soft expression. "You can be honest with me, Heath."

He's still got a grip on my shoulder, so I can't turn away. I feel tears welling up in my eyes, but I force myself to tell the truth.

"Fine. Yeah, it's worse than that. It's been hurting for the past couple of months, and I've just been trying to stretch more before pitching, but every time we play it gets worse.

"It used to only hurt when I was training, but over the past few weeks it's been hurting when I wake up and randomly throughout the day. Tylenol does nothing. It's driving me freaking bonkers all the time, and I can't… insurance stuff is complicated, so I haven't even told my dad. I know he'd insist I go to the doctor, and I just… what if I need surgery, Coach? We can't afford that, and then I couldn't play for the rest of the season, and *then* I couldn't play at Vanderbilt, and—"

"*Heath*," Coach Lee says. "You're hurt. The only way this is going to get better is if you get it diagnosed correctly, so we can start treatment and get you back on the field."

He finally lets go of my good arm, and I turn and start to walk back.

"You don't understand," I say. I know I'm not making much sense, but he doesn't get it. "What's that saying? The only way out is through."

He catches up with me. "Sure, but that doesn't apply to *everything*. You can't use a shitty saying to justify killing yourself out there."

"Then what do I do?"

I turn to see him massaging his temples slowly, lost in thought. Even through the throbbing, and the vulnerability of telling him that I'm hurt, there's a small piece of me that feels relieved.

"I know a good sports medicine doctor. Let me see if she can do a house call and come to practice next week—I can get the school to pay for her to come out and see everyone and give them tips on how to prevent injuries. While she's here, I'll have her sneak you in for a visit." He sighs. "Tell your dad. Figure out what your insurance options *are*. If she says we can take care of it through rest, massage, medicine, whatever it might be—then we might be okay." A seriousness takes over his expression. "But if she wants you to get X-rayed, or suggests surgery, I can't let you play until you get yourself fixed. It's not ethical, and I'm not going to let some game give you a lifelong injury."

"What do I do until then?" I ask.

"Warm the bench," he says, and my heart falls to the ground. "*For now*. Rest. Use ice packs or heating pads or whatever eases the pain."

"But if I don't play—"

"You will play. When you're ready."

I turn away from the dugout as I start to cry, and I'm not sure if they're tears of pain or stress or relief—probably all three—but I know he's right.

He sees me start to tear up again, so he pulls me into a one-armed hug.

"We'll get through this, bud. Here," he says, taking his sunglasses off his hat and passing them to me. I quickly put them on to hide the tears.

"Thanks, Coach."

• Golden Boys •

GABRIEL + HEATH + REESE + SAL

I GOT IN!!!!!

THE Ohio State University
here I come!!!!!!!!!

G

lol they sent an acceptance
letter at 8 am on a saturday??

H regardless OMG YOU DID IT!!!!

Yes! No surprise here, but
S congrats!

R 🎉 🎉 🎉

Your dad must be losing his
mind right now. Are the OSU
S flags out front yet?

That's an understatement...
I've never seen him so happy   G

R   Did you tell Matt? I can't
remember, was this on his
list of schools too???

He's so happy for me, but
no it's not. But he might go
to Pitt, which isn't far.

A lot closer than now, at
least...

ANYWAY Dad's throwing
an impromptu party for the
fam tonight. Please come!!!   G

CHAPTER FORTY-FOUR

SAL

WHEN I SHOW UP to Gabe's, I can hear the party from the other side of the front door. They've had a few parties each year, but as they're all sports oriented, I usually find a way to skip them.

As I reach for the doorbell, the door flies open, and a beaming, OSU-hoodie-clad Gabriel stares back at me. His smile is so sweet, and his eyes are so full of joy, I get the urge to close the distance and say hello with a kiss. The thought surprises me, but old habits die hard.

"Congrats, Gabe! Looking good."

"Oh, please," he says, running his hand through his short hair. "I'm in a hoodie, and you're in a button-up with a bow tie. Side note—I didn't realize you had any red clothing."

"Just the one red bow tie, which I never wear because it makes me look like a Republican."

"Fair," Gabe says with a laugh. "Well, it fits the theme today. I'm glad you came—come on in!"

I wave to Gabe's mom as I enter the living room, and as I scan the house, I recognize most of the relatives and family friends. Of course, they're all in OSU gear, but none of them seem to bat an eye at my outfit—they've all seen me enough to know this is how I roll.

"Sal!" A deep, booming voice comes from the stairwell behind me. "Glad you could make it."

Gabe's dad crosses over to me and wraps me in a hug. They've always been a hugging family, but I'm not used to this kind of welcome. They must really be excited.

Enjoying this moment feels like a momentary betrayal, since I can barely remember my own dad, but I'm so used to their family's touchy-feely love for one another that I savor the moment.

As soon as I let go, someone jumps in and hugs me from behind—from the long hair fanning around my face, I'm guessing it's his sister.

"Katie, I didn't realize you'd be here!" I say.

"Couldn't miss this," she says. "I can skip one weekend of college parties to come celebrate with my little bro."

"That's big of you," Gabe says, rolling his eyes.

"Sal, how are you?" she asks. "Did you ever figure out your whole college dilemma?"

I laugh. "I did, but Gabe will have to fill you in on this one. It's a long story, and today is his day. Oh, Gabe, Mom says congrats—she sent me over with these chocolate buckeyes. Our neighbor makes them all the time, and they're really good."

"I'll take those," his dad says. "And I will taste test them immediately."

He leaves, and Gabe's sister follows so she can snag one too.

"I didn't think your mom was talking to me," Gabe says.

"Maybe she's just glad one of us is going to college," I say. "But no, she's been better lately. And she is genuinely happy for you."

He sighs. "She won't be for long. Remember that banned books list Cassie and I found in the library? We've got to confront her about it. We're just trying to find a way to do it that doesn't get us suspended."

"Whoa," I say. "That's big. But dealing with this stuff is her job. Hopefully she can keep it separate from how she likes you as a person. But don't think about that now—just enjoy your party."

"You're right," he replies, and pulls me into a one-armed hug. "Once my relatives go home, my sister brought us some booze to celebrate. Want to see if you can stay over?"

The last time I stayed over, we were fully into our friends-with-benefits thing. The idea of drinking knowing I have to stay away from him sounds impossible, but I don't have a choice. I can be strong. I always am.

"Of course. I'll call Mom and tell her not to pick me up until tomorrow morning."

CHAPTER FORTY-FIVE

GABRIEL

IT'S AMAZING HOW QUICKLY a party can come together. It's also amazing that none of these people had plans before this morning.

Though we don't plan on drinking until tonight, the same can't be said for my dad and a few of his alumni friends. Heath and Reese have spent most of the party in the dining room, away from all the festivities, but Sal's stuck by my side through it all.

Dad brought out his old college graduation video, and as the images fly by, it starts to settle in just how much this is going to change my life. My sister always says that some people peak in high school, some people in college, and some people in the real world, but it's clear that Dad peaked in college.

"There we are! All four roommates in one photo, finally," Dad shouts, pausing the DVD on a photo from one of the OSU/Michigan rivalry games. Four guys are all decked out in OSU gear, holding red beaded necklaces, waving flags, with a touch of red and white face paint on their cheeks.

"I wonder how Greg's doing," Dad asks his friend who's in the shot, and they launch into a conversation about what's been going on with their old roommates.

As I look to my own four-person crew, I wonder what it'd be like if we were all roommates in college. It might be a little more complicated when two of us are dating, and two of us have dated, but it must be so nice to be surrounded by your best friends all the time.

My sister nods toward the basement door, giving me the signal that we can probably excuse ourselves from the party since it's no longer about me and is fully about Dad and his college friends now.

I take all the boys downstairs while Katie goes to lift plastic cups and mixers for the booze she brought. Once we're all downstairs, Reese puts on an upbeat playlist while Heath and Sal settle into the couches.

"We'll never have that, will we?" I gesture upstairs. "It's kind of a bummer. I'm so glad we're all pursuing our own passions, but college is going to be so hard without you guys. And, like, we're never going to be in the same place at the same time anymore, are we?"

"We'll have the summers, won't we?" Heath says. "And we'll all visit each other. Reese can put a schedule together for us. And when we graduate, we can plan entire vacations together."

"It won't be the same," Reese says a little sadly. "Do you

think we'll be like that? Do you think *these* are our 'golden days,' and we'll come together just to reminisce on who we were in high school?"

"God, I hope not," my sister says as she comes down the stairs and passes out cups. She pulls out handles of rum and vodka from the bathroom, where she was hiding it. As we fill up our drinks, she continues. "You remember last year's valedictorian? Loved that girl, but her whole speech had nothing to do with the future. She kept going on about how we'll look back on *these days* like they were perfect. If any of you become valedictorian, let's workshop your speech so it doesn't get so sappy, okay?"

I laugh. "Agreed."

Sal grabs a blanket and curls up across from me on the love seat. I pull my feet up and cover them with the other end of the blanket. As my sister gets into an in-depth conversation with Reese about his new drag persona and how he *needs* to borrow some of her heels, I turn to Sal.

"For what it's worth, I'm glad you'll be in Ohio after all this." I smile. "I know I'll be busy with college and stuff, and you'll be busy running the whole town, but you and I won't be as alone."

"I'm glad too," Sal says simply.

We sit and chat for a while, until the alcohol makes my cheeks flush. I'm not drunk, but I've just hit that moment when things feel a little off, a little different. My sister hands me a water bottle, so I down that.

"Have you heard any more about prom?" Reese asks. "It's not going to be a problem when Heath and I go, right?"

"The LGBTQ+ Advocacy Group has got your back," I say. "Cassie and I are well versed on your rights. If you have any issue, just come right to one of us. We'll make sure Sal's mom knows we'll be watching too."

"Good," Heath says, putting an arm around his boyfriend. "They can't stop us. Plus, I think the whole school knows about us and no one's made it an issue."

"It's not usually the students," Katie says. "Though we had a few dicks in my grade, as you and Sal know. The superintendent is a piece of work, from what I've heard, but again. You have rights."

Reese leans into Heath, who strokes his hair softly.

"It's not fair," Reese says. "No one else even has to talk about this stuff."

All this talk about prom has tears coming to my eyes. I've been so focused on my advocacy group, I haven't given enough thought to what prom is going to be like for me. But it's staring me in the face: I've got a boyfriend, but because he's hours away, I'll be going to prom alone.

Sal kicks me lightly under the covers. He mouths, "You okay?"

I shrug. "It's just...the alcohol is hitting. I'm lonely. I wish Matt could come to prom with me."

"Have you asked him?" Sal asks.

I shake my head. "We talked about it at the beginning of the year, but I don't think it'll work out. It wouldn't make sense. He'd have to drive all the way here, or fly, and I don't think my parents would let him stay here."

"I think they would. He could stay in my room." Katie drops

her voice to a conspiratorial whisper. "Or that's what you can tell them."

I laugh. "Really?"

"You'll be eighteen by then, so you can always play that card. They really lightened up with me when I reminded them I was an adult."

"Ask him!" Heath says, and Reese nods alongside him. Sal looks hesitant, only offering me a light nod.

"I'm going to do it," I say, and I take the phone into the bathroom so I can have a little bit of silence.

I sit on the edge of the bathtub and send him a FaceTime request. I wait, and wait, and wait for the call to connect. Just when I'm about to give up, it does.

"Gabe!" he says. "How are you doing, my love?"

My whole body melts into a puddle when I see his face on the other end of the screen. It looks like he's at a party too—there's a lot of ambient noise, but it's muffled.

"Are you drunk and in a bathroom too?"

He laughs. "Yeah, I'm at a friend's house."

"I miss you, Matt."

"I miss you too. Sorry I keep missing your calls—it's been so hectic with school and band and everything, but enough of that. How is my soon-to-be-collegiate boyfriend doing?"

I blush. "Good! Really good. We were all just talking about high school and college and prom and a bunch of other stuff. Matt, would you want to come to prom with me?"

"Oh," he says. "I mean, I'd love to, but I don't know if I can swing it."

CHAPTER FORTY-SIX

REESE

SINCE WE'VE ALL HAD a little too much to drink, the party ends quickly. Within a matter of minutes, the four of us are all spread out on the basement floor. Sal and Gabriel take the two couches, while Heath and I split an old mattress pad and a knitted blanket.

We're far enough from the others that we can steal a few kisses in the dark without thinking we're putting on some sort of public show. We're both in athletic shorts, and as we hold each other tightly, I feel so much of him press into me.

"I hope one day we're able to just spend the night together *alone*," I whisper to Heath. "Because dear god is there a lot I want to do to you right now."

He chuckles. "I know, I know. But we can't do anything here, because Sal and Gabe would one hundred percent hear us and they would never be able to look us in the eyes again."

"Hey, now. We dealt with their PDA for years."

"I didn't even tell you the date," I say, and he shrugs.

"Text me the date and I'll check my calendar, but all of May is such a mess. We have two big band performances, and I don't want to miss my own prom of course. It's just..." He sighs. "God, I miss you."

"Then let's plan something. Even if we just meet halfway some weekend."

"Yeah!" he says excitedly. "If we can get our parents to sign off on a three-hour drive. But I bet they would."

"I think so too," I say. "I wish you were here now."

"I wish you were *here* now." He sighs, again. "This is just going to get more complicated, isn't it? Once we're in college, and our lives are even more hectic."

"I know. I hate it," I say. "But I love you."

A pounding noise comes from the phone, and I see him look up to the door. "Crap, I'm getting kicked out of the bathroom. Let's talk later, okay? Congrats again, I'm so proud of you!"

The call disconnects, and even though nothing particularly bad even happened, I start crying.

After a few minutes, Sal pokes his head into the restroom. I look up, bleary eyed, and he quickly darts in and closes the door. He lifts me off the edge of the bathtub and onto the ground opposite the toilet, then sits next to me.

I find myself falling into his lap, as he puts a supportive arm around my waist. He strokes my hair with his free hand and just repeats: *It's going to be okay. It's going to be okay. It's going to be okay.*

And despite myself, a part of me believes him.

He kisses me softly all over my face, up my cheek, down my nose, finally stopping at my lips.

"Well, what *I* want to do is a few steps past PDA."

"Same," I say. I force myself to give us a few inches of space between us. "Maybe we could figure something out for prom?"

"Very cliché," he says in a cheeky tone. "But I'm starting to understand why it's a cliché."

I rub my forehead into his chest and breathe him in.

"You okay?" he asks.

"What if all we have is prom? What if we look back on high school and that's when we peaked? When *you and I* peaked, I mean."

"You have this habit of mourning things before you lose them," Heath replies, and his drunken wisdom makes me feel sober. "We have all the time in the world, okay?"

"I got into Parsons," I say. "I haven't told anyone. Not even my parents. I know everyone will make a big deal out of it, but I can't pretend to be happy about it, not now."

"Oh," he says. "Oh wow, okay. Um...but that's great. That's like a dream, right? Why aren't you happy?"

"You *know* why," I say, resting my forehead into his.

He pulls me into a kiss. "Let's not talk about us, okay? Let's just celebrate you. Tomorrow, after baseball practice, let me take you out for dinner."

I blush, because even four months into a relationship with Heath, the number of butterflies flooding my body have only increased. And that's so special, right? That's not normal, right?

It means we should stay together, right? No matter what?

"I love you, Heath." I roll over, and he wraps me into a tight hug. It's his injured shoulder, but you'd never know it by how secure he makes me feel in his arms. "No matter what happens, you know I'll always love you."

CHAPTER FORTY-SEVEN

HEATH

I HOLD HIM AS tightly as I can, even when my shoulder starts aching.

I never want to let go of him. I know that. But I also know I'm going to have to, someday. Slowly, my shoulder ache turns into a sobering pain, but I still won't let go.

It's worth the pain.

CHAPTER FORTY-EIGHT

HEATH

"ALL RIGHT," COACH ADDRESSES the whole baseball team. "I've asked Dr. Sands to come here and talk with everyone about how to safely warm up, how to reduce injuries, and what to do if you do experience any injuries throughout the season."

"Thanks for having me. Assistant Coach Roberts, would you mind taking me through your usual warm-ups with the team?"

"We usually just start by running laps," James says, earning an angry glance from Coach Roberts. "Sorry, it's true!"

The doctor laughs. "Okay, well here—I'll show you a few warm-ups that you should do before every practice. *Before* you run laps."

She takes us through a few leg stretches, focusing especially on our hamstrings. She teaches us how to breathe through our stretches.

"Everyone grab a partner, and you're going to want to press

your shoes together. Since you all do a lot of sprinting, this kind of stretch is really going to help you prevent shin splints."

We walk through a few arm stretches, which I do as well as I can. I see her eyes on me the whole time, and I feel a little embarrassed.

"I'm going to do a couple one-on-ones with the pitchers, since they're at a higher risk for injury." She turns to Assistant Coach Roberts. "You should run them through an entire warm-up now. Have them stretch, then send them on a run. Okay?"

"Got it," he grumbles.

"You," she points to me. "And you," she points to Coach Lee. "Let's talk about that shoulder."

Coach Lee leads us to his office, and as soon as the door shuts, the doctor releases a long sigh.

"Coach Lee, if you and Assistant Coach Roberts keep this up, you're going to end up losing half the team to injury," she says. "People always think that you need less stretching for baseball, but I always think you need *more*. It's a game where you should be as warmed up as possible, since you go from zero to a full sprint fifty times a game."

"Huh," I say. "I don't think I've ever warmed up like that."

She points to my shoulder. "I can tell. All right, take your shirt off and let's take a look at this shoulder."

I do, and I sit in one of the chairs in front of Coach's desk. She gently pulls my head one way and pushes on my shoulder. She follows the neck muscle down to my shoulder blade. I wince a couple of times, but she hasn't exactly hit—

"*Ow!*" I shout. "There it is."

I'm used to seeing Coach Lee so composed, but in this moment, he's biting his nails, wincing along with me.

"I see," she says. "How long has this been hurting?"

"A few months. I first noticed it in early January, I think? I was practicing a lot that week."

"How much?" she asks.

"Well, let's see. I was going to the batting cages for a few hours about three or four times a week. Then I'd go practice pitching with my dad in the park a few times a week. Then we had weight training every Monday, Wednesday, and Friday."

"Did you rest at all during this time?"

I shake my head. "It's just, I have this big scholarship opportunity with Vanderbilt."

"Oh, I love Vanderbilt," she says. "I did my residency there; they have a great sports medicine practice there."

"Like, as a major?"

She shakes her head. "No, I don't think so. They just have a good hospital and good sports medicine doctors there. But, I mean, you don't need to be a sports medicine major. I studied biology. You learn the good stuff in med school anyway."

"Huh," I say. "I never knew that."

"Were there any weeks that you did some sort of training every single day, no breaks?"

I shrug. "Most weeks, I guess? Sometimes I'd take a day off, but I figured that I could do a little bit of something every day."

She pokes and prods me a little bit more, then tosses me my shirt before leaning on Coach's desk. I slowly pull my shirt on, wincing when I have to raise my arm.

"Well, if this were a real doctor's appointment, which it isn't, officially"—she gives Coach a wink—"I'd say that you have over-training syndrome. I'm going to talk to your dad and suggest he pick you up some over-the-counter muscle relaxers and a heating pad, if you don't already have one."

"I have one here he can use," Coach Lee says. He digs it out of a drawer and hands it to me.

"I will insist that you come into my office to get a cortisone shot. Have your dad check about insurance, but it'll really help the inflammation. Take the next two weeks off—no games, no train-ing, no lifting, nothing," she continues. "Use the heating pad as necessary, drink a ton of water, and generally take it easy. If it gets better, then give me a call and we'll talk through your options, and Coach Lee and I will discuss how to slowly reintroduce baseball into your routine.

"If it doesn't…" She hesitates. "It could be a torn rotator cuff. And you'd need to get an MRI to check it out. If it's a small tear, then you'll need a little more time off. A corticosteroid injection can help, and we have a few more things we can try. Surgery isn't out of the question, but I think we caught this early enough—if you'd have pushed it much further, we'd be having a very different conversation."

I take in all the information, then turn to Coach. "What about Vanderbilt?"

"I'll have to report it to them," he says. "They'll be expecting your midseason stats."

"Does that put me out of the running for the scholarship?"

He shakes his head. "No, injuries happen, I'm sure they'll

understand. They want to make sure you can *actually* play. I'll talk to the coaches about it. Trust me."

And even though he's asking for my trust, he sounds so unsure of himself that I'm not sure I can. But I have no choice. Whether I like it or not, I'm officially going on the injured reserve list. My entire future is going to be decided by what happens in the next two weeks.

"Heath," Coach says, "you might also want to talk to a therapist who works with athletes, though finding one in-network is hard. But it sounds like you're carrying a lot of this Vanderbilt stress with you, and I think that's what led you to overtrain yourself like this. It's completely natural for you to feel some anxiety around this, but they can help. Do you mind if I suggest this to your dad as well?"

"Let me talk to my friend first, if that's okay." I sigh. I *don't* say how there's no way we could afford it. "I'm not sure how I feel about therapy, but my friend has it every week and always says good things. Maybe he can talk me through it."

She nods. "You got it."

"I guess you're dismissed," Coach Lee says. "I don't want to see you in the weight room for two weeks. You can warm the bench for the next few games, and we'll have James sub in as the starting pitcher, since he's the best we've got. Text me and keep me updated with your progress, and be honest, okay? I'll talk to Vanderbilt."

I thank them both, stand, and walk to the door.

Coach calls after me, "We'll get through this, buddy."

"You know, I almost believe that." I smirk. "Thanks, Coach."

• Facetime •

GABRIEL + HEATH

H Hey, serious talk for a sec. Could you tell me a little bit about why you started therapy?

G Oh, sure. I mean, I started noticing that I was experiencing all this anxiety about the time we started high school. At first it was just before exams or other stressful things, but then I started feeling uneasy all the time. I would have all these dark, pessimistic thoughts. I started avoiding social events entirely.

H And it got all better once you talked to a therapist?

G God, I wish. It took me a long time to sort through my experiences with anxiety and unlearn some of the behaviors that were causing me stress. But some things helped right away, like how my therapist introduced me to these guided meditation apps that help me calm down when I'm in a moment of panic. It's not perfect, even still, but it's helped a lot. Do you want to start going to therapy?

H◀ Maybe. I don't know. I think all this pressure has really gotten to me, and I might have a serious shoulder injury, so I'm freaking out about Vanderbilt and everything. My doctor said that I have overtraining syndrome, and that a therapist who works with athletes might be able to help me through it.

G◀ Well I'm here if you ever need to talk through therapy stuff. I know it can feel weird the first time you go, but it's worth a shot.

H◀ Yeah. I think so too.

CHAPTER FORTY-NINE

GABRIEL

WHEN I CALL THE next LGBTQ+ Advocacy Group meeting to order, I start to wonder what's the point. Due to "scheduling conflicts" it's just me and Cassie, again, and we're no closer to figuring out the cryptic list that we lifted from the library.

"Maybe I should take it to Mrs. Camilleri," Cassie says. "She's always extra formal around you, like she has to prove that you've caught her in work mode, not Sal's mom mode."

"Yeah, but we're still going to have the same problem: she's not going to be honest with us."

"I tried searching for this list online, just in case the librarian picked it up somewhere. Like, I thought maybe there was this hidden underground network of book-banning jerks out there sharing books they needed to investigate."

"Really?" a voice sounds out from the doorway. When I lean over to peek, all the blood drains from my face. The librarian,

Miss Orly, scowls as she shuts the door behind her and crosses the room to where Cassie and I are seated.

"How much did you hear?" I ask.

"Plenty." She shrugs. "But that's why I'm here, so I'm glad we can get through this conversation without you denying what you stole from me."

"But we didn't—" Cassie starts.

"Don't. Mrs. Camilleri has been talking to me for weeks about how you two won't stop asking her about the books I've taken off the shelves. You could imagine my surprise when I came back from the pep rally to see my list had been taken—not to mention, I'm pretty sure I saw two teens sneaking loudly out of the library."

"You saw us?" I ask.

Cassie leans forward. "And you didn't get us in trouble?"

"Not yet," she says. "Because I think you can help me. I know I'm new here, and you were all probably fast friends with the last librarian, but unfortunately that doesn't make me an enemy."

"But you just admitted you took the books off the shelves," I tell her.

"I did. That list was provided to me by the superintendent—who is truly one of the most hateful people I've ever met. It's a list he got from your mayor." She shakes her head. "The last librarian was let go because parents complained about her displays, and I'm doing everything I can to keep these books on the shelves."

"Then why didn't you push back?" Cassie asks. "Instead of just taking them off the shelves."

"I did at first, but then I realized what he was asking—I needed to pull every book and personally review them before putting them back on the shelves." She throws her hands in the air. "That's why I tried to do it in batches, so I wasn't taking everything off the shelves at the same time. I have to read every single one and report back. I feel like I'm back in middle school, writing book reports."

She sighs. "Writing these makes my blood boil. But he seems to trust me, which is why some of the books are already back. But he keeps sending me new lists. He and the mayor keep finding new books to 'investigate.' It's only going to get worse, unless..."

"Unless what?" I ask after silence fills the room.

"Unless you were to find a way to leak that anonymously."

I look to Cassie, who offers me a shrug.

"What if that makes it worse?" Cassie asks.

"It will, at first, but it needs to be out there. Someone is literally trying to ban books. They'll investigate *me* when this gets out, but if I'm able to honestly deny it, and they find no instance of tampering on my computer, I think I'll be okay."

"Sure, I'll do it," I say. "I'm about to graduate anyway, so even if they trace it back to me, what's the worst they can do?"

"Stop you from walking in graduation?" Cassie says, pulling me aside.

"If that's why I don't walk, then it'll be for a good reason. They can make your senior year hell, but I've got one foot out the door."

"You're not doing it alone," Cassie says. "I might be able to anonymously reach out to a few reporters, or something."

"Once it goes live, Sal's mom is going to know it's us."

"She won't have any proof," the librarian says, cutting into our private aside, "but just so you know—she's on our side. She doesn't always show it, but she's also torn between doing her job and resisting our awful superintendent. Even if she has to look like she's on the school's side, behind the scenes she's pushed back a lot. But while she seems happy to keep pushing back, I want real change to happen."

We agree, and before long, Miss Orly leaves us alone in the room.

"Think we can trust her?" I finally ask.

Cassie shakes her head. "I wish we had a librarian and a vice principal who just stood up to them, publicly. Who didn't have to play both sides, because that's absolutely what they're doing."

"Yeah, 'working behind the scenes' sometimes means they're just too scared to do it in front of the camera." I smile. "But she did give us permission to blow this whole thing up, and I'm taking it."

"Maybe one day they'll be able to handle things without getting a bunch of teenagers to do their bidding," she says with a laugh. "But I'm so in. We're going to leak it anonymously, so no one tries to make it about us stealing school property, but if you're going public with the fight, then I am too."

I give her a high five. "Looks like our advocacy group is about to make the news."

CHAPTER FIFTY

REESE

EVERY DAY, I GO through the same routine. I wake up, text Heath good morning, and spend a half hour in the design world. Sometimes, that means sewing a new panel onto a dress I'm working on. Other times, that means sketching.

Some days, like today, I only have the energy to dick around on social media. I've been maintaining my drag alt on Instagram, and I'm starting to get a little bit of attention. Nothing viral, nothing particularly successful, but I get to show off some of my designs. I've gotten a couple hundred followers out of it, and I hope that'll grow, but for now I've just been interacting with other designers and showing off my work.

In my latest post, I shared a few drawings of the design I'm working on. This one's a little out of my comfort zone—it's a bright yellow Marilyn Monroe look, a classic Hollywood silhouette that reminds me of some of the projects my summer classmate Philip worked on.

When you search for "Marilyn Monroe wigs" you'll get about a billion results, and they all look the same, but I've been striking out on good wigs lately. I haven't been spending much money on them, though, which is probably why.

I'm not sure I have enough fabric for this one, but I still decided to post the look, along with the caption, "Some news! Your girl just got into The New School for the Parsons Fashion Design BFA. I have a few other applications out, but I'm feeling really good about this opportunity."

I use the acceptance hashtags that the school suggested in their email and call it a day. I head for the shower, since Heath will be here to pick me up in about fifteen minutes.

"Hey, babe," I say to him as he opens my car door from the inside. As he pulls his arm back, I see him wince.

"Reesey," he says, patching on a quick smile. "How's it going?"

"Has it gotten better at all?" I say, asking about his shoulder. "You've been resting it for a week, right?"

He shakes his head. "No, but Coach doesn't seem worried. Yet."

"Okay. Well, I'm glad you're taking it easy."

He shrugs as we head toward the school. "Don't have a choice. Coach said I can't come back unless I do what the doctor says. I've been googling shoulder ligament tears so much all my targeted ads are pain relievers."

"Yeah, the algorithm will get you." I laugh, but an awkward silence fills the truck. "Are you worried?"

He pulls up to a stoplight and wipes his sweaty palms on his jeans. He turns to me with a neutral look on his face before saying,

"I am. Really worried, actually. But I reached out to a therapist, and I have an intro call with him next week."

"That's great! Maybe rest and managing your stress is all you need to patch this up," I offer.

I wish I could tell him that everything was going to be just fine, but we don't know that. So, instead, I just put my hand on his leg and hold it there until we get to school.

The day goes slowly, and I keep distractedly checking my Instagram notifications. By lunchtime, I can safely say my latest post has started to receive some attention, and I've gotten about ten new followers from using the New School's hashtags. A few DMs have even come in, with other newbies asking me where I plan to live when I get there, what classes I'm taking, and whether we can meet for coffee at one of the upcoming orientation days.

As I walk the halls, I realize for the first time just how small they are. How during the school year my whole life is contained in this building. Last summer, I got to see just how big the real world was. And even today, I've had more conversations with literal strangers through a school's incoming class hashtag than I did at school.

These strangers...we're all doing the same thing. We're moving on from our high schools to explore something more exciting. A program that's tailored perfectly to us. And I realize that in a few months, I might not ever see a lot of these people again.

I also realize that, aside from the boys, I'm one hundred percent okay with that.

CHAPTER FIFTY-ONE

SAL

"IS IT UP YET?" my mom asks as soon as I walk into her office.

"Not yet," I say, balancing my laptop on one hand as I close the door with my other. "Reese said he'd do it as soon as he got home, though."

I refresh the page again and again: SalForMayor.com, but each time it just brings up an error message. Once the website is live, my campaign has officially started.

Mom reaches into her mini fridge and pulls out two Cokes, passing one to me. I take it and crack it open. I'm going to need as much caffeine as possible for this. Not that *this* means anything. We still have to, you know, direct people to the site. But still, it's exciting.

And it's got my mom talking to me again. She's still harassing me about college—begging me to go somewhere local, since being the mayor of a village isn't exactly a full-time job—but she's coming around to the idea, at least. And I'm coming around to the idea of taking a few classes at the community college nearby.

We're meeting each other halfway, which is something I never expected out of either of us.

"Check it again," she says impatiently.

"Reese just left!" I say. "Give the guy a break."

"Fine. I have all my press release emails queued up to go out to all the local journalists I know."

My cheeks burn with embarrassment. "Do you think they'll wonder why my *mom* is doing my press?"

She thinks for a second. "No, I don't think so. And even if they do, it's better that the story is that I'm helping you. Sometimes silence speaks louder than words, so if they found out and I wasn't publicly advocating for it, they could easily question whether I was on board or not."

I nod my head, thinking through the small but mighty plan I have laid out on my website. After discussing it with Mom and Betty, we narrowed it down to three key talking points.

1) I will use my experience leading the school as student council president to solve the many issues facing our village. The previous mayor hasn't signed an open license in the past six weeks, and I will never let important requests pile up on my desk.

2) In response to the dwindling population numbers in our village, I will strive to make Gracemont a more

welcoming place by expanding our library's diversity and inclusion resources, creating Gracemont's first Pride Festival as early as next June, and more.

3) Our village's parks are in disrepair. Within my first year in office, I aim to lead *and participate in* a volunteer program to clean up the parks, work with local nurseries to plant more trees, and bring the community together. (With Gabriel's help!)

Easy enough. I had more ideas, but Betty forced me to cap it at three. I can reveal more throughout my campaign, but she said that focusing on a few key messages in the early stages should get me the signatures—all three hundred of them—that I'll need to get my name on the ballot.

"What about now?" Mom asks, and I groan. She's never been the impatient type, so this must really be getting to her.

"Let's see." I refresh the page, and my *Sal for Mayor* logo stares me back in the face. "Oh! It's up!"

"Let me see!" Mom says, before typing the link into her browser. "Well. I'll be."

"It's really happening."

"This looks really professional. I don't even think our current mayor *has* a website." She smirks. "He's going to need one after this."

"Is it go-time?" I ask, and Mom agrees.

We put our heads down, and the rapid typing from my and mom's computers reminds me a little bit of the energy on the Hill— just without all the trauma and pretty architecture.

I send links to the group chat and instruct them to **Go! Go! Go!** They all respond immediately, saying they're sharing with everyone they know.

My phone buzzes, and I see Gabe's calling me. I answer the call.

"Sal! Just want you to know you already have four signatures on the online form."

I look to my mom in confusion. "It's only been two minutes!"

"Let me read the list to you: Gabe, Heath, Reese…"

"And me," Mom says with a smile.

"Four down, two hundred and ninety-six to go!" I say.

"Two hundred and ninety-five! My sister just signed it." He laughs. "Reese and I will get our whole families to do it. They just have to be turning eighteen by November, and they have to live in the village, right?"

"That's it," I say.

"We'll have it in no time," Mom says.

I hang up the phone, and a flurry of excited butterflies jolts straight into my stomach for the first time since I left DC. This feels like something I can accomplish. This feels like the right move.

Everything… just feels right.

• iMessage •

GABRIEL + SAL

> All right, I'm off to Pittsburgh now to meet up with Matt (YAY!)

> I won't be able to check the signatures for a while, but after one full week, we are at 185! We've just got to knock on a few doors and we'll be at 300 in no time! G

Thank you, but stop checking! You're about to go see your boyfriend. You're officially off S the clock. Go have fun!

I can't believe it's really happening.

It doesn't feel real.

But god I miss him.

Sorry! Too much?

S • • •

Sal?

S I'm just really happy for you.

CHAPTER FIFTY-TWO

GABRIEL

EVEN THOUGH IT'S A three-hour drive to Pittsburgh, more or less, I find myself nervously packing the car with everything I could possibly need. I'm in a T-shirt now—it's unseasonably warm, which gives me hope for the coming spring—but I still throw a hoodie and a sweater in the car. (Thought process: if I'm cold in the car, I throw on the hoodie; if I'm cold on the date, I throw on the sweater. Genius.)

Mom and Dad keep pointing out various snacks I might want or need, and I find myself packing them all. Just in case. As I zip up the duffel bag of goodies, I give them a quick wave before starting the trip to meet Matt.

From the very start, my palms are sweaty. I consider giving one of the boys a call, just to keep my nerves in check, but before I can do that, I get an incoming call from Cassie.

"Perfect timing," I say. "I just got on the road to Pittsburgh, and I'm already bored."

She laughs. "Just wanted to give you an update on the whole library-book-banning-bonanza thing."

"Okay, shoot."

She clears her throat. "Well, last night I started collecting a list of local reporters who have written about this kind of thing. School issues, social justice issues, things like that. The list wasn't very big, to be honest, but I still sent them a quick note from a burner email address with a rundown of what's going on."

"Any luck?" I ask, hopeful.

"Actually, yes. I was going to create a whole website for this, but it looks like Channel Four news wants to run the story and agreed to post the full spreadsheet on their website, anonymizing the source."

"But Miss Orly wrote all over that piece of paper, right? Won't it be obvious that either she leaked it or someone stole it from the library?" I swallow hard. "And if they decide to look at the tapes..."

She laughs. "We worked that out too. I agreed to send them a picture of the list for proof, and they agreed to retype it completely."

"Oh well, that takes care of that. Are we missing anything?"

"Mrs. Camilleri is a bit of a wild card. She could probably put the pieces together quickly." She sighs. "But she wouldn't have proof, so I don't think she can do anything to us based on a hunch, right?"

I ease onto the highway, the sound of my blinker filling the silence as I think through the scenario.

"Sal's mom can do whatever she wants, I'm sure."

"There's one other thing. It also has to do with his mom."

"Oh?" I ask.

"The reporter who's interested in this is the same one who

did that news story when Sal's mom committed to advancing LGBTQ rights in the school. He's going to ask her for a comment, and the angle might not be the best for her." She pauses. "I know Sal's your friend. I just wanted to make sure you knew."

"That's a good point, but I don't think we have a choice. I mean, it's the strongest angle there is—she promised to fight for us, then immediately backpedals? We'll just have to see if she sides with the superintendent or with us."

The pause from the other end of the phone is long, but once Cassie speaks again, the uncertainty is gone from her voice.

"Let's do it, then," she says.

"Let's do it. Here's to maybe getting expelled!"

She laughs. "Don't even *joke* about that."

We end our conversation, and I put on one of Reese's playlists. This one's titled *RomCom Dreams*, and it's one he created when he and Heath started dating. It's actually really cute, bordering on cringe, and it's the kind of joy that I need injected into my veins right now.

Because, for the second time since we said goodbye last summer, I'm getting to see my boyfriend.

• • •

I park in a garage in Pittsburgh. Matt's waiting for me out front, so I chomp on my granola bar, grab my sweater, and head toward the entrance.

As I exit, I glance up and down the street until I see him. Golden-red hair, piercing blue eyes, and the kind smile that always makes me a little weak in the knees. It hasn't been easy, but the rush of excitement and pure joy I get from seeing him in the flesh is unlike anything I've ever felt before.

I run to him and throw myself into his arms, which instantly squeeze me close to him. I bury my face in the soft spot between his neck and shoulder, before pulling back to meet him face-to-face.

He plants a sweet kiss on me, and I can't fight the smile that breaks my pucker.

"You're here," he says.

"And so are you," I reply.

"Coffee?"

"*Please*," I beg.

We walk the streets of Pittsburgh, passing no fewer than twenty people in Pittsburgh Steelers jerseys, despite the fact that it isn't football season and it's also a workday. (Or maybe this is considered work attire in Pittsburgh? Who am I to judge other cultures?)

Once we finally come across a coffee shop, Matt opens the door for me. I step in and throw my sweater over a two-seater near the window, while Matt goes to order our drinks.

He passes me mine, and I hold it tightly, hoping some of the warmth returns to my fingers. It was a long drive, and I have a habit of white-knuckling it even when the drive isn't particularly stressful, so this is key for getting the blood back into my extremities.

"How was your drive?" he asks.

I shrug. "Long, but pretty smooth. Yours?"

He sighs. "Not great. A lot of accidents today, and traffic is wild."

"I'm sorry." I place my hand on his and offer him a smile. "But at least we're together now, finally."

He smiles too, and we sip our coffees in silence. We talk to each other every day, in one form or another, and we never have problems finding something to talk about, but today's a little different. It's full of the same awkward pauses, the stops and starts that we had when we very first started dating.

"Sorry about prom," he says. "I finally looked it up, and ours are both on the same exact day in May, so we couldn't have made it work anyway. I assume you wouldn't want to miss the last big dance with the boys, and I'm feeling the same way with my friends."

"It's fine. Realistic, I guess." I force a dry laugh.

"Have you talked to Art or Tiffany lately?" he says, referencing our friends from the volunteer program. "I haven't spoken to them in ages. Oh! But I did just talk to our old Save the Trees boss, Ali. She's writing a recommendation letter for one of my applications."

"Oh, that's great!" I say. "I had Laura write one for me back when I applied to Ohio State."

He raises his coffee cup in a "cheers" motion. "Congrats on that, by the way."

"Thanks. But . . . no, I haven't talked to Art or Tiffany in a long time. It's sad, isn't it?" I sigh. "These people were our lifelines for three months, and now it's like . . . okay, back to our previous lives."

"It's a part of life, I guess?" A sad expression comes over his face. "People move on. That summer was so special, but it's hard keeping up with people when you're applying to colleges and planning your whole lives out."

"At least I can see what Tiffany's up to. Art doesn't have social media—how am I supposed to check in on them? *Email???*"

Matt laughs. "We could text, but they weren't much of a texter last year."

Once we get that conversation out of the way, Matt suggests we take a walk through one of the local parks. He pats his backpack and gives me a wink, and that reminds me of the picnics we used to do back with the whole gang.

Our first date was even in a city park.

"Do all city parks just look the same?" I say. "I know it's not Boston, but the big trees and tall buildings…and you. I don't know, it all feels so familiar."

We find a patch of lawn in the sun, and Matt throws a blanket over it. He sets out a full lunch spread.

"Did you bring me chicken parm?"

"I did," he says with a laugh. "I got here early and got takeout from a restaurant a couple miles out. It's lukewarm and, of course, not from our favorite cheap restaurant in Boston, *but* chicken parm is chicken parm."

We eat and talk and laugh and sneak kisses in between bites. It reminds me of why I fell for him in the first place. But I still can't silence the voice in my head, reminding me that the sun will be setting soon. That it'll all be over again soon. That we'll never be in the same place at the same time.

"You okay?" Matt asks, pulling out a container of chopped-up fruit for dessert.

I look to him as he pops a cube of honeydew in his mouth, and

I feel the tears come to my eyes. Startled, he comes around to my side of the blanket and puts an arm around me cautiously.

He doesn't push it, or ask me over and over and over again what's wrong, he just gives me time to breathe and figure out what I'm even upset about. I appreciate that more than I even do the picnic.

"I love you," I say.

"I love you too, but I feel like there's a 'but' coming after that…"

"No. No buts." I sigh. "I love you *and* that's why this has been so hard. This sucks."

"This date?" he says.

"Don't joke," I say.

He squeezes me hard. "Yeah, I probably shouldn't."

"I think you're perfect for me," I say. "I really, *really* believe that."

"Is this where the 'but' comes in?"

"Yeah. You're perfect for me, but you're so far away."

"About that," he says. "I guess now's as good a time to tell you as any. The letter of recommendation that Ali wrote me? That was for Berkeley. They have this awesome environmental sciences program as part of their College of Natural Resources."

I look to him. "You didn't tell me you applied to Berkeley."

"I didn't think I would get in, honestly." He shrugs. "But someone from the program just reached out to schedule a virtual interview with me this week, so it looks like they're seriously considering me. If they accepted me, I would go."

"Fuck," I say. "California?"

I look to him, and the tears in his eyes must match my own. My mind's just an endless loop of *no, no, no*. This can't be true.

"I got into Pitt, but I don't think I want to go here. I mean, the farthest I've ever been from my parents was when we went to Boston." He sighs. "I want to be close to you so badly."

"Same."

"But I can't make that the deciding factor here."

I shrug. "I wouldn't want you to either."

He leans his head into mine, and I let it rest there for a while. We don't say anything, both of us afraid to shatter this moment. This perfectly tragic moment on this perfectly tragic date.

"Where does that leave us?" he asks.

"I think we both know. We can either stay together and slowly drift apart—"

"—or start to resent each other."

"Yep, that too," I say. "Or we could..."

"Can you just not say it?" he says with a grimace on his face. "Just, don't say the words. Not right now."

"But we are," I say sadly.

He replies with a soft, "Yeah."

We've kept the PDA to a minimum on the streets of Pittsburgh, presumably to not get hate crimed, but we hang off each other for the entirety of the last block. The walk to the garage is slow and agonizing, and it really starts to sink in as my car comes into view.

I give him one last kiss, and try to force my brain to remember everything about this moment. Everything about him—the feel of his lips, how he tastes, how his hands feel on my back, how his cologne fills my nose.

"I love you," I say.

"No buts?" he says with a smirk, and I shake my head. "I love you too."

I cling to him for a few more moments, but we ultimately have to pull apart.

"'Bye," I say. "Let's keep in touch, okay? None of this 'I'm busy' business. I want to be a part of your life."

"Likewise," he says. "'Bye, Gabe."

GABRIEL + HEATH + REESE + SAL

How's Pittsburgh? **R**

G I'm already back.

Oh... short trip? **R**

H everything ok???

G It's over. It's fine.
It was mutual.

Shit, seriously?? I'm so sorry.
Do you need us to come
over? **R**

G No, I just want to be alone.

S I'm sorry, Gabe.

• Breakup Mobilizers •

HEATH + REESE + SAL

we're not going to listen to him about leaving him alone right?

Absolutely not.

I'm already looking for ice cream lol. I think we have a whole gallon in the freezer.

Perfect. I think I have some of his favorite jerky on hand.

i love you guys

i'll pick yall up in 5

CHAPTER FIFTY-THREE

HEATH

"GABE?" I ASK, KNOCKING lightly on his bedroom door. I turn to the other boys, who are packed into his upstairs hallway. "Gabe, we're here. Can you open up?"

"I said I didn't need you to come over," Gabe says from behind his closed door.

"We didn't listen," Sal says.

"Let us in!" Reese demands. "Unless you want all this ice cream to melt."

He opens the door, and we all slowly pile into his room. The room reeks of mourning, which seems impossible since the breakup only happened a few hours ago. But the bed is fully unmade, his overnight bag is spilling sweaters, snacks, and other random clothes all over the floor of the bedroom.

He makes his way to the bed, pulling his heart-shaped plushie into his grip.

"Have you been crying?" Reese asks.

"No," he says. "I can't. How can I be *so sad*, but I can't even shed a tear? Is something wrong with me?"

"Nothing's wrong with you," Sal says reassuringly.

"Easy for you to say, you're a robot. You've never cried in front of us!" Gabe huffs. "You never let us know how you're feeling."

"Ouch," Sal responds. "I thought I've been better about that. Sorry?"

Gabe waves his hand dismissively. "It's fine, I'm just being snippy."

"It's still a little sunny out," I say. "Do you want to go to the baseball diamond with us? We can take our blanket out there, just like old times?"

He looks to me and nods slightly.

"All right, it's settled," I say. "Reese, salvage whatever snacks you can from Gabe's bag; I'll grab some bowls and silverware and bring the ice cream down."

"What do I do?" Sal asks, a little desperately, as he takes a seat next to Gabe on the bed.

"Just . . . be here for me," Gabe says, leaning on him softly.

"Oh. Okay." Sal's smile is soft. "I can do that."

• • •

I load up my left arm with as many goodies as I can, since my right one's out of commission, and I lead the group down to the baseball diamond. It's chilly out, but not freezing. We're able to get by with just a few sweaters, though we know that with how unpredictable March is, that might not be enough when the sun goes down, especially while eating ice cream.

The things we do for our friends.

CHAPTER FIFTY-FOUR

REESE

THINGS FEEL ODDLY NORMAL once we all take our seats on the corners of the blanket. This tradition is something that always brings us comfort, so when Heath brought up the idea, we were all in agreement. It helps that the baseball diamond basically touches Gabriel's backyard, so we can walk there quickly.

We take turns eating ice cream out of the tub with a spoon, ignoring the bowls that Heath brought out, and eventually, Gabriel loosens up and starts to smile more.

"I just wish we had more time in Boston," he says. "Like, I really think we were something special. I hate that none of you got to see it."

"I got to see it, briefly," Sal says. "Even though I almost messed everything up, I knew he was a good fit for you. And he cared so much about you."

"And he still does," Heath says. "He already texted me to see if you were okay."

Gabriel's eyes glisten. "I think we really will be better about being friends after this. It's so hard to keep in touch with people, but we have all the same interests, and he's going to have this awesome life in California. I'm just... not going to be a part of it in that way."

"Seems like it really was mutual," I say. "Not that that makes it much better, but still."

"I think we both could have kept up the charade for a while, but that would have just hurt more. I mean, we've been so busy lately we haven't even gotten to FaceTime in a couple of weeks. I was holding that silly pillow Heath got us, but it's not like we ever used it. With all the drama in the school library, and thinking about Ohio State, I guess he stopped being a priority for me a long time ago." He sighs. "And now I know—I'm just not a long-distance guy. At least I'm not kidding myself about it anymore."

Heath and I meet eyes across the picnic blanket, and I see a dark expression come over his face. With his eyes, he asks the question—*Are we kidding ourselves?*—and I wish I could honestly answer no.

I can't compare what we have to what Gabriel and Matt had, but it was certainly something special.

I just hope what we have is more special.

CHAPTER FIFTY-FIVE

SAL

ONE WEEK AFTER GABE'S big breakup, things have slowly gotten back to normal. He seems okay with how things ended, but still disappointed that they had to end at all. I've had to console him as a friend, but it's been hard not to lean on how we used to be. We really did have to relearn how to be friends over the summer, and it only got harder once the school year started.

But we're in a good place. Finally.

I haven't crossed the line, and I won't.

Even though I kind of want to.

Just before physics starts, Heath and I get individual pieces of paper passed to us from the student aide, with instructions to skip next period to see the vice principal—my mom—in her office.

"What's this about?" Heath asks, and I shrug.

"She's never pulled us out of class before," I say.

I feel my anxiety spike, and I wonder what could cause Mom

to call me and Heath—and presumably, the other boys—into her office. Have we messed up? Or maybe this is a good thing. They should be announcing valedictorian and salutatorian soon—maybe that's why Heath and I were chosen.

Either way, it's hard to concentrate through class.

Once the bell rings, Heath and I both release a long sigh. As our other classmates all scramble to their next class, we walk slowly down the hall toward Mom's office. Ahead of us, I see Reese and Gabriel open the door, and that's when I know this has nothing to do with valedictorian announcements.

"Wait up!" Cassie says as she runs up behind us. "What's going on? Did you all get called to Mrs. Camilleri's office too?"

"Yeah," Heath says. "The whole LGBTQ+ Advocacy Group did."

"Plus Reese," I say.

"Well, this isn't good." Cassie walks ahead of us and opens the door. "You first. She loves you guys, but she's likely to kill me."

"We'll protect you," Heath says with a chuckle, and anxieties aside, we step in.

The five of us cram into her office, each taking a chair across from her. She smiles at us, wearily, and hands me a printout of a news article.

"What's this?" I ask.

"You should read it," she says. "But I'll summarize. Basically, one of the reporters I pitched about your mayoral run decided to cover it. But he was also approached by an anonymous student who had proof that LGBTQ+ discrimination was happening in these halls." She sighs. "This Frankenstein of a piece is what resulted. Essentially, it announces your run, but the focus is on me: how I could be supportive of my son's campaign that's focused on diversity and inclusion, but behind the scenes, how I'm orchestrating the county's biggest book ban in secret."

"You … what?" Gabe asks. "I thought it was the superintendent."

"It *is* the superintendent. But to some journalists, checking their facts isn't as exciting as publishing a story like this."

I finish scanning the article. It's full of mockery, and it paints my mom in a really challenging light. Though, for what it's worth, he doesn't mock my campaign. He actually supports it.

But as I scan the list of books that have been pulled from our school library, I feel my cheeks flush. Gabriel wasn't kidding, this is majorly screwed up.

"I want to know who leaked that list," Mom says. "I know it's one of you in this room, and I need you to tell me who it was."

CHAPTER FIFTY-SIX

GABRIEL

I'M OFFICIALLY OUT OF fucks to give.

"It was me. I stole it from Miss Orly, and I told the press about it. Last year, you promised to protect LGBTQ+ kids at this school, and you haven't held up that promise. It's about time someone called you out on it."

"Gabriel," Cassie snaps.

"No, no, let him continue," Sal's mom says.

"These books were being pulled all year, and you knew about it. You made me and Cassie out to be paranoid liars when we first brought the issue to you, just like you debated us about our rights for prom." I sigh. "You think we're doing this for attention? You're *right*. If the people who are supposed to help us can't, or won't, this kind of attention is the only thing that's going to work."

"Heath, Sal, Reese," she starts, "you're dismissed. I need to talk to Gabriel and Cassandra alone, now that I know who did this."

"I'm not leaving," Sal says. "I'm a part of the LGBTQ+ Advocacy Group, *and* I'm student council pres—"

"Sal, I know you're the president, I'm your mom. Also, I work at the school." She clears her throat. "Reese, Heath, please leave us to chat."

They do, after I give them the okay.

"The superintendent makes these decisions. He has the backing of the mayor. There's nothing we can do, except what I've been planning to do all along." She sighs. "The superintendent is speaking at town hall next week for his annual education update. This is usually when he gets to brag about test scores, but I plan to be there to give him hell. Miss Orly is joining too. I have everything documented meticulously. *This* was the right way to go about it."

"Respectfully," I say, feeling Cassie's and Sal's eyes on me, "I don't agree. Sometimes things can't be taken care of behind closed doors. Sometimes it's not about logic, or personal appeals. Sometimes it's about numbers. And by leaking this, I think we'll have the numbers to really push back—maybe even at the town council meeting. We'll all go."

"I have a better idea," Sal's mom says. "Could you get your parents to come instead? Could we get as many supportive parents in the stands there? If the school board sees a league of parents standing against the superintendent, we might have a chance with all this."

"So I'm not in trouble?" I ask.

"I'm not going to punish you for this," she says with a chuckle. "And not because you don't deserve it—theft of school property, taking private school emails...that's not a small offense. But for this to work, I'll need to say that I don't know who leaked it."

She pauses, then looks to Sal. "You'll need to respond to this on your own. Maybe on your new Facebook page? But I can't coach you through it. Just be honest, and if you can, make an appeal for parents to come to the next meeting to confront the school board."

"I'm on it. I even have a hundred people on my mailing list who I can reach out to about it." Sal smiles at me, and I smile back.

"All right. So we're doing this?" I ask, to subtle nods from everyone in the room. "Then let's go."

Sal for Mayor

To the Village of Gracemont:

Many of you have reached out to discuss reporter Brandon
Davis's recent article announcing my bid for candidacy.
Although the article focused on controversy, I truly believe this
article captured the spirit of my campaign, and detailed my
goals for Gracemont in a hopeful way. Of course, I'd expected
the jabs at my age and supposed lack of experience, but I
didn't expect my mother to be the real target of this article.
I don't think our relationship was fairly portrayed, but the issue
brought up *is* a huge one: Are LGBTQ+ people protected in
our towns, and in our schools?

Unlike Mayor Green, I know that protecting our LGBTQ+
youth means keeping diverse books on shelves, and I want
you to fight with me.

Next Monday, my mother will file a formal petition to stop
this constant surveillance of our libraries and to return all the
investigated books to the shelves. The mayor, should he agree

to open it to a vote, will want to hear from any concerned parent out there. Of course, he'll be expecting a wave of support for these bans, but I know there's more acceptance in our village than there is hate. Please attend the town hall meeting on Tuesday, and together, let's show Mayor Green he does have something to worry about—Gracemont turning against him in November.

Thank you. See you on Tuesday.
Sal

CHAPTER FIFTY-SEVEN

HEATH

DAD AND I HAVEN'T gotten to know much about our neighbors since we moved, as we've really just kept to ourselves. I'm always in and out with baseball, and Dad works so much that we don't really have time to go around and make friends.

And based on how today's going, it looks like we're making more enemies than we are friends.

"Thanks for coming with me to get these signatures for Sal," I say. "I had no idea Mayor Green had all these fierce supporters in our apartment complex."

Dad nods. "I'm just glad you've got something going on that isn't about baseball."

"What do you mean?" I ask. "It's, like, baseball is everything to you."

He looks at me oddly. "*You're* everything to me, bud. And yes, I love watching you play and practicing with you and reliving my own glory days from the bleachers, but baseball is definitely not everything to me. And it shouldn't be everything to you either."

"It's not," I say quickly.

He laughs. "It's okay. I know this scholarship has really been weighing on you. But I think we're doing better, right?"

"Yep." I nod. "Almost got the full range of motion back. The cortisone shot really helped, and so has working with that rehab doctor. I know we've already spent enough money, so if we wanted to stop with rehab we could; I already know all the stretches—"

"Heath," Dad says in an unusually stern voice. "It's fine. We have the money, I promise. You just need to get back into top shape."

"Oh . . . okay."

We knock on another door, and the door opens to reveal Lyla, one of my classmates who's on student council with Reese.

"Ooh, I bet I know what this is about," she says. "Hey, Mom, get over here!"

We hand out Sal's flyer and talk about his vision for the village, carefully going through all the key talking points Sal wanted us to say.

"Would you two like to sign this petition to get Sal on the ballot?" Dad says. "Mayor Green's run unopposed for more than a decade now, and we think it's time he had a real challenge."

Lyla's mom looks at each of us slowly, eventually pausing on my dad. "You really think this kid can do it?"

"You'll see," Dad says.

Lyla laughs. "You should see how he runs student council meetings, Mom! Remember when you filed to have your crafts table at the farmers' market last year and he never approved it, returned your calls, or got back to you? That's something Sal would never do."

"It's true," Heath says. "He's really organized and excited to help this town. Especially small businesses like yours."

We talk them both through the process of signing the e-petition to get Sal on the ballot, and after the positive interaction, we wave goodbye. I sigh in relief before they can even close the door.

"Finally, someone normal," I say.

Dad nods. "And two more signatures."

We meander through the apartment complex, and our conversation turns again to money. Insurance, doctors' appointments, narrowly avoiding surgery—all of it.

"Can we talk about something else?" Dad asks.

"Sure," I say. "Oh, right, I forgot to tell you—I FaceTimed Uncle Rick, and he showed me how to fix the leaky pipe under the kitchen sink, so that's all taken care of. I could even do it with one arm!"

"Thanks, bud." Dad sighs. "I'm sorry I can't be around more. You know how busy season is at the factory—they've got me working ten-hour days and weekends, and I'm about tired of it. You shouldn't have to take care of all that."

I shrug. "Nah, it's fine."

"Your friends don't have to do this stuff, do they? They don't worry about money like we do; they don't have to work themselves until they crash just for a scholarship. God, Heath, I couldn't even help you pay to fix up your truck. I'm really sorry."

"Dad, it's okay. Really." I look at him. "I don't compare myself to them like that, at least not anymore. I . . . I appreciate what we have. And I wouldn't trade you and Mom and Jeanie and Diana for any of what they have. It's hard sometimes, but I mean that."

Dad's eyes start to water, so I see him pull his shades from his head to cover his eyes.

"Aw, is someone getting emotional?" I tease. "Come on, let's find someone else to yell at us, I'm sure that'll snap us right back into reality."

He laughs as I knock on the next door.

CHAPTER FIFTY-EIGHT

GABRIEL

CASSIE AND I DECIDED to take the plats around our village, not far from where I live. While Sal and Reese live a bit farther out into the country, Cassie and I live in the more densely populated streets just outside the school.

I've always liked the area. Heath's old street was deathly quiet in the evenings, and his new place is a little too noisy, being on Main Street. Here, all we have to deal with are some yappy dogs and the occasional loud passerby.

"Is this kind of like what you did over the summer?" Cassie asks, and I nod.

"This seems even more invasive, actually. I would just stop people walking on the street when I was canvassing for donations to the Boston Save the Trees Foundation; this one I have to go to their homes. It's a whole new kind of anxiety."

She shrugs. "At least people have been nice so far."

"We even got a few signatures. I hope we can get more, though."

"We will. Plus I have my parents telling all their friends and spreading the word. They know just about everyone, and I think they know Gracemont's ready for a change. I'm so pissed I'll only be seventeen on election day, though."

"Maybe when he runs for reelection," I say with a chuckle. "Well. One thing at a time I guess."

We go from house to house, interrupting people's days—for some people, they'll invite us in, listen to our plea, and offer us water, even if they don't end up signing on the spot. For others, they slam the door in our faces. The feeling of rejection, and the feeling of success too, really does feel like Boston, which makes my heart ache when I think about Matt.

"Oh no, you're looking sad again." Cassie takes me to a bench near a path that leads into a hiking trail I've never been on. "Talk to me."

"It's nothing new. Just postbreakup stuff."

"Do you feel like you have closure? I'm still a novice at this whole dating thing, but I hear that's kind of important."

"Yes and no," I say. "Getting to break up in person was really nice. And it *was* mutual. It just sucks, and I don't think either of us knows how to be just friends. But it's okay, because I am throwing myself into helping Sal get elected and making sure this town hall meeting goes off without a hitch. I have a whole speech prepared, and a presentation, and—"

"Gabe, Sal told us not to interfere. It's our fight, I know it's our fight, but right now the mayor on the podium doesn't give a shit

AFTERGLOW 🎓 321

what we say. We need to get our parents and their friends to show up in big numbers. If Mayor Green walks into a room with even a dozen parents who are angry with him, it could make him pause. But he's already shown he doesn't care about us teens."

I sigh. "But I feel like I could make him understand."

"Honey, no one can make that man understand anything. He's been in that cushy spot as unopposed mayor for ages, and he doesn't see us as a threat. But if we come with some major backup, that'll change. I mean, have you seen the comments on Sal's post already? It looks like a lot of the town is fired up."

"I've seen them," I say. "I just wish I could do more, you know?"

"We are. Literally, we're doing it right now. Getting people to check out his website, to learn more about his campaign, getting him on the ballot. Change isn't easy, but it feels like there's been a shift, and we just have to keep riding that wave."

I laugh. "I find the surfing terminology very appropriate for a girl who's going to crush it in California after high school."

"Oh em gee, like *totally*," she says with a fake Valley girl accent while flipping her hair. She laughs. "Sorry, that was cringey."

I shake my head. "Please, this is all cringey. Let's keep going, though. He's getting so close to three hundred signatures, and I think we can pass it today."

CHAPTER FIFTY-NINE

REESE

WHILE THE OTHERS CANVASS for votes on this gorgeous sunny day, Sal and I are trapped inside.

"All right, and here are the assets—"

"What?" Sal asks.

"Images? Logos? Things like that," I explain. "These are all the assets for your campaign. I also uploaded all the designs for the pamphlets, yard signs, banners, and anything else we might need in this folder. Of course, we'll need to pull through on some more donations before we can afford anything beyond the pamphlets, but we have time."

"So I can go ahead and start sending out my newsletter, right? Gabriel helped me come up with all the content; I just want to make sure it looks right before sending."

I click through and adjust the code for the email slightly, moving the logo to the top, changing the font to our "official campaign font" that I picked out, and making sure the color scheme suggests Sal's political affiliations without it being too in your face.

"This is perfect," he says.

"I can't believe your aunt is hosting this fundraiser party for you," I say, reading the email in more depth. "I haven't been to her house in ages. Does she still have that pool?"

"Technically, yes, but it was all scummy last I saw it, and had all these cracks in there too. No pool parties for us anymore, I fear."

I sigh. "God, those were fun when we were kids."

"This is starting to feel real, isn't it?" he asks. "Like, *really* real."

"That's because it is," I say with a laugh.

"No, I know, but this all feels next level. I couldn't have done any of this stuff without you guys. I don't know how to thank you."

"Thank us by winning," I say. "Here, let's check the counts again and see if the boys and Cassie were able to work their magic yet. We were at, what, two hundred and twenty-five this morning?"

"Two hundred and twenty-seven," he corrects me.

I open the official petition and go into the back end to see how many have signed. The number that pops up barely seems real.

"Three hundred and four?" I ask. "Holy shit, Sal. Three hundred and four!"

I turn to him, and I can't decipher his expression.

"I think my brain just short circuited. I, *we* did it. I'm going to be on the ballot. Holy . . ." He trails off.

"I understand your mom really drilled this no-cursing thing into your soul, but of all the times to say it, now is the time."

"*Holy fucking shit.*"

• Golden Boys •

GABRIEL + HEATH + REESE + SAL

> Can you all make it to my virtual drag show late tonight?

> I'm doing an Instagram Live with this guy who goes to Parsons, and he has like 5k followers.

(R)

> this is huge! you know I'll be there

> you're all coming to the game first right?

(H) > i'm finally in the clear to pitch a few innings!!

Wouldn't miss it.

(The game or the show.) Ⓢ

I think I'm going to get nachos.
Or a pretzel?

Ⓖ Thank god you have baseball
again, Heath, concessions food
can't be beat.

Ⓗ if baseball games didn't have
food would any of you come?

Probably. Ⓡ

Ⓖ Maybe.

Ⓢ No. ♥

CHAPTER SIXTY

HEATH

THE SUN IS WARM, and the smell of dirt and grass flood my nose as I step on the field as a player for the first time in weeks. I've followed the rules to a tee. I've taken my anti-inflammatories, I've narrowly avoided going to the doctor, but it's wild that all I really needed was some rest. Well, that and a cortisone shot.

I do my warm-ups, which consist of the same movements that I've been doing to recover from my injury. There's still a tightness there. Something off that strikes me with the slightest bit of insecurity. A hint of anxiety.

"You doing okay?" James asks as he pats me not so softly on the shoulder.

I flinch out of habit, waiting for the pain. But it never comes, so I breathe a sigh of relief.

"James, I'm going to need you to pay attention to which shoulder you slap next time."

He yanks his hand away. "Oh, fuck, sorry, bro. But you didn't scream or punch me, so at least that means you're doing okay?"

"Yeah," I laugh. "We'll see."

Assistant Coach Roberts leads the team in warm-ups—normally on a game day, they'd only last about five minutes. But these are more thorough, so it looks like he's been listening to the doctor's advice. Everyone takes the field and starts passing to one another; a couple of our strongest batters warm up with weights on their bat.

"Heath—got a second?" Coach Lee asks, and I nod.

He walks me to the dugout, and we sit on the bench. He always gets a little erratic before games, calling out commands and changing his mind mid-warm-up, but his presence is a steady one today, which I appreciate.

"We're going to take it slow and steady. This is a big game for us, but I don't want you pushing it and getting hurt."

I nod. Even if it's a little disappointing, I never expected to play six innings right after an injury.

"James is going to be the starting pitcher today, but we'll bring you in around the fourth inning. I know our last couple practices went okay, but if you feel any pain, let me pull you out immediately. Promise me that."

I nod. "Absolutely, Coach."

Before the game starts, I reach in my equipment bag and check out my phone, where I have a slew of texts from the boys wishing me luck. I don't have a great view of the stands from the dugout, but I know that Dad and Reese are there, and the other boys might stop by later.

At the end of the third inning, Coach gives me a signal, and I start warming up with one of the backup pitchers off to the side. When I emerge into the sun, I hear roaring applause from the stands—all the boys are there. I blush and give them a quick wave, then focus on the pitches.

My range of motion isn't what it used to be, but it's getting better. My fastballs are a little less quick, but still quicker than most. My curveball doesn't snap into the strike zone exactly like I'd like it to, but the bones are good. This probably won't be my best game, but by the end of the season, I know that I can impress Vanderbilt enough to lock in my scholarship.

Suddenly, it's time. Coach goes out to the mound, the umpire joining him, and James gives me a wink. Anxiety floods my body, and I think of the many, *many* things that could go wrong here. What if my arm starts getting sore again? What if my now-slow fastballs give up hit after hit?

What if everyone sees me fail?

When I take steps toward the mound, the cheers block out some of that anxiety, but my hands are too sweaty. My breaths are too short. I can't do this. I take a few deep breaths, thinking of the advice my new therapist gave me in our first session.

My mind quiets once I take my spot on the mound and dig my cleats into the hard rubber. While the ump goes back to his spot behind the catcher, I scan the crowd. It's an intimidating crowd, our biggest yet of the season thanks to the warm weather. Fifth row back, Reese sits there with a hot dog in hand, waving frantically.

I give him a quick nod. When I turn back to the batter, I try to focus on Reese in my brain. If I think of him, and how great things are going with us, I won't be worried about all this. But that reminds me how close we are to graduation. How so much about us is up in the air.

I can't get enough air. But I also need to pitch *now*.

I square up and shift my body weight to my back leg. I pull my arm back and, using all my body weight, launch a baseball toward the batter.

Immediately, I know something's wrong. A flare of pain explodes from my shoulder, and the rest of my body pulses with pain. Since my brain is a little too blocked to think of anything but *extreme fucking pain* I let momentum carry me forward and down, into the dirt.

My face skids across the ground, and in that moment, I lose all shame and despite my surroundings I just keep shouting, "No, no, no, no, no, n—"

There are so many noises. The shuffling of cleats in grass, worried chatter from my teammates as they approach, the sounds of various baseball equipment thudding on the soft ground. I gasp in pain just as I hear Reese scream, "Heath!"

I want to stand up, show him I'm okay. Grit my teeth and push through, like I always do. But I can't.

I let the pain take over, and I black out.

CHAPTER SIXTY-ONE

REESE

THE MEDICS COME QUICKLY. At least, I think they do—to tell the truth, I'm not sure how much time has passed since I watched Heath collapse into the ground. I've been stuck here, gripping the bench beneath me for dear life, ever since.

When it happened, Sal snapped into action. He said something about how an EMT is always nearby during games in case of injury. I'd never noticed that—I'd never thought of baseball as a particularly dangerous sport—but he knew exactly where they were.

"Are you okay?" Gabriel asks, putting his arm around me.

"He just...dropped. I've never seen anything like it. I never thought anything could take down someone like him."

He's the strongest person I know, both mentally and physically. He's the perfect big spoon, the kind of cuddler who no matter what happens, makes you feel like everything will be okay. And he's just...out like a light.

"He's awake, at least," Gabriel says, but it's hard to confirm with his whole team around him. "See, the medics are talking to him."

"I have to stand up," I say.

"They won't let you onto the field, though."

"I know that," I snap, then shake my head. "Sorry, I didn't mean—"

"—It's fine," he says with a nod. "Let's see how close we can get."

We take the steps down to the front of the stands. There's a paved path in between the stands and the fence, netting, and field that looks out into the neighborhood.

"Heath is going to be okay," I say with a wavering voice.

"He will," Gabriel confirms.

As we make it to the fence—as close as we can be to our friend without getting in the way—I feel a hand wrap around my waist. Sal, Gabriel, and I hold one another. Or maybe they're just holding me. But we're here, helpless, as Heath shakily gets to his feet.

His arm is in a makeshift sling, and he makes his way toward the gate in the fence. Scratches and rug burn line his face from the way he fell into the hard dirt; he can barely keep his eyes open from the pain. His dad leads the way, opening the gate as Heath's coach holds up his body weight. The EMTs on duty are rattling off medical terminology to the group, but no one seems to be listening.

Because everyone knows what it means: a career-ending injury, surgery—and his future at Vanderbilt? It seems impossible now.

I leave the other boys and follow behind the group. I see

Heath's coach press his forehead to Heath's, with tears in his eyes, and I get the sense he's blaming himself for this. Once Heath's in the ambulance, his dad steps in. I inch closer, just wanting to make eye contact with him one more time.

They go to close the doors, but Heath snaps out of his pain-induced stupor enough to shout, "Where is he?"

Slowly, all eyes turn to me. I can't say anything, because anything I do say will make the tears pour from my eyes.

"Reese," his dad says. "Do you want to come to the hospital with us?"

I nod quickly and brush my runny nose with a folded-up napkin that's thankfully in my pocket. I climb into the ambulance. Heath and I make eye contact as they prep him for an IV. He doesn't flinch when the needle enters his veins, but I do.

"I'm so sorry," I say to him.

His dad puts a palm on my back, and for a moment, I feel like a part of *his* family.

• • •

The wait in the hospital is excruciating, but I spend the time chatting nervously with his dad. He and I never really get one-on-one time, and this might not be the best circumstances to have that time, but at least we're not waiting alone.

Eventually, the doctor comes out and asks for us to follow her. We trail her to a hospital room where Heath is, and as I step into the room, I almost faint. He's hooked up to so many machines, he's wearing a hospital gown, and he seems so weak.

I zone out at the beginning of the conversation, but snap back in as soon as I pull my eyes away from him.

"Look, you're young and your tendon tissue is strong and healthy," the doctor explains to Heath. "The MRI shows a pretty substantial tear, and it's only going to get worse over time." She sighs. "I know you don't want to hear this, but if you want baseball to be a part of your life again, you'll need to have surgery—and in the next few weeks."

Heath's face falls, but he just nods. "Dad, will we have enough—"

"That's not for you to worry about," he says quickly. "Your health comes first, end of story. Let's schedule the surgery."

"Okay," the doctor says. "We can get you in as early as next week."

Heath's eyes widen, and he looks to me. "But prom's next week."

"It's okay," I say, though it kills me to watch my dream of going to senior prom with Heath, the love of my life, just flutter away. "This is more important."

"It's not," he says. "Can we schedule it for Monday? Right after prom?"

The doctor smiles. "A week from Monday is fine. Until then, you'll be in a sling, and putting that tux on is going to be pretty painful, but the extra week won't matter much—you're already going to miss the rest of the season."

They go over the logistics for a while. The doctor leaves and says a pain management doctor would be in to talk about what the next few days will look like. Heath asks his dad to leave, and we're alone.

"I'm sorry," he says. "I heard you scream."

I come around and sit on the hospital bed with him, leaning my head on his good shoulder. "Don't be sorry. I'm just so glad you're okay."

"Wait, it's already seven? Don't you have that drag thing tonight?"

I shake my head. "There will be other things. This is more important."

"But this is your future," he says. "I don't want to get in the way of that."

Seconds of silence pass. There's a double meaning here, and it feels intentional. He doesn't want to get in the way of me and my exciting new life in New York, and he's not just talking about today's show.

"But you're my present. *And* my future," I say.

He smiles for a moment, before his expression falls.

And I think it's because we both know that's not exactly true.

CHAPTER SIXTY-TWO

SAL

I HONESTLY DIDN'T THINK Gabe and I would ever be in bed together again.

Of course, it's not like *that*, but still, I made such an effort to put up my own boundaries—and respect his own—but there's a familiar comfort in lying next to him like this. Shoulder to shoulder. Hip to hip. Just staring at my ceiling.

"Remember when we were ten, and you tried to climb that huge tree?" I ask. "That's the last time I think any of us got hurt. Like, call-the-ambulance hurt."

"I still blame you for that," he says.

I scoff. "For making you fall?"

"You kept daring me to go higher," he says. "I just wanted to impress you."

I roll over, leaning on my elbow as I look to him. He's never told me *that* before. Of course, I felt a little guilty after, but I thought I was pushing him higher because he wanted to get higher.

"You don't have to impress me," I say.

He laughs. "Well, I know that *now*. I was always trying to get your attention when we were younger, before we started...you know. It took me way too long to stop being dependent on your approval. Until this summer, really."

"What do you mean?"

He sighs, then runs a hand through his short hair. "My therapist...we've been talking about you lately. What you and I had wasn't toxic, exactly, but we were so codependent—like your approval was all that mattered. You were the one who could push me out of my shell; I was the only one who you came to with your problems."

"Oh wow." I gulp. "I'm sorry, I never meant—"

"I know, it's fine. It was all me."

"But I took advantage of it. Last summer, after I had that breakdown, I needed you, and I knew you'd drop everything to be with me."

"You did, but you were a mess, you apologized for it, and I can't pretend I didn't enjoy spending that time with you too. Sure, I should have kicked you out—and I eventually did—but at the end of the day Matt was understanding about it." He turns to me, so we're both on our sides staring at each other. "So, no harm."

"Are you okay?" I ask. "We haven't really gotten a chance to talk about you and him in a while."

This yearning hits my chest when I mention him. This irritating sort of jealousy that's followed me through their entire relationship. I'm protective of Gabe—he's my boy. But under it all, I'm fighting the truth that maybe it's not protection—maybe it's something real.

"I'm sad," he says plainly. "Of course, I'm sad. I spent an entire week holding that light-up plushie hoping it would just glow once—just show me that he's thinking of me. Of course, we've texted, but it's oddly formal. Like we're distant friends."

He puts an arm on my shoulder, and my whole body lights up at the sensation. This touch is like our old ones, but different at the same time.

To me, these feelings are real. *Crap.*

"We should ask Reese how Heath's doing," I say, quickly brushing his hand off me.

"Oh!" He sits up in bed quickly. "Right, definitely."

"I'll start a chat with just the three of us."

"Sal," Gabe says, then points to my shoulder. "With that, I wasn't—"

"—No, obviously, yeah, of course, right." I get out of bed. "I was just thinking of Heath."

He looks at me, and so many emotions fall across his face. Confusion, hesitation, and a hint of enjoyment. I'm never the flustered one, and here I am acting like I have this boyish crush?

Our eyes meet, and we break into awkward laughter. This friendship has never really worked. This friendship is too complicated. But god, I wouldn't trade it for the fucking world.

CHAPTER SIXTY-THREE

GABRIEL

THAT WAS FUCKING *WEIRD*. Not that anything about us has ever been truly normal.

Back at home, I sit on my bed and look around my bedroom. It's adorned with just about every item that the OSU online store has in stock: jerseys, flags, and even a stack of shot glasses from my sister. My desk, though, is covered with various social justice bumper stickers, pride flags, and a whole lot of stuff from my time at Boston Save the Trees.

My bedside table is a little harder to look at. It's got three things: a framed picture of me and Matt kissing at one of our outdoor movie-in-the-park nights, the light-up plushie that used to glow every night before bed—a sign that Matt was thinking of me, and the bracelet with the sapling charm that Reese made for me this summer.

I haven't worn it since Matt and I broke up. That bracelet was supposed to remind me of my best friends, but it reminds me of that summer: of Matt, of Sal, of the new experiences that changed my whole life.

I know I shouldn't call Matt, but I feel our friendship fading away. And maybe that's what's supposed to happen, but maybe I can stop it. I pick up the phone and scroll through my recent FaceTimes, my heart falling when I realize how low he is on the list.

He picks up almost immediately.

"Gabe! How's my favorite . . . Ohioan?" He laughs. "I started that sentence and had no idea where I was going with it. But I think it's true. I don't know many other Ohioans."

"Thanks, I think?"

"Well, at least this isn't awkward at all," he says in a sarcastic tone. "How are you doing, b—"

He shakes his head. Blushes.

"Did you almost call me babe?" I say, and my heart melts a bit.

In this bizarre relationship that we had, summer fling to falling in love to living off long-distance love, it was easy to convince myself that I meant less to him than he did to me.

"I'm trying to get over you," he says, "but it's not always easy."

"I know what you mean."

"Can I ask you something that's been bugging me? Like, full transparency, no judgment, just trying to tell you the thoughts in my brain?" I nod, so he continues. "Do you think we'll ever be just friends?"

"I do," I say. "I think a long-distance friendship is going to be even harder for us, but I think we can do it."

We talk more and fill each other in on our lives—and I take the time to talk about Heath's injury, Sal's mayoral run, and force Matt to follow Reese's drag account while we're talking.

As he fills me in on his life, his friends, his college prep, I realize that what I said earlier was true. What we had happened so quickly, from strangers to crushes to lovers all in one summer, but despite all that, I'm excited to get to know him as a friend. It's a new dynamic for us, and it's so much less complicated than what I had—have—with Sal.

"I'll be thinking of you," Matt says as we end the call.

Though we already broke up, this call feels like the real turning point in our new friendship. I think we can do this.

I charge my phone, turn off my lamp, and bury myself in my covers, and a feeling of peace comes over me for the first time in a while. It was a dramatic day, but Heath is going to be okay, Sal and I are okay, and I can honestly say I have a new friend.

The plushie on my bedside starts glowing, and the smile that hits my face is so sudden and intense it almost hurts. I reach over and give it a squeeze back, letting Matt know I'm thinking of him too.

CHAPTER SIXTY-FOUR

GABRIEL

WITH T-MINUS THREE HOURS to prom, all the boys and I are in the basement putting the finishing touches on our outfits. Mine's pretty simple—I'm wearing a maroon tuxedo over a black button-up shirt. Sal lent me one of his floral patterned neck ties (not of the bow tie variety), which brings the whole look together way better than the silk white one that came with the rental.

Sal and Reese are, of course, dressed impeccably. Sal's in an emerald tux with black lapels, a classic white tuxedo shirt under it with a simple black bow tie. Though all the tuxedo wearers I know rented tuxes and suits with varying levels of formality, Sal looks so adult. So grown-up, even though he's the only one of us who's still seventeen!

Reese is in this shimmering blue tuxedo with a paisley pattern. He found it at a thrift shop earlier this year, and after some alterations, it fits him perfectly. He put his own touch on it, hand stoning the paisley details to make them stand out. His undershirt is white, simple, and clean, and he buttons it to the top without wearing a tie.

Heath's in his dad's old tux. It's a simple tux, but it's in a metallic ochre color that makes it look far more vintage than it is. Everything about him is classic, from the black bow tie to the ribbed undershirt. Even the sling his arm is in matches, but that's because Reese found matching fabric and crafted it for him.

"Why didn't you two match, again?" I ask Heath as I brush a piece of fuzz from Heath's shoulder.

Heath shrugs. "I wanted to wear Dad's tux. Reese wanted to do his own thing. Everyone already knows we're together anyway."

"Exactly," Reese says as he comes in for a kiss. "And I do have something that matches, but you'll have to wait for the after-party at Cassie's to see that look."

Sal laughs. "Reese, you're the only human I know who would have two prom suits."

"You're just jealous you didn't think of it first," he says. "Plus, this suit is super tight—if we're going to dance all night, I want to be able to breathe a bit."

"Fair," I say with a laugh. "All right, if we don't go upstairs soon, our parents are going to kill us."

Above us, I hear the makings of a miniparty for the adults. Our parents are rarely in the same room together, but our final prom is a little special, I guess. When we're all ready, we go upstairs to the oohs and aahs of our parents—and the high-pitched catcall whistle from my sister.

I roll my eyes. "Why did you come back again?"

"Couldn't miss my baby bro's final prom!" she says cheerily, then leans in and drops her voice to a whisper. "Plus, *someone* has a trunk full of booze for a certain high school party."

"Shh," I say. "You're going to drop it off later, right?"

"Naturally." She pulls me into a hug. "You do look great, bro. I'm really proud of you, you know?"

"For wearing a suit? Anyone can do that."

She punches me in the arm. "You used to be so…dependent. On me, on your friends, especially on Sal, but I don't know, something changed. You're so confident. You've always wanted to fight for people, but you've been too scared to put yourself out there."

I want to respond, to tell her that I still don't know how to put in the work when it counts, that sure I'm not a kid, but I'm not exactly a grown-up either. But I can't respond, because suddenly the adults start clamoring for pictures of us all dressed up.

Reese follows me out front. "Mamma's going to take like fifty pictures, get ready."

"I think all our parents are."

Heath's dad and Reese's parents get dozens of pictures of them standing stiffly next to each other. Eventually, Heath wraps Reese in a hug with his good shoulder, and they get more comfortable with the photo session.

We all get solo pictures, and the whole time, I keep making eyes with Sal. He looks so hot in his tux, and it reminds me of the times he wore a suit on the Hill, sending these beautiful, sun-filled selfies with him wearing a suit jacket, bow tie, and sunglasses to the group chat.

"One with Sal and Gabriel!" my sister says, nearly shoving us together. "Or should I call you Gabe now? Seems like everyone calls you that now."

I look at her, surprised, then I realize that somewhere over the past few months, I *have* become Gabe. The bold, confident guy I wanted to become last summer.

"Yeah. Call me Gabe," I say, before putting my arm around Sal and pulling him in to me for the picture.

"You're going to wrinkle my suit!" he says, laughing, but I still hold him tightly.

After our photo shoot, we pile into Heath's truck, and Reese hops into the driver's seat. Heath's been driving his dad's car recently, but Reese learned how to drive a stick shift for this moment, and from how it's almost stalled eight times since we got on the road, maybe we made a mistake.

Reese's moms offered to splurge and rent a limo for us, like a few other students are doing, but we all felt like that was too much. If this is our last hurrah, we want it to feel like old times.

"I'm about to destroy some mozzarella sticks," Heath says. "Which is unfortunate, since I barely fit into Dad's old suit as it is."

"I'm so glad we're going to the diner for this," I say with a laugh.

"James and his girlfriend are at Olive Garden," Heath replies. "He says, like, everyone is dressed up for prom and the wait is over an hour."

"Oh god. Cassie said her crew were going there too."

"I'm not sure what the draw is," Sal says. "Olive Garden is great, but how many people are going to stain their rentals with pasta sauce?"

Everyone else laughs. "I don't know if I'd laugh—we're all about to be covered in grease."

CHAPTER SIXTY-FIVE

SAL

WE SHOW UP TO the art institute where prom is being hosted, and something just feels right about us arriving in an old truck with stomachs full of greasy diner food. Being an all-queer group of friends, we get to pick and choose what traditions mean the most to us.

Heath and Reese didn't want to match? Then who cares—they'll be making out the whole night, so there will be no confusion that they came together. We didn't want to take a limo? Again, who cares?

As we pull up to the venue, it's clear we've outdone ourselves this year. Ambient music hits our ears as we enter the museum, and after we turn our tickets in to Miss H, we walk slowly down the corridor and toward the ballroom, the bass thudding through our dress shoes as we walk.

Busts, paintings, and various art pieces line the halls, and the excitement builds as we cross toward the music. Gabe grabs my hand and squeezes as we get close.

We step into the art institute's event space, and I look to Reese, who mouths, "Oh my god!"

Earlier today, he and I started setting up the space with the rest of student council. While Mom and I took care of the operational logistics: meeting with the caterers, the DJ, and the venue's A/V and lighting teams, Reese managed the volunteer student decorators, who got to work hanging string lights, draping a Parisian cityscape over the back wall, and setting up the photo booth. With the lights on and everything half set up, I wasn't sure things would click, and I certainly wasn't feeling the Parisian magic. But with our vision fully executed, with the atrium lights off and the party lights on, it feels... perfect.

"Holy crap, this is nice," Heath says with a wink. "Just like Paris, I'm sure. Good work, guys."

Sure, it's kind of corny, and it doesn't feel like we're *actually* in Paris, but it sure as hell doesn't feel like Gracemont, Ohio. I look to Reese and smile. It's like our summer experiences combined: his design inspiration, my event-planning experience, all in one. Thankfully our class has been raising funds for it for years, because this was *not* cheap.

The four of us spend the first thirty minutes or so lingering awkwardly around the refreshments, waiting for more people to come in. Eventually, Principal Gallagher gets on the microphone and welcomes us all, goes through a list of rules and guidelines, and lets us know when the prom court needs to report to the stage.

Heath's the only one of us who has to worry about that, but it'll still be a while.

They turn the lights down, and we dance. Though it starts off a little cliquey—people dancing only in the groups they came with—eventually people start to loosen up and we're all talking and vibing with one another like we've all been best friends.

"There's something weird happening," Gabe says. "Have you noticed that everyone's been so nice lately? To us, to everyone else. Lyla just came up to me and told me she's going to miss me so much, and I can only remember talking to her once...ever. And it was about math homework."

"Must've been a pretty impactful conversation," I say with a laugh.

"Hardly. Everyone's getting really sappy and nostalgic, though. Did you see that slideshow they played when we walked in? I swear I saw a few football guys crying while watching it."

"Yeah, did you also notice none of us are in that slideshow? I should have known putting our star quarterback in charge of the slideshow was a mistake." I chuckle. "Maybe once I'm mayor I'll be smarter about who I delegate things to."

Gabe shrugs. "Whatever. Let them have their fun; we can make our own slideshows."

"But you're right—it really is the end of an era," I say. We're still dancing to the upbeat song that's playing, but my heart's not fully in it. I'm feeling nostalgic, and it feels like our time is running out. I've been so focused on this pending mayoral campaign and what happens next that I don't know if I took enough time to cherish what I had here.

"It is," Gabriel says. The music changes to a slow song, the first of the night, and people start coupling, holding each other on the dance floor. "It's also the start of something new."

He puts his arm around my waist and looks at me with an expression I haven't seen from him in so long. Tears prick at my eyes, and I look down at his hand on my hip.

"Can we dance?" he asks, and I nod.

He takes the lead, for once, and I get wrapped up in his embrace. I drape my hands around his neck and look up into those eyes. We sway back and forth, barely enough to count as a dance, and I gently rest my head on his neck.

His hands slide up my back as he pulls me closer to him. I look up to him, and as he licks his lips, I see the question in his eyes. I nod, and smile, and he brings his lips to mine. We kiss, and we kiss, and we kiss, like there's no time left.

But really, we have all the time in the world.

CHAPTER SIXTY-SIX

REESE

"I CAN'T BELIEVE THEY'RE doing it again," I say, nodding over toward Sal and Gabe, who are in a full-on make out. "Think it's real this time?"

Heath laughs. "Who knows with them."

We dance, as well as two people can when one of them is in a sling. He's got his arm around me, and I reach my arm around his waist. It probably looks awkward, but it feels somehow natural for us. We rock back and forth slowly, but we really just use this as a time to hold each other, feeling both like it's just the two of us and like we're putting our love on show.

"True," I say.

"So tell me about this second suit," Heath says, and from how he narrows his eyes, I sense he might suspect what the surprise really is.

"You'll see it tonight." I laugh. "It matches your suit, though. Vanderbilt yellow."

As soon as the words leave my mouth, I flinch. We've been so good at not bringing it up, but the closer we get to graduation, the harder it becomes. All Heath is thinking about is his uncertain future at Vanderbilt. All I'm thinking about is my future in New York.

We're not thinking about our future together, but that's because it can't exist. When I look up to try to change the topic, the reflection in Heath's glossy eyes stops me.

"Heath, are you—"

"Yeah," he says between gasps. "Maybe it's just the pain pills. They make me feel a little loopy sometimes."

"You're not 'loopy,' Heath." I sigh.

Tears start streaming down his face, and I bury my face into his chest as the tears come to my eyes as well. He grips me tightly with his good hand, bunching the fabric so hard he might pop one of the stones off. But I don't care.

"We're running out of time, aren't we?" I say.

"No," he says quickly. "We can't be."

"But we are!" I pull his chin up so he makes eye contact with me. "This is it. At some point, we can't keep ignoring it, we have to make a plan, we have to—"

"Can I ask you something?" he asks, and I nod. "In your journal, do you have a pros and cons list for . . . for us? It's all right if you do. I just want to know."

"You know me well," I say. "But I have lists for everything."

"For us staying together after graduation, were there more pros or cons?"

I press my face into his chest again, but he pulls away.

"Please?" he says. "Can we just be open about this?"

"Fine. There were a lot of cons." Our eyes meet. "But the pros matter more, because I can still be with you. I've wanted this for so long, we're so good together, I love you so much."

He smiles, but it's such a sad smile I drop eye contact.

"I love you too," he says.

"I mean, I flew to *Florida* to confess my love for you—you're so special, and perfect, and I know everyone says that your first love is never the real one, but what if it *is* for us?"

We resume dancing, and despite the conversation, I find myself smiling. Until Heath starts talking again.

"I think it's real," Heath says. "But I mean, look at Gabe and Matt—maybe it was real for them too! That doesn't mean it'll work out."

"Well, then, let's make it work out," I plead.

He holds me tightly. "I love you. But—"

"Don't say but."

"*However*—" he starts.

"Heath!"

"Reese! I can't hold you back. You're going to be a fucking star, and I want you to live your life without me attached to it. We could try everything: long distance, an open relationship, a total breakup, we could even plot out our entire lives together if we wanted to, but all the options suck."

"I just want to be with you," I say.

"Enough to give up your dreams?"

The answer is, of course, no. If I gave up these dreams just to be with him, I'd hate myself for it, and I might even resent him for it, which would just lead to a breakup anyway. I rest my forehead into him instead of a response.

"I feel the same way," he says. "I hate that I do, but I do! I don't want to be in New York—not now, at least. If I can somehow make it onto the Vanderbilt team after I recover from all this, I want to see where baseball takes me. I'm even thinking of studying biology so I can maybe even go to med school. I've done so much research on injury recovery that I think I might actually want to go into sports medicine or become an orthopedist or something."

"You're declaring a major?" I say. "That's huge, Heath."

"It might change, but that's where I'm leaning. And I'm excited about the future—I hate that I'm excited about a future without you there by my side, though."

The music shifts to a recent pop anthem, and groups of friends start forming dance circles, scream-singing the music. But Heath and I just sway back and forth. Back and forth.

"I don't want this to be it for us, though," I finally say. "Maybe we don't have to have all the answers right now?"

"I think we have all the answers," Heath says. "But maybe we can ignore them for a few more weeks."

We sway to the music, in our forced blissful ignorance, holding tighter and tighter to each other, terrified about who is going to let go of the other first.

CHAPTER SIXTY-SEVEN

HEATH

ALTHOUGH THE FIRST HALF of prom was pretty dramatic, things started to pick up once the other boys convinced us to put a pause on slow dancing to rap and pop songs and, instead, dance like normal people.

Reese dropped me and Gabe off at Cassie's, then went back to get into his second outfit of the evening. He also went back to switch out cars, since I'm the designated driver of the evening and driving a stick shift with only one usable hand is . . . well, frowned upon, to say the least. And so is taking pain pills while driving, so I take a couple of Tylenol to help get me through the night. I'll be a little uncomfortable, but it'll be worth it.

Cassie welcomes us into her house. After short introductions with her parents, she ushers us through to her huge backyard. Stacks and stacks of long branches, two-by-fours, and random scraps of wood lie in a big pile in the middle of the yard.

"Gabe tells me you're good at starting bonfires," Cassie says.

"He's the best," Gabe chimes in.

"Could you two get this started? I've got to set out the coolers—including the, um, special one Gabe's sister got ready for us—and people will start getting here any minute."

"Sure," I say. "Who else is coming?"

"Everyone who's ever attended a GSA meeting," Gabe replies. "Plus a few other people. Nary a homophobe in sight for this occasion."

"The homophobes can all go to the official afterprom," Cassie says with a laugh. "I'd prefer this anyway."

She leaves to go set up the refreshments, while Gabe hands me the lighter fluid. I get started building the fire, though it's a bit slower than expected due to my use of only one arm, so Gabe becomes my second arm.

"So you and Sal, huh?" I say. I feel like I need to say something, to at least get enough details to gossip about it with Reese later, but I'm not sure how to ask if this is just them being ... them, again.

"I'm not sure what happened, exactly, but it really feels right this time."

"And you'll both be in Ohio after graduation," I say. "Not that I mean that resentfully or anything. I just mean that you have some time to figure it out. Unlike ... well, yeah, okay, maybe there's some resentment there."

"You two really are made for each other," Gabe says. "The timing's just off, I guess."

"That's one way to put it. But seriously, if what you two have is real, don't take this for granted, okay?" I wipe a tear from my eyes. "You have a real shot at this, and I just…"

Gabe wraps me in a hug.

"I just wish we did too," I say, burying my face into his shoulder. "I'm sorry."

He lets me cry it out for a bit. The good thing about being out here, it's quiet and remote, the only one who could find us is Cassie, and no one else has really shown up yet.

"Thanks for that," I say. "I hope you know I'm not mad at you or anything. Just… a little jealous, maybe."

"You two are going to figure it out, I know it." He sighs, then hands me a pack of industrial matches. "In the meantime, let's burn this shit to the ground."

• • •

Within the next thirty minutes, the party really gets going. Gabe puts on one of Reese's party mixes, even though he and Sal still haven't made it back to the party. Other people have come, though. Like James, who's kept me up to speed on all the baseball drama that I've missed this week and has a hundred questions about my surgery on Monday.

"I have no idea how you dealt with the pressure," James says. "I know you didn't pitch every game, but still. Coming in as a relief pitcher, I had a very clear job—close out the game. But now, I have to control the entire pace of the game, and each time someone hits off my pitches I get more frazzled."

I laugh, and I gesture to my sling. "I didn't deal with the

pressure well, obviously. But you can't take the guilt on yourself. We're a team, and you're doing the best you can—Coach Lee keeps saying you're doing well."

We keep talking baseball as a few others join us. I look around, and Cassie and another junior girl are sitting on a bench by the fire, a little too close for them to be just friends. I marvel at how everyone here is so comfortable being themselves.

Is this what life will be like after high school? Will we all find these big groups of people who don't care who you are, instead of us having to thrive in these little pockets of rural acceptance?

The music gets quiet, and across the fire I see Sal at the Bluetooth speaker. My chest flutters, because if Sal's here, Reese must be too.

"All right, everyone, it's time for a show!"

And though it's supposed to be a surprise, I have a pretty strong suspicion I know what's about to happen. Gabe and Cassie start hooting, and everyone else slowly joins in, though no one else seems to know exactly why.

And then I see him. *Her.*

"We have a *very* special guest tonight," Sal announces. "Gracemont's own Reesey Piecey!"

"Oh my god, Sal, that's not my drag name!" Reese shouts from the darkness. "That's so cringey. Just call me Reese."

Sal's voice is mocking. "Your fans are waiting, Miss Piecey!"

I hear Reese groan before taking a big breath in. I walk toward him just as he starts walking down the strip of dirt that leads to the firepit from the house. The first thing I notice is the flash of white heels with each step. *Since when can Reese walk in heels?!*

The dress he's wearing is made out of the same fabric as my sling, I can tell immediately. Somewhere between a golden yellow and a burnt orange, the below-knee-length dress flows behind him as he walks, no, *struts* the runway.

The shape of his body is completely different—he seems to have padded his hips, but the dress still flows swiftly from the bottom. It's a V-neck dress, with ruching at the top and pleats down the front. His caramel-colored shoulder-length hair bounces along with him.

He stops in front of the fire, and everyone erupts in applause. He's captivating, showcasing how drag really is an art—but there's so much artistry in that dress as well, since I know he made that from scratch.

Sal clears his throat. "And now, with a sickening lip-sync performance to Dua Lipa's latest, here is R—"

"*—don't say that name!*"

"Fine," he says with a sigh. "Here's Reese. Just, Reese."

He's kept so much of his work private from us—the only previews we get are in the posts he makes on his drag Instagram account.

But this is different. As he performs, Reese is alive with the kind of fire that we all knew was inside him all along. The kind of fire that will take him far in New York City, or Paris, or wherever he ends up.

James comes up to me and puts a palm on my good shoulder. "One of these days, he's going to be a famous drag queen and you're going to be a famous pitcher—wouldn't that be so cool? Like, talk about power couples."

I laugh. "Yeah, maybe."

I can't take my eyes off Reese as he twirls, only losing his balance in those heels once or twice through the entire performance. The whole crowd's into it—even Gabe found a few dollar bills in his wallet and throws the money at Reese, who rolls his eyes... before picking it up and stuffing it down his dress.

After the performance, Reese takes a seat next to me and warms himself by the fire. He curls up with me.

"Unless this is too weird?" he asks, and I laugh.

"Oh, it's weird. Weird that you sprang an *entire drag performance on us!*"

He laughs. "Sal and I have been working on that for a while."

"You look great," I say, and give him a peck on the lips.

"And now, we match."

• iMessage •

HEATH + REESE

Hey, love. I'm not sure when you'll get this, hopefully before the procedure, but I don't know, maybe they already took your phone away. I just wanted you to know I'll be by your side as soon as I can. This surgery is going to go great, and you're going to be back to pitching in no time. Wow, this might be the longest text I've ever sent. Maybe I should stop. Anyway. I love you!

R

going back soon

H love you too, Reesey

CHAPTER SIXTY-EIGHT

HEATH

WHEN I WAKE UP, everything feels . . . fuzzy. Weird. Wrong.

Why can't I open my eyes? What's that beeping? I try to say the words out loud, but my lips won't move right. Am I drunk? I can't be—I couldn't partake at the party because of the pain meds I was on anyway.

That's right, I haven't drunk since way before the injury.

My shoulder! I had surgery today!

I force my eyes open, but everything's a little blurry. The heart rate monitor near me starts beeping faster, which gets the attention of a nurse nearby.

"Heath, you with me, dear?" she asks, and I nod as much as I can, which is . . . not much at all. "Let me go get the doctor."

She leaves, and I drift back off to sleep two or three more times in the time it takes the doctor to come back along with Dad.

"Dad!" I say, but it comes out as a whisper since my throat is raw.

"Your throat's going to be sore for a little while from the breathing tube," the doctor says. "But don't worry, the surgery went perfectly. You're going to need a couple days of bed rest, and then you can start to go about your life."

He rattles off a list of things I can't do (shower, move my arm, lift anything) and the things I can ("live your life as normal"... just smellier, I guess?). He keeps talking, but I drift off to sleep. I feel the slight pressure of my dad holding my hand as I rest, and even though the pain is starting to radiate from my shoulder, there's this brief moment when I feel like everything's going to be all right.

• • •

Once I'm back home from the hospital, Dad helps me from the car and into the apartment. When we enter, Diana and Reese jump up from the couch and start coming over to me, asking me a zillion questions.

"I said you two could come over under one condition," Dad says. "And what was that?"

"That we don't overwhelm Heath," Reese says.

He and Diana back off, but I give them a smile. "Babe! Have you ever been under anesthesia? It's...really weird."

"You're not even going to say hi to me?" Diana huffs.

"Hey, cuz," I say, then hobble into my bedroom. "Wait, you don't live here?"

"He's still a little loopy from the meds," Dad says, and I sneer at him in protest.

Once I'm in bed, Diana and Reese come into my room to hang

out. I said I was *not* going to sleep because I just had the deepest, most medically induced sleep of my life and I didn't need it.

"Sorry, I think I'm starting to get more…what's the word… lucid?" I say.

"It's fine, it's fine." Diana says. "How did everything go?"

I feel the pressure of Reese's grip on my foot, and it makes me smile. Even when he's trying to give me space, he's reminding me that he's here. He's nice like that.

"Well, obviously, I'm all healed." I laugh, but they don't. "Oh come on, that was funny. Anyway, they reattached my shoulder to my, um, shoulder. And now I just have to not bathe for three weeks."

"Maybe we should have asked his dad for details," Reese says, and we all laugh.

"It's all good news, right?"

Heath nods. "I'm gonna be okay. They set me up with an athletic rehab place, so I'll be good as new. Someday. Once this stops hurting. Diana, did you see Reese in that dress? He looked so cute."

Reese squeezes my foot harder, and my eyes snap to him.

"What? You did!"

"He posted it to his Instagram, so you know I saw it. I was the first comment!"

"You're always the first comment," Reese says.

Diana shrugs. "Well, one of these days you'll have fans that I'm going to have to compete with, so I'd like to say I supported you first."

"I'm glad you're here," I say, interrupting them both. "I'm… I'm glad you're both here."

As I start to sober up a little more, and Diana tells me about her flight in, and how she got the whole week off school for this trip because she convinced her teachers a close family member had surgery and she needed to take care of them. It's not exactly a lie, but not exactly the truth either.

Our doorbell rings, and I can't hide the confused expression on my face. The other boys are busy today, though they checked in via text about a billion times. My mom called me while I was in the car, and she was very much still in New Mexico, though she said she'll see me soon, when she comes up for graduation. Aunt Jeanie didn't come with Diana on this trip, and Dad and Reese are in the house with me.

I see Dad cross past the door in my room, toward the front door. I hear a short conversation, though I don't hear the voice.

"Heath, are you up for seeing another visitor?" Dad asks. "Coach Lee just stopped by."

"Coach? Uh . . . sure."

Diana and Reese leave the room just before Coach enters. He sits on the edge of my bed and stares at me for a second, and I know I must look like a wreck, because his face is white.

"Heath, I'm so sorry about all of this. If I hadn't pushed you so much, or maybe if we'd have done more stretches or—"

"It's fine, Coach. It's not your fault. I pushed it. I was in pain, but I just kept pushing it." I sigh. "I can't believe I ruined everything."

He looks at me. "You didn't ruin everything. It sounds like you're going to be fine to play in a few months—after the season, of course, but it won't get in the way of college."

"If I can make it on the team," I say. "Or if I can even find the funds to replace the athletic scholarship."

"That's just it," Coach says. "You didn't lose the scholarship. I've been talking with the coaching staff there, and they'd like to extend a formal offer. The full amount we discussed earlier. They have a really good sports medicine practice at Vanderbilt, and as soon as you move in you'll start a really thorough rehab program there. They saw your talent last year, they were impressed with your stats so far this year, and they wanted to make sure you knew they offered the scholarship based on that. They know how committed you are; they just need you to take your time. Get back slowly. And you'll be more than ready by next spring."

Tears flood my eyes. "Really?"

"Really."

Just beyond Coach, I see Reese peek his head into the room. He must have heard everything, and I search for any hint of sadness in his eyes, knowing that now, beyond a doubt, I'm going to Vanderbilt.

But there's none. Just pure joy.

He mouths the words, but I still know what he's saying: *You did it!*

CHAPTER SIXTY-NINE

GABRIEL

"I WISH WE COULD be with Heath right now," I say as we pull into the parking lot of the town hall building. "But at least I know Reese and Diana are taking care of him."

"I do too," Sal says, "but he was very clear about wanting us to see this town hall issue through to the very end."

We walk side by side into the hall. I've been here before a few times—most recently, I came to lobby for Mayor Green to start an initiative to clean up the parks, which was promised to me by the mayor but never actually scheduled.

Sal's been here a few times, and based on his recent research on how the meetings go, I know he understands the process way more than I do.

Once we enter the hall, I'm surprised by how many people are in attendance. Way more than when I came last time.

"Let's grab a seat over here," Sal says, gesturing to a line of seats in the back row.

"The back row?" I say in a harsh whisper. "What if we need to go up there?"

"We're not going up there," Sal says.

We take our seats, but I eye him suspiciously. "What do you mean, exactly?"

He sighs. "I . . . trust my mom. She said she would take care of this, and if we interject or make her seem not supportive enough, it could hurt our chances even more. The school board is in attendance, and they're going to want to end the conflict as smoothly as possible. Mom thinks that as long she presents a united front with the many parents who came today, then things will be okay."

"And you believe her?" I say, in the gentlest tone I can muster. "She's basically saying not to worry, and to let the adults handle it. Honestly, the adults haven't been handling it correctly."

Sal grabs my hand, squeezes it, and pulls it onto his lap.

"I have to trust her," he says. "This is her last chance, as far as I'm concerned."

"So we stay quiet?"

"I'm not going to stop you from speaking if you feel like you must, but give my mom a chance first, okay?"

I nod. I can at least promise that. As much as I hate the idea of letting the adults in the room handle a situation, I know this is a big moment for Sal as well. If someone like him can take the back seat on this, maybe I can too.

More people pile in. Mom and Dad take seats near the front; Reese's moms slide into the seats next to them. Heath's dad even offered to come, but we all assured him that tending to Heath was more important. Cassie's parents make their way in, along with a few other familiar faces that I've seen over the years.

One face I'm not exactly *thrilled* to see.

"That's the reporter who posted that shitty story about your mom," I say. "If you're not going to let me speak up here, can I at least go give that guy a piece of my mind?"

Sal laughs and gives me the go-ahead, and I step down the stairs to meet him. Just as I'm about to tap on his shoulder and give him a talking-to, Sal's mom steps in front of him.

"Brandon Davis," she says in a polite but firm voice. "Always a pleasure."

"Rachel Camilleri," he says, a little uneasily.

"I'm so glad you accepted my offer to come hear me speak at this meeting. I understand all the pressures you're under to get the full story, but I do think this will be helpful for your readers."

"You invited him?" I ask, and they both turn to see me.

"Oh, have you met? Gabriel, this is Mr. Davis. Brandon, Gabriel is the leader of our new LGBTQ+ Advocacy Group at Gracemont High."

"Nice to meet you," he says, still a little flustered. "It looks like we're about to get started, but would you mind if I interviewed you after the meeting? I'd love to get your perspective on everything."

"Gladly," I say. "I'll get my classmate Cassie to join us as well."

We say our goodbyes, and he takes a seat. Mrs. Camilleri looks at me and shrugs. "You can't always trust the media, Gabriel. I learned that during my public relations days. Be honest with him, but keep your wits about you. You're a smart kid, and I think he's on our side, just be careful. You've seen what he can do."

"I will," I say. "Thank you."

"Thank you, Gabriel. I know this hasn't been easy for any of us, but it'll all be out in the open today. I don't know how this will go, but either way, I think we'll get some closure."

"Okay," I say with a light smile. "Good luck."

I return to my seat just as the mayor walks into the room. The vibes are *tense*, and even Mayor Green looks a little disoriented—I've never seen so many people turn out for a meeting like this. Based on the comments on Sal's post, there's a lot of support in this town, and a lot of the parents stepped in, but there's a lot of pushback too.

And we're all in one room together.

"Thank you all for coming. We've cleared the agenda today, so if you're here waiting on permit requests, you'll need to wait a little bit longer."

Sal scoffs, and whispers to me, "This man will do anything to avoid doing work."

"If you want to file a complaint, I would be glad to send it to my political adversary," he says with a smirk. "I'm sure he'll get you a response soon, if his mom can get him some crayons."

I squirm in my seat, but Sal just puts his hand on my knee.

"Mayor Green," Sal's mom says firmly as she stands from her front-row seat, "as you've been in this position for decades, you should know it's against our village bylaws to discuss an upcoming election or its candidates."

"Just a joke," he says smugly. "Besides, who here would be the one to enforce such a law?"

Sal's mom nods slowly and takes a seat.

"Why did your mom back off?" I ask, still fuming, until Sal points to Brandon Davis, who's furiously typing on his iPad.

"The mayor just said he was above the law." He smiles.

Shortly after, the mayor starts the discussion about the books being removed from the library. He lets the superintendent speak first, and he goes on a ten-minute rant about *protecting our kids*. None of it really makes sense, but it's met with some very clear applause from half of the audience.

Anxiety claws at my chest again, and I feel like the outcast here, again. I felt so safe in this town, dancing with Sal at prom, but here it's a completely different story. These sharks sense blood in the water, and they're attacking. I turn to Sal, who looks a little concerned, but he just grabs my hand and squeezes it tightly.

Mayor Green opens the floor for public comment, and Reese's Mamma jumps up immediately to take the mic. She explains, in detail, how she never had these kinds of books growing up, and how fears about protecting children are nothing but homophobia. She passes the mic to her wife, who reinforces everything she says.

The mic gets passed back and forth, and it seems like there's an even split of opinions. Eventually, Miss Orly takes the floor.

"I've reviewed every single one of the books that Superintendent Charles has brought to my attention. Each one, he and the mayor claimed, should be investigated and removed from shelves. I have a list of every report I've ever sent him, and there was not one book that was 'pornographic' or 'lewd'—to quote Mr. Charles's concerns." She clears her throat. "I know speaking here puts my job at risk, but I can only tell you the facts: none of these books have anything objectionable in them, unless you object to the fact that LGBTQ+ people exist, that is."

With that, she leaves the stage. We sit through a few more speeches that take us well into the evening—this has got to be the longest meeting of our town's history. Sal's mom speaks last.

"It's almost time for the town council to vote on whether these books should be removed from our shelves, but I speak to you now as an administrator for this school. If you want to protect our kids, keep these books on shelves."

With that, Mayor Green opens the floor to voting. He casts his vote first, choosing to—of course—permanently remove the books from the library. One by one, the town council starts to vote.

"We only need four votes," Sal says.

The first two votes, though, only reinforce the mayor's agenda. But even though the council members are all close to the mayor, a shift happens. The remaining four people on the council vote for the books to remain. It's swift, it's quick, and it's clear they are avoiding eye contact with the mayor the entire time.

"Well, that settles it. Four to three, these books will remain on shelves, for now." He looks to the rest of the room. "But trust me, I will keep a close eye on this. Per county bylaws, we will revisit this issue at the earliest date possible, in six months."

"Right after election day," Sal says with a grin.

CHAPTER SEVENTY

SAL

FOR A MOMENT, I feel like I'm in DC again. Hours of meetings
and debates followed by a fundraising event. Only this time, it's
my fundraising event. Gabe and I pull up to my aunt's house and
see a dozen or so cars in her long driveway. This won't be like the
galas I went to as a senator's intern, that's for sure, but I just hope
Aunt Lily's finally got her Christmas tree down.

"A good turnout," I say. "Right?"

"Absolutely," Gabe says. "The party just started. More will
come, especially after that spectacle."

My chest is tight. "Can I be honest with you for a second?" He
nods, so I continue, "I didn't think it would go our way."

"It's all because of your mom," Gabe says, and I scoff.

"Please, if you and Cassie hadn't put the pressure on her like
you did. Hell, if you two didn't steal that list from Miss Orly,
there's no way it would have even come to a vote."

He blushes. "Yeah, I guess you're right. It was a group effort."

"And not just us, it was the whole town," I say as we slowly walk up the gravel driveway.

We hold hands, and I feel comfort in having him by my side. He's got to play many roles tonight—the politician's boyfriend who schmoozes with everyone, the fundraiser who asks for campaign donations, the event planner, the person I rehearse my speeches with.

I realize, then, how he really is my everything.

"Thank you," I say. "Thank you so much."

He blushes again, and lightly pushes me away. "Please don't be sappy right now."

We walk into my aunt's house, and for a moment, I don't recognize the place. The furniture's been rearranged, so there's a makeshift podium where the Christmas tree once was. The entire place is spotless, and as I cross out to the patio, I see the pool—completely fixed. Patched up, cleaned, and filled with crystal blue water.

"Gabriel promised me you boys would use it this summer," Aunt Lily says from behind me.

"Aunt Lily!" I say, giving her a hug. "You've really outdone yourself here."

"Your mom and I worked for days to get this ready." She smirks. "Seems like she finally came around to your plan."

"And I came around to hers, though I haven't told her yet." I laugh. "I applied to the community college in Mansfield. I figure that, while I'm campaigning here and living with Mom, I have time to take a few classes."

"That seems like a smart use of your time. But enough about that—we're thinking about thirty minutes of you working the crowd, then you'll come onstage for your speech, then we'll have an hour or so for people to get their donations in before we start kicking them out."

I smile. "Sounds good. I'm ready."

Alone, I work the crowd. I speak to Reese's parents briefly, and they let me know they were so inspired by the town hall meeting that they're considering running for a council position themselves.

"This is going to be a long battle," I say. "But it's like Gabriel always says: we can't be complacent, we have to keep fighting."

"We will, and we know you will too."

I have a longer conversation with Mr. Davis, the reporter who dropped that awful article about my mom, but he seems to support me more as a candidate. We talk off the record for a while, and he says that even though he's still very skeptical an eighteen-year-old can be an effective mayor, I'm starting to change his mind.

Before my big speech, I meet Gabriel just off the podium.

"Are you ready for this?" he asks.

I give him a quick kiss. "As ready as I'll ever be."

My mom takes the podium and introduces me, and just from the way she talks, I get this true feeling of pride from her that I've never felt before. I think it's because she's not just proud of a version of me she's made up in her head—she finally sees the real me, and better yet, she fully supports the real me.

I take my speech out of my breast pocket, adjust my bow tie, and take the stage to raucous applause.

• Golden Boys •

GABRIEL + HEATH + REESE + SAL

GRADUATION DAYYYYYY **H**

S Finally!

I can't believe it's finally here!!!

G I can't stop crying you guys we did it!!!

R Sal, Heath, you two ready for your speeches?

more or less. if my valedictorian speech flops at least I can play the surgery card if Sal's intro speech flops he has no excuse! he's known the student council pres speaks at graduation ever since he got elected H

Thanks for the vote of confidence . . .
S

G You'll both be great!

CHAPTER SEVENTY-ONE

REESE

"I CAN'T BELIEVE THIS is it," Heath says as he delicately leans into my car.

A sweet scent hits my nose, and I turn to him in surprise. "Ooh, you smell nice considering you haven't showered since prom night."

"I took the most detailed sponge bath you could imagine." He shakes his head. "God, please don't imagine that, it was *very* unsexy."

"Too late! And I agree. Very unsexy."

He scoffs, and we wave to Heath's dad as I pull out of their apartment building's parking lot. All the parents plan to meet us at the ceremony, but since the students have to get there hours early for a run-through, we're all riding to the venue together on school buses. At first, I thought it'd be super cheesy, but riding a school bus for the last time actually seems fun.

We make it to the high school and pick one of the buses. Sal and Gabe got there early to stake out the back few rows for ourselves. We each take a big green seat and face into each other.

You can feel the heaviness of this moment. In a few weeks, I'll be moving up to New York City, into a tiny Hell's Kitchen apartment I'll be sharing with three other freshman designers. We all found one another through Instagram, so who knows if we'll even get along, but it'll be fun to have people to share this whole new experience with.

Then, Heath will leave for Vanderbilt. They want him on campus early to do some athletic training so they make sure he'll be at his best once baseball season starts in the spring. He's not so sad about it, since he'd rather be gone experiencing new things rather than waiting around Gracemont missing me—his words, not mine.

Then, Gabe will move into his dorm at Ohio State at the end of summer. It still feels weird to call him Gabe, but that's who he's become, who he's happy with. He and Sal are inseparable again. Even though that was something that drove me nuts back when I was pining for Heath, I can't deny that they fit together better now. Whatever they have, it's real, and it's special, and . . . okay, fine, I'm a little envious of it.

Sal will be the last to go, but that's because he's not going anywhere right now. He's been working on his campaign lately, spending every week in town hall pushing for more changes while gaining new supporters. The papers still don't seem convinced that he'll have a chance, and maybe Sal doesn't believe so either, but according to Brandon Davis's latest report, "sources say" Sal's campaign has scared Mayor Green into approving permits at a rapid pace. So, in a way, Sal's already changed Gracemont for the better.

Heath scoots next to me on our seat and puts his arm around my shoulders.

"It's finally time," he says.

"You never really answered my text. Are you ready for your speech?"

He laughs. "I guess so. It was unfortunately written under the influence of painkillers, so whatever I say can't be held against me, right?"

"Right," I say. "No matter what you say, I'm still going to be so proud to say that my boyfriend is the valedictorian."

He holds me tighter. "We're all about to do it, huh? We're going to take over the fucking world, Reese, I know it."

I kiss him, softly at first, but growing in intensity. That is, until I open my eyes and see Sal and Gabe hanging over the backs of their bus seats.

"Kissing on the school bus?" Sal says. "What is this—seventh grade?"

"That's what *you two* did in seventh grade." Heath laughs. "We're still catching up."

"Oh! Did everyone bring their bracelets?" Gabe asks.

Heath, Sal, and I all show ours off. They're the copper bracelets from last year, the ones I gave to them just before the summer when everything changed. The charms dangle off their bracelets, and I'm stunned by how little our charms fit us anymore.

Sal's bow tie showed how he wanted to present himself as this perfect, polished person to the world, but this year's been nothing like that. His grades have slipped, he's found a new passion, and he's getting mayoral votes based on that passion—not based on his bow ties.

Heath's bonfire still makes sense, but he's so much more than that now. He's going off on his own—he's no longer a contained fire, he's a raging wildfire, about to take over the world. Mine were the four dots from my planner—though I still journal and sketch, I don't live my life by my schedule anymore. And Gabe? He's no longer a sapling. He's a full-grown tree.

But it's good to remember where we started.

Our hands reach out to one another, and it kind of looks like we're going to do one of those chants athletes do at sports games. But we just hold them there, together, for one of the final times.

The bus pulls up to the ceremony space, and people start gathering their gowns and heading out the door. We finally break apart.

"Time to graduate, I guess," Sal says.

"Let's do this thing!" Gabe shouts.

Heath clears his throat. "Make way for the valedictorian!"

I laugh. "Here goes nothing."

CHAPTER SEVENTY-TWO

SAL

WE ARRIVE TO THE venue, and though there's a lot of excitement in the air, the morning is filled with a lot of boring things. We do a full dress rehearsal of the graduation, which honestly doesn't take very long since there are only eighty of us in the graduating class, and once we've all got the run-through down, we are ushered back into an empty ballroom to put our gowns on and chat nervously until it's time.

I hear the clacking of shoes behind me, and I turn to find my mom alongside Congresswoman Caudill, the guest speaker for today's ceremonies. I give the congresswoman—Betty, I mean—a quick hug and look to Mom. I gesture to my gown and give her a big smile.

"You ready for your speech?" Mom asks, wiping a tear from her eyes. "I think you're going to do great. Just remember—you can't mention the election at all. I know you'll want to, but I would get in so much trouble since it's against the—"

"Mom," I say. "Don't worry. I'll inspire the audience with my speech so they won't have any choice but to vote for me, but I won't make it about me. I only have five minutes, remember? Hardly enough to welcome everyone. Heath's got the big speech."

"Yes, he does."

I pause. "Are...you okay with that?"

She shrugs. "I think I've been a little too hands-on with your high school career. I know this is the worst time to come to that realization, but you have a lot of exciting things in your future, and just know I support you one hundred percent. Okay?"

"Thanks, Mom." I give her a hug.

"I'm looking forward to your speech too," Mom says to Betty. "Nothing political from you either?"

She laughs and gives me a wink. "You don't seem to trust us politicians very much."

"Oh fine, you all do whatever you want. I need to go talk to Principal Gallagher about us starting soon."

Mom leaves, and Betty puts a hand on my shoulder. "I'm really proud of you, Sal. I know your mom is too, even if she doesn't say it much." She sighs. "And I want you to know, I've been watching your campaign very closely. I think you're going to do great. And, just so you know, if you want some part-time work while you sort out the city, Senator Wright is about to announce his campaign for president, and I know they'll need some help in the local office. It won't be the nightmare that last summer was, but it might help you figure out more about your career aspirations."

I smile. "I'd love that. Thanks so much."

A teacher comes into the room and claps to get our attention. We start filing up by last name, and as Gabe passes me, I pull him in for a kiss.

"Love you," I say.

He smiles. "Love you."

CHAPTER SEVENTY-THREE

HEATH

"THANK YOU TO PRINCIPAL Gallagher, Vice Principal Camilleri, and to all the Gracemont High teachers and faculty for giving me the opportunity to give this speech today. I pitch a ninety-mile-per-hour fastball. I'm a good batter too. With baseball, it's always been easy to know what to do, how to improve, what choices to make. But I made so many mistakes over the past year, it was like I didn't even know the basics of the sport. You might have noticed that I'm sporting this very fashionable sling—this isn't just to get some sympathy laughs from the crowd either. I overtrained myself, repeatedly injured myself, and ended up tearing my rotator cuff in the very first scrimmage in the year . . . and if you look closely at my cheek, I even got scuffed up when I fell directly into the ground after the pitch that could have ended my career.

"That pitch was a strike, by the way.

"But I think that's what we all end up doing a lot. Pushing

ourselves too far, thinking that we only have one shot to make it. Thinking that we can plan, or debate, or care our way into the perfect life. But that's not how it works. It takes slow dedication, it takes flexibility.

"Does anyone else here want everything they've been working for to just happen to them immediately? Who wants to wait for the good part, when you can just skip to it?

"I'm glad I didn't skip. I fell in love with my boyfriend back when we were kids, though I didn't realize it until last summer, when we were thousands of miles apart. Now, of course, we're destined for different places. But if we'd have found each other when I was thirteen, we wouldn't have become the people we are today. And I love who we are today.

"That's ... enough of my personal life. Yes, I'm blushing; let's not read into it.

"But for everyone here, I know we're in such a hurry to get to the rest of our lives. And we should go! No matter where we go, we should go boldly into the future without looking back on our past. Without letting the past disrupt who we can be.

"Sure, maybe it's a little cringey for me to stand on this podium, say, 'Make good choices, sweeties!' and then go off to college, but it's so important that we keep our hearts open as we move forward.

"My closest friends and I are some of the most ambitious people you'll ever meet. I used to think they were so much better and smarter and cooler than me—but hey, look which one of us is valedictorian, *ha!*—but I realized we all were just excited about our lives. Having a friend group like this is rare, especially when we're four queer boys in a rural town, but because we had one another, we could keep pushing ourselves.

"So my advice to you is not to shoot for the stars or try to become president or anything. My advice to you is to surround yourself with good friends. Those who make you want to be a better person. Those who you want to spend all the good times, the bad times, and every time in between with, even if they drive you bonkers sometimes.

"If you didn't make many friends in high school, keep yourself open to making new friends out in the real world. If you're going to college, join every extracurricular group you can and find the people who are just like you as well as the people who couldn't be more different from you. Learn from each other. Build up each other. Celebrate each other's wins.

"I know I'm celebrating the wins of every person on this stage tonight.

"Because, Gracemont High, we deserve it."

• • •

The adrenaline's still pumping through my body as I return to my seat, the muffled sound of applause and cheers, the pats on my back, everything making me feel like I crushed it. Of course, there's still a lot of programming to go, so I uncomfortably shift in my seat along with everyone else while we sit through a speech from our superintendent that sounds like a bad stand-up set, a choir performance, and somehow two more speeches.

Vice Principal Camilleri steps up to the podium and pauses

thoughtfully as she scans our faces—presumably looking for Sal. She gives a soft nod, and the band starts to play "Pomp and Circumstance." The hairs on the back of my neck stand up, because I know *this is the moment.* But I also know there's still a lot of waiting, and also, I can't help but think how I'd rather be hanging out with my friends and spending our final days together than going through the motions here.

But then I think of Mom, Dad, Jeanie, and Diana all out there in the audience somewhere, and I smile. Graduation is for them as much as it is for me, I guess.

Sal's mom reads the names in alphabetical order, and a steady stream of blue and silver gowns line up to greet her, shake hands with the administration, smile for the cameras, then get back in their seats.

Salvatore Camilleri

Her voice cracks as she reads her son's name. Sal's got a huge grin on his face as he runs up to give his mom a big hug—she laughs and puts her arm around him, and without coordinating it, Reese, Gabe, and I cheer for him as he gives the crowd a dramatic bow.

Reese Hoffman-Russo

Reese stands up and nods to the crowd, showing off his bedazzled graduation cap. The spotlights bounce off the rhinestones, and little dots of light scatter across the room. He walks slowly up to accept his diploma and gives a shy wave to the crowd. He turns back to me and blows me a kiss.

Gabriel—excuse me—Gabe Kroeger

Confidently, maybe a little overconfidently, Gabe strides up to the podium to accept his diploma. He's got two honors cords on, but I see he's added a third, rainbow one, sometime in the past few minutes. He gives the crowd a dramatic curtsy as he leaves, and from the crowd, I hear the faint chant of his family shouting *O-H! I-O!*

My palms are sweaty, but the closer they get to me, the more ready I am to get this over with. To be honest, all this for one piece of paper is a little extra, but I can't help but give in to the joy of the moment.

Heath Shepard

I take my diploma without much aplomb or fanfare. I've already had my moment onstage, so I just give the crowd a quick wave—mostly to appease Diana, who keeps chanting my name for some reason—and walk back. I pass the other boys and give them each a smile. As I file back to my seat, I pass Reese, who's on the corner of the row in front of me. He grabs me and pulls me in for a quick kiss.

"Love you," he says.

I smile. "Love you back."

We take hundreds of pics with our families, friends, and pretty much everyone we can in the parking lot of the graduation venue, but after a while, it's clear that our parents are getting impatient.

"I'll try to stop by your places if I can," I tell everyone.

Gabe sighs. "Why do we all have to have our graduation parties at the same time?"

"Because... it's right after graduation," Sal says. "When else would we have them?"

"I think that was rhetorical," Reese says, nudging him with his elbow.

Sal laughs. "I know, just giving him a hard time."

An awkward silence follows, as the four of us look to one another. I can't help but think how handsome these boys look in their caps and gowns, and how much we've had to work to get to this moment. Sure, what comes next will probably be bigger and more exciting, but it's hard to believe any of us will ever forget the gravity of this moment—the gravity of *us*, right here, right now.

We pile into one last group hug, and I squeeze them as tight as my injury will allow. Things will change after this moment, I'm sure, but I don't think any of us are scared of that change anymore.

We may be going different places, but at least we're growing together.

EPILOGUE

GABRIEL

"ACTIVITY TIME!" I SHOUT as I float around the deep end of Sal's aunt's pool.

It's about eighty-five degrees this sunny day in late June, and I couldn't be happier. When it gets too hot, I take a dip. When it gets too cold, I sun myself like a lizard on rocks. Sal's mom made us all virgin piña coladas—side note, ours are absolutely not virgin anymore, but she doesn't have to know that.

"This is an activity," Sal says. "It's a pool day, what more do you want?"

"And this is an effective exercise program," Heath says while slowly rotating his arm in the pool.

Although he leaves tomorrow to head to Vanderbilt for his rehab and training journey to start, our moods are distinctly not low. Back forever ago, when we all were worried about one summer tearing us apart, or wondering how we'd make it on our own, we had so much to worry about. But today? Everything feels right. Like we're exactly where we're supposed to be. Each of us.

"What's the activity?" Reese asks.

I clear my throat. "What else? I want to know your rose and thorn for the whole school year."

"Maybe we could just do roses," Heath says. "I think we've had enough thorns for a century."

"Fine. Only roses," I say. "That work for everyone?"

Once the others agree to my sappy game, I go first.

"My rose was Reese's drag show, I think," I say, surprising myself. "I mean, so many great things happened this year, but in that moment, I realized just how accepting our community was. We had so many people there, but we knew everyone was either queer or a fierce ally, so when Reese hit the stage and everyone started cheering, I wanted to cry I was so happy. I bet that was Gracemont's first drag show, ever."

Reese laughs. "That was a big high for me too. I think my rose was the first time Sal helped me put on makeup, in that shop in Paris. I took these photos of it that I never shared with anyone, but I'll send them to you. But it was the first time I looked at my face and thought of it as a canvas, and it was like this whole world just... unlocked."

"I enjoyed our little makeup dates," Sal says. "My rose was Heath's valedictorian speech. We've had to listen to so many bad, self-absorbed speeches over the years, and I looked back at the one I was drafting in case I made it and it was just as bad as the rest. But seeing someone finally getting the credit he deserved, and in that moment, him turning it into a speech about friendship? It was honestly inspirational."

"Sometimes, I felt like the odd man out in this group," Heath admits. "I didn't realize how insecure I was about my living environment until it felt like everything was crashing down. But this year really showed me how wrong I was. My rose was you, Reese. Every single minute we spent together. Every time we cried wondering how we were going to make this work. The highest highs and lowest lows. I can't just pick one rose. With you, it's a whole bouquet."

It's silent for a while, until Sal makes a gagging sound.

"You two make me sick," he says.

Heath splashes water at him. "Ask a sappy question, get a sappy answer."

And even though this is the last time the four of us will be together for god knows how long, I'm not worried. Hell, I don't think any of us are worried. The friendship we have is more than just proximity, and when one of us changes, the rest of us will grow with him. Because that's what best friendship is all about.

So don't worry about us.

We're golden.

ACKNOWLEDGMENTS

Writing the first book in this duology, *Golden Boys*, was the most challenging endeavor I'd made in my author career. That is... until I had to write the sequel. Planning, writing, and editing four interlocking character arcs through a two-book series was unlike anything I've ever done before, and I'm so grateful I had the opportunity to spend more time in Gracemont, Ohio, with these boys. As always, some thank-yous are in order:

To my agent, Brent Taylor. This career brings so much uncertainty, but your guidance always keeps me focused and clearheaded, and I absolutely couldn't do any of this without your hard work and steadfast support.

To my editor, Mary Kate Castellani, for talking me off the ledge (more than a few times) as I brought this ambitious duology to a close. From our first call about *Golden Boys* through the final edits of *Afterglow*, you never once doubted that I could pull it off.

Thank you to my team at Bloomsbury for all their work to put this book in the hands of readers all over the world: Lily Yengle, Lex Higbee, Phoebe Dyer, Erica Barmash, Beth Eller, Kei Nakatsuka,

Donna Mark, John Candell, Laura Phillips, Diane Aronson, Pat McHugh, Jill Amack, Katie Ager, Bea Cross, and Mattea Barnes.

To May van Millingen, who illustrated the US cover, and to Patrick Leger, who illustrated the UK cover.

To my author friends, for keeping me grounded when deadlines had me spiraling out of control. And to my non-author friends, for reminding me it's sometimes okay to step away from my writing, log out of social media, and breathe.

And finally, to Jonathan, for everything. I feel so lucky to have you by my side through our many, many adventures.